DARK PASSION

A strange warmth gleamed in the depths of Jared's fever-bright eyes as they traveled over me quite frankly. "You're very beautiful," he whispered thickly. "A lovely redhaired angel."

Swiftly bending over him, I pressed his shoulders back against the cushions and felt the flushed skin of his forehead with alarm. "Please don't try to talk. You have to conserve your strength."

Suddenly he caught my arms and pushed himself upright on the pillows.

"Stop! Please," I cried, trying to loosen the strong grip of his dragging fingers. "You'll start to bleed again!"

In spite of my struggles, he forced me down against him and both arms went around me, hard and fierce. One arm clamped me to his hard, broad chest while the other hand wound painfully in my tangled waves of hair and brought my gasping mouth to meet his own, cutting off my protests in full cry.

My blood rose, enveloping me in fire and pounding in my ears like the roar of an ocean tidal wave. My vision blurred, becoming a red haze.

For the first time in my life, I was about to faint. . . .

THE BEST IN GOTHICS FROM ZEBRA

THE BLOODSTONE INHERITANCE   (1560, $2.95)
by Serita Deborah Stevens

The exquisite Parkland pendant, the sole treasure remaining to lovely Elizabeth from her mother's fortune, was missing a matching jewel. Finding it in a ring worn by the handsome, brooding Peter Parkisham, Elizabeth couldn't deny the blaze of emotions he ignited in her. But how could she love the man who had stolen THE BLOODSTONE INHERITANCE!

THE SHRIEKING SHADOWS OF
PENPORTH ISLAND   (1344, $2.95)
by Serita Deborah Stevens

Seeking her missing sister, Victoria had come to Lord Hawley's manor on Penporth Island, but now the screeching gulls seemed to be warning her to flee. Seeing Julian's dark, brooding eyes watching her every move, and seeing his ghost-like silhouette on her bedroom wall, Victoria knew she would share her sister's fate—knew she would never escape!

THE HOUSE OF SHADOWED ROSES   (1447, $2.95)
by Carol Warburton

Penniless and alone, Heather was thrilled when the Ashleys hired her as a companion and brought her to their magnificent Cornwall estate, Rosemerryn. But soon Heather learned that danger lurked amid the beauty there—in ghosts long dead and mysteries unsolved, and even in the arms of Geoffrey Ashley, the enigmatic master of Rosemerryn.

CRYSTAL DESTINY   (1394, $2.95)
by Christina Blair

Lydia knew she belonged to the high, hidden valley in the Rockies that her father had claimed, but the infamous Aaron Stone lived there now in the forbidding Stonehurst mansion. Vowing to get what was hers, Lydia would confront the satanic master of Stonehurst—and find herself trapped in a battle for her very life!

Available wherever paperbacks are sold, or order direct from the Publisher. Send cover price plus 50¢ per copy for mailing and handling to Zebra Books, Dept. 1650, 475 Park Avenue South, New York, N.Y. 10016. DO NOT SEND CASH.

THE MASTER OF BRENDAN'S ISLE

Marion Clarke

ZEBRA BOOKS
KENSINGTON PUBLISHING CORP.

ZEBRA BOOKS

are published by

Kensington Publishing Corp.
475 Park Avenue South
New York, NY 10016

First printing: August 1985

Printed in the United States of America

Chapter One

The strange sound came again, a little fainter . . . almost like a scratching at the door.

Engrossed as I was in Dickens's latest novel, I felt most reluctant to forsake the comfort of the fireside on this raw and chilly night. Therefore, I only turned my head aside to listen, mildly curious, fingering the dark red braid that fell across the bosom of my robe.

I bit my lip. Was that a moan or whimper? Perhaps some poor animal, cold and friendless, huddled on the doorstep, seeking warmth and food. Cousin Octavia wasn't home tonight to scold me for supplying a starving dog with scraps of meat or a mangy cat with a saucer of milk. Betty Ann, our one servant, was no doubt using the heavy yellow fog as an excuse to dally on her monthly visit home. I, alone, must heed that importuning sound.

I regret to say that still I hesitated. One did not open the door recklessly at night, especially in this end of London, so near the slums of Holborn. There was the dangerous, creeping fog to keep at bay, as well as unknown human terrors who used the swirling mists to slink out of their lairs. Creatures driven by a misery greater than that of dogs and cats. Men, women, and even children used the fog to steal and plunder in an effort to keep starvation away for just a few short hours.

How much more fortunate was I in my cozy—albeit shabby—room. The drawn red drapes, the glowing lamp, the crackling fireside—all represented escape from the dreary world outside. But when I heard the sounds again, a little fainter, a little more despairing, I sighed and realized there was no help for it. I must see who scratched against my door.

Relinquishing the world of *David Copperfield*, I stepped into the tiny vestibule and peered cautiously through the heavy curtains masking the window beside our narrow door.

A gasp burst from my parted lips and I stared in mounting horror and dismay. A dark shape, too large for cat or dog, lay huddled on the steps. A hand clutched desperately at the black iron balustrade, and a face, death-white, stared blindly back at me.

It was a man! A human being needing help.

The next instant, his head fell forward and he slumped into a heap. A scarlet wetness spread across the back of his dark coat. All too often I had seen such signs before. Giving an inarticulate cry, I twisted the key in the lock and flung the door wide open.

The fog, silent and thick as damp, grey wool, was a chilled menace all about me, and, quickly, I bent to drag the big man inside the house. I had handled invalids at the hospital where I worked, and, although I might appear too slender, my muscles had grown strong and I had learned the technique of moving inert bodies.

However, even exerting all my skill, I was only able to drag the injured man into the hall. Immediately, I closed and locked the door, then bent closer to examine him. How white he looked! Fearfully, I felt his pulse and found a heart still beating. Thank goodness! But blood seeped ominously from his wound and had rendered him unconscious. He was in grave danger, that I knew full well.

I flew to bring clean towels, thrusting them beneath his jacket and pressing hard until I felt the viscid red flow begin to lessen.

The man stirred and he eased himself against the wall. "How bad is it?" he muttered huskily.

Quickly, I looked at him and noticed that his black eyes were fixed on me with a controlled fear lurking in their pain-glazed depths.

Inwardly, I applauded him. He wanted to know if he would live or die, and so he came right to the point, wasting no time on moans or groans.

How could I answer? How could I know? Matching his calm tones as best I could, I said, "Someone stabbed you. It appears to be quite deep, but I think I've stopped the bleeding for the moment. Can you move? I'd like to get you into the parlor on the couch."

"I can move." With my help, he struggled to his feet. But before he took a step, he said most strangely, "Have you locked the door?"

"In this neighborhood we always lock the door. Now, please come this way."

He clamped his lips together, and, with a great effort on his part, we moved across the carpet where he collapsed, almost fainting, onto the couch.

"I will get my nursing kit," I said, starting from the room.

"Who—who—" He tried to form a question. "Where—"

"I am a nurse at Women's General Hospital. You can trust me, sir. Oh, my name is Margaret Mac-Neil, and you are in my home."

"A female nurse! A gentlewoman and so young . . ."

Perhaps my braids, now unraveling into curls upon the shoulders of my robe, gave me a more youthful aspect than my twenty-four years deserved. He had rallied briefly, and manlike, his black eyes swept me curiously.

I drew the gaping edges of my robe together hastily, aware that I wore just a low-cut nightshift underneath.

"Don't try to talk. Not now," I told him. "I must bind your wound at once and get you something for the pain."

"Yes." He grimaced. "Now that you mention it—" His full, firm mouth, the best feature in a rather rough-hewn face, thinned tautly and he bit back a groan, clenching his big hands. He seemed to try with all the strength at his command to staunch the waves of pain.

I knew what he was going through and I hurried to my room, tightening the sash on my blue robe.

Ordinarily, I would have been in bed by now, but it certainly was a blessing that I had not retired. The man might have bled to death if it had not been for my intervention.

When I returned, he opened pain-filled eyes.

"Drink this; it's laudanum." I held the cloudy mixture to his lips, my other arm supporting the broad shoulders clad in a fine, grey serge jacket now ruined beyond repair. He wore a satin waistcoat underneath it, with a gold watch looped across the front. He certainly looked like a well-to-do gentleman, I thought, wondering why he had been on foot in such a neighborhood as this.

"Do you know who attacked you?" I inquired.

"No, he came up from behind. I didn't see a thing." He drained the medicine and ran a tongue across his lips. "Some street thug, I suppose." He leaned back with a deep sigh of relief.

"Well, we'll worry about that later. Now, I fear we must remove your coat so that I can dress your wound." This was accomplished with some difficulty, and, when I turned him on his side, his upper torso clad only in the blood-stained shirt, the man's face was grey and dripping, a muscle jerking in his tightly clenched jaw.

I discovered that the wound was deep but narrow, fortunately high enough to have missed the heart. Carefully, I bathed the blood from his back, squeezing out a cloth into a little pan of tepid water from the kitchen kettle. All I could do after that was apply a soothing ointment and bind a pad in place with strips torn from a clean muslin sheet. Then I buttoned him into his vest and jacket and covered him

9

with a blanket. He now seemed exhausted and immediately fell into a heavy, unconscious sleep as the laudanum took control.

I drew a ragged breath. It was a good thing he was fairly young and strong. His age might be somewhere in the middle thirties, and his face showed no signs of dissipation. His chest was well-muscled and his heartbeat now pulsed steadily. I decided he probably had a very healthy constitution, based on his clear-grained skin and thick, springing waves of midnight hair. Healthy he might be, but just now he had lost a lot of blood and I would have to watch him closely.

It was unfortunate that we couldn't get a doctor, but in these fogs no one could venture more than a few feet outside without becoming lost. I would just have to care for him the best I could alone.

I added a shovelful of coals to the small fire in the grate and sank into a chair close beside the couch. Chin in hand, I prepared to watch my patient through the night.

Who was he? I pondered this big, dark stranger with his expensive clothing and chased-gold watch now winking on a nearby table. His harsh face somehow belied his clothes and upper class accent. There was a certain toughness stamped upon his features, harsh grooves beside the studied control of a tautly held, firm mouth. I had seen that look a hundred times in the poor section that was so close to where I lived and worked. I knew that guarded look so well. Rough men, coarse, even cruel they often were. Dedicated to survival and a certain code that bound them all together. Recognized because of my work at the hospital, I walked in safety during daylight hours. But never would I venture out in Holborn after dark without an orderly or doctor at my side.

I knew it was the height of impropriety to be alone in my house with any strange man, but tonight that didn't bother me at all. I was simply acting as a nurse, as I had for the past six years. My father, Dr. Angus MacNeil, working among the poor in Edinburgh, had taught me all I knew of medicine. I had often accompanied him on his rounds, and, when he died, I was forced to find a home in London with my cousin and employment at the local women's hospital. Tonight my father's teaching probably had helped me save a life, I mused, as my thoughts drifted on the edge of sleep, recalling memories both fond and sad. . . .

I started when a voice spoke indistinctly from the couch. "My dear girl, have I th-thanked you yet? You surely saved my l-life." His speech was slurred, his eyes heavy-lidded from the laudanum. But a strange warmth gleamed in their dark depths as they traveled over me quite frankly. "You—you're very beautiful," he whispered thickly. "A lovely, red-haired angel."

"Indeed, I'm not! You must be feverish. Please don't try to talk. You have to conserve your strength." Swiftly bending over him, I pressed his shoulders back against the cushions and felt the flushed skin of his forehead with alarm.

Suddenly, with an astonishing show of strength, he caught my arms and pushed himself upright on the pillows. "Of course you're beautiful! That un-

11

bound hair gleams just l-like copper fire. Your eyes are grey, I think. Deep pools to quench my thirst. And, ah, those cherry lips — come closer, angel — "

"Stop! Please," I cried, trying to loosen the strong grip of his dragging fingers. "You'll start to bleed again!"

But in spite of my struggles — which seemed to give him an added zest for conquering — he forced me down against him and both arms went around me, hard and fierce.

"What ails you?" I shrieked. "Let me up at once — "

He paid my words not the slightest heed. I doubt if he even heard them. One arm clamped me to his hard, broad chest, while the other hand wound painfully in my tangled waves of hair and brought my gasping mouth to meet his own, cutting off my protests in full cry.

He ground against my lips, moving back and forth until they parted and he was able to delve deeper. Never had I encountered such a thing! For the first time in my life, I felt invaded by a domineering, lustful male. I could feel the thundering heartbeats in his heaving chest, the heat of his hard body as his hands worked feverishly up and down my back beneath my opened robe. His panting breath mingled with my stifled cries until I knew not which was which.

My blood rose, enveloping me in fire and pounding in my ears like the roar of an ocean tidal wave. My vision blurred, becoming a red haze, and I knew I was as close to fainting as I had ever come.

Then, as suddenly as it started, the passionate onslaught ended. His hold grew slack. His eyes

12

drooped shut. Gathering all my strength, I thrust him off and sprang across the room out of his reach.

Pulling up my robe, I cried out wildly, my voice choked and cracked beyond all recognition. "Is this the th-thanks I get? Is this the way you show your gratitude after I saved your life? With loathsome, shameful advances to me? You—you—monster!"

He didn't move or speak. His eyes were closed and he only muttered incoherently. I realized then that he was under the influence of the laudanum, drugged from shock and loss of blood. He was completely unconscious of what he'd done.

Chapter Two

It was quite some time before my racing heartbeats became normal. Hands pressed to my chest, I stood across the room and stared at my unconscious patient, now relaxed in a state of complete peace, his face once more grave and sober. It was almost impossible to realize that, moments before, he had been so wild—so passionate—and so strong. But I had seen the effects of laudanum many times and I knew he was not responsible for his actions. No, the man was sick, and I felt certain that when he regained consciousness he would never know what he had said or done. I wouldn't tell him, either. However, I would stay alert and be prepared for any return of such dismaying conduct.

While he was at rest, I would take the opportunity to don some clothes. A robe and nightgown might have stimulated him to errant thoughts. I could take no chances.

I sped upstairs to the little room beneath the eaves that Cousin Octavia's meager income had furnished for me to the best of her ability. A fringed spread covered the cot, and white, starched curtains graced the single window. A bureau held a jug and basin; books and pictures of my parents reposed on a small table. From a row of hooks within a standing wardrobe, I selected petticoats, a dress, and so forth, feeling more secure when I had buttoned up a brown merino gown topped by a snowy apron to my ankles. I brushed my tangled hair severely and fastened it closely with a plain black ribbon tied behind my head.

I stared into the round, wall mirror, smoothing down my collar. Did my face bear signs of its recent experience? Except for reddened lips, I just looked pale and rather worried. Why be upset? I was a nurse, after all, used to the strange effects of drugs and the wild emotions of people close to death. Still, I had never been subjected to such a violent, amorous attack before.

It had been most curious . . . the man downstairs had seemed to think me beautiful. No one had ever called me that before. Not even Dr. David Wainright, to whom I had been engaged for several years. Of course, he usually had seen me when my hair was covered by a concealing cap and my person by a large, rough apron. And the other times — when we went strolling in Hyde Park or boating on the Thames — his mind had usually been concentrated on the world of medicine. He had worked beside me in the hospital, a gentle, dedicated man, saving for our marriage, when illness had struck him swiftly, and he had died. That was two years ago now, and the quiet, serious young man was only a sad, blurred image in my memory. Often I felt a wave of guilt that I no long suffered over poor David's passing.

Even now, his image faded swiftly from my mind as I recalled my duty to the patient in my parlor. I hesitated on the stairs and bit my lip. He was a gravely injured man, but he still was possessed of an uncommon strength, with a mind clouded so that his natural restraints were blurred—or even swept away completely. I was sure there would be no repetition of his frightening conduct, but, just as a precaution, I picked up a stout wooden rolling pin from our little kitchen and placed it near at hand when I returned to observe my patient's progress.

He was shifting restlessly upon the couch, although still unconscious. His fingers clenched and unclenched and he gave a groan of pain. Nothing mattered now to me except my training as a nurse. I felt the racing pulse below his thumb. Dear heaven, was he worse?

Swiftly, I brought a bowl of water and sponged the perspiration from his pain-wracked face, pushing back the waves of dark, tousled hair with a stab of pity. Such a strong, vital creature to be laid so low! As my father had often said, nothing was more important than preserving life. Fame, wealth, youth, and beauty, all faded into nothing when living was at stake.

At last, satisfied that I had done all I could for the time being, I saw my patient settle down into quiet oblivion once more. Recklessly, I dumped another shovelful of coal into the grate, then made myself as comfortable as possible. I soon slept lightly in my armchair, as I had been wont to do so many times while on nursing duty.

Habit made me waken quickly at any change, and, near dawn, my patient stirred and muttered. Springing up, I bent above him, feeling for his pulse a little

16

apprehensively. Thank heaven, it was steady. And his color was a little better, too. I had been right in diagnosing him as a healthy specimen of manhood with remarkable powers of recovery.

As I watched him, his eyes opened fully, clear, black, and alert. "Where am I? Who are you?" His voice was low, but quite a lot stronger, with a rather attractive husky timbre. "Wait, now—I remember—you're the nurse."

"Margaret MacNeil." I nodded, moving to sit upon the edge of my chair. "You are in my home. Someone stabbed you near my doorstep. Can you tell me how it happened?"

He passed a hand across his brow and frowned. "I had gone to meet—someone—in a Holborn tavern. When he didn't appear after I had waited quite a while, I finally left and found that a fog had settled in. All I could do was hurry from the area, hoping to find a cruising cabby. Then, suddenly, I heard a footfall. There was a sharp pain in my back that drove me to my knees. As I fell, someone ran, but I didn't catch a glimpse of him."

"And somehow you crawled onto my doorstep," I added.

He nodded carefully, his dark eyes on my face. "You saved my life, Miss MacNeil, and you don't even know my name."

I raised my brows inquiringly.

He gave a brief dip of his head. "Jared Warwick, at your service, of Brendan's Isle. Ever hear of it?"

I shook my head.

Before he could continue speaking, a cloud of pain swept his face and he shut his eyes and winced.

"Your wound was very deep, I'm afraid. I wish that we could have had a doctor, but there's none close by." I leaned toward him anxiously. "I'm sure it pains you a great deal."

"Like the very devil," he ground out. "But it comes and goes. And I'm sure, dear lady, that you have done the best thing possible for me. How fortunate that I landed on your doorstep."

"I could give you another drop of laudanum in some water," I said reluctantly. "But it might make you feel worse after it wears off." And it might make *me* feel worse *before* it does, I thought, recalling my recent frightening experience on his couch.

He drew a rasping breath and then relaxed. "No, thank you. It's better now. You saved my life with your quick and generous care, so I should be able to endure an occasional twinge of pain." He smiled a little thinly. "And I should be glad that I'm alive to feel it."

"Well, you must see a doctor as soon as this fog lifts. And we also should summon the police."

He shook his head decisively. "No police. What good would they do now?"

I gave an exclamation of surprise. "But weren't you robbed? Don't you wish to report the theft in case some of it can be recovered?"

He gestured toward the small table near the sofa. "I see my gold watch there. That wasn't taken, and it was the only thing I was carrying that really mattered. My grandfather gave it to me when I turned sixteen."

"Strange that it wasn't stolen," I murmured.

He thrust his hand into his jacket pocket, drawing out a bulging wallet. "Neither was this. It seems that I was somewhat lucky, after all."

"I wonder why you were stabbed, then?"

He shrugged, then winced and caught his shoulder in his hand. "Probably something scared the thief away before he 'glomed the swag,' which I believe is thieves' cant for a robbery."

His fingers strayed among the banknotes. "How can I ever repay you, Miss MacNeil? Most people wouldn't take an injured stranger into their homes—not in this part of town." He leaned forward, speaking with strong emphasis. "Ask me any favor and I promise you, if it is within my power, I will grant it with the greatest joy."

I raised my hand and spoke as emphatically as he had. "Nothing, nothing! Your recovery will be reward enough."

A warm light filled his eyes as they searched my face. The next minute, his gaze turned to rove around the shabby sitting room with its faded Turkey carpet and crocheted doilies covering worn spots in the horsehair chairs and sofa. I knew he even saw the stains of mildew on the floral-papered walls.

I sat up straighter and raised my chin, defying any pity. Our home was clean and neat, we paid our rent, and always there was substantial food upon the table. If there was nothing over for refurbishing, it was through no fault of mine. I worked long, hard hours for small wages because I felt that I could do some good. And Octavia took in a little sewing.

He put the wallet back. "Very well," he sighed. "We'll let it go for now. But I will just say this: I think you are a most remarkable, young woman, Margaret MacNeil."

I felt my cheeks turn pink, and, giving a disclaiming gesture, I jumped up hurriedly to peer out of the windows. "I think the fog is finally thinning. It's growing lighter and it will soon be morning. Do you think that you could take some nourishment, Mr. Warwick?"

"A little hot tea, if it's not too much trouble. Laced with plenty of brandy and sugar."

"Oh, dear, I'm afraid there is only cooking sherry."

"Never mind, that will be fine."

I hurried to the kitchen, feeling my own hunger stir, and made a pot of strong, black tea. After that, I toasted bread, buttered it liberally, then set everything—including the sherry bottle—on a table by my patient's side. With good appetite, he downed several cups of hot, dark liquid and crunched the honey-buttered toast with strong, white teeth. Afterward, he appeared greatly fortified and in considerably less pain.

I, too, was refreshed after my toast and tea, and, while we ate, we talked. From him, I only learned that he was a writer and lived on an island off the southern coast of England with his wife and daughter. A shadow seemed to cross his face when he spoke of the latter individuals, and he quickly turned the conversation in my direction.

"Could I ask you why you took up the exacting profession of public nursing? It is scarcely the province of a gentlewoman such as yourself. The wards are usually tended by tough old hags or prostitutes. Surely parents, sweetheart, someone must have tried to stop you?"

I shook my head with a slight smile. "No one tried to stop me. Actually, my only relative now is my Cousin Octavia, with whom I live. My mother died when I was born, and, while my father was alive, he encouraged my career. He was a very dedicated doctor in Edinburgh and taught me all I know. He believed it would be a fine thing if trained women of good character could be nurses in our hospitals. He used to say that someday they even might become doctors."

Jared Warwick raised his eyebrows, then nodded thoughtfully. "Your father was a man before his time. And I think that I agree with him. A woman's touch certainly is needed in those pits of hell called hospitals."

His harsh, dark face was grim as he stared into the flames flickering in the grate and I wondered what knowledge a well-dressed, wealthy man could have of public wards and thieves' cant. And why had he been meeting someone in the slums?

Perhaps he was not what he seemed . . . gentlemen had been rogues before this time. There was some mystery behind his closed, hard face, that much was certain.

I tried to thrust away the uneasy stirrings of suspicion, only to have them flare up when I realized his slitted gaze was riveted on my face. Nervously, I brushed the curls clinging to my brow, remembering with a pang of fear how his drug-induced ardor had been turned in my direction. Was it possible he remembered? Could his lust be stirring once again? My hand closed on the nearby rolling pin with a convulsive grip. His next words set the seal of terror on me.

"God, how I could use someone like you!" he muttered to himself, his black eyes sweeping me from top to toe with the strangest expression I had yet seen on his face.

A suffocating breath seemed lodged somewhere in my throat, but I found the strength to press one hand against my heart while my other fingers whitened on

21

the rolling pin.

In the heavy, waiting silence, I thought how isolated we were in this empty house with the street outside deserted in the chilly predawn. There was not a soul to help me anywhere if he . . . if he . . .

Our glances clung for several minutes — to me it seemed much longer — then the coals snapped sharply and a fountain of red sparks exploded up the chimney.

With a labored sigh, the man's eyes turned away, filled now with a brooding sorrow. "My daughter fell from a horse six months ago. She hasn't walked a single step since then."

I expelled my breath and sank back in my chair, the rolling pin forgotten, as well as all my fears. "Oh, how dreadful," I whispered. "Surely there's some hope for her recovery? What do the doctors say?"

His voice came low and harsh. "They say she simply doesn't want to walk and cannot give a reason. Her mother has very little understanding of the child, and I — to my regret — have spared insufficient time for my daughter in the past. Now, my efforts meet with a blank wall, and I realize we need an outside person, someone who could devote herself to Harriet with encouragement and companionship. A sensible, kind young person, one who also knows the art of nursing."

He lifted his dark head and looked at me levelly. "A person such as you."

"What — what do you mean?"

He leaned forward, stretching out his hand imploringly. "I'm asking you to come and nurse my child. This is your profession. It would just be for a little while, I think. And I would pay you handsomely."

My heart began to pound again, this time with an

uncontrolled excitement. His request was so startling—so unexpected! I jumped up and went to stand before the fire. "Mr. Warwick, I know nothing about caring for a crippled person. It's a terrible thing to happen to a child. I feel so sorry but . . ." I turned to face him slowly. "I truly don't see how I could do your daughter any good."

"I disagree."

"Another thing . . ." I cleared my throat. "You—you are a complete stranger to me."

"My dear girl, that's one area in which I can set your mind at rest. I can furnish impeccable references from banks, my publisher, the local clergy. . . ."

He sat up eagerly, as though he sensed a weakening in me. "If you came to us, your status would be that of a companion to my daughter. I'm sure that you could lift her spirits while you use whatever therapy you deem best. You are both strong and brave—you've proven that tonight. My daughter needs to have her own low spirits bolstered, and I know that you would help her."

He named a sum for my services that made me catch my breath in astonishment, then he continued his entreaty with all the force at his command, which was considerable. "You would have a large room next to my daughter's and the services of a maid. There is swimming in the sea cove, a boat to sail, and horseback riding in the island meadows. You would be given every comfort and consideration within our power to provide."

I faced the couch, looking down uncertainly, when, to my surprise, he suddenly reached up and caught my hand in his. Not roughly, just a warm clasp of entreaty.

For some reason, I didn't pull away.

"I think that Providence sent me to your door, Miss MacNeil," he said with that strange, attractive huskiness in his voice. "If I had to be stabbed as part of the plan, it would be well worth it if I have found an answer for my daughter."

"You really know nothing about me," I protested, aware that something was drawing me nearer and nearer to a commitment. Something? Or someone? A strong, hard-featured man whose face grew wracked and vulnerable when he spoke about his daughter. A man of great persuasive powers . . .

"I think I know a lot about you," he replied, his black eyes boring into mine. "Never have I learned so much about a person in so short a time. You have courage, compassion, and intelligence. And you are ready to tread new paths. That much is obvious from your pioneering work at Women's Hospital."

I withdrew my hand and returned to a chair, nervously pleating my long white apron. "How long would it be for?"

"I hope that you will stay as long as needed. But whenever you wish to end your time with us, I'll understand and provide you with a first-class return ticket on the railway and another month's full pay. All this will be put in writing if you decide to come."

"Well . . . my cousin and I had planned to attend the Great Exhibition in Hyde Park next month." Even as I said it, I knew it was but a flimsy excuse thrown up to barricade my tottering willpower.

"I will bring you back for a day or two to spend at the affair." When his mouth softened, as it did just now, I realized that his face was almost handsome. The lower

24

lip was sensuously full, the upper lip a contrast of firmly indented self-control. Two warring factors in his nature? I remembered the feel of his ruthless, demanding kisses with a little quickening of my heartbeats. But I felt no fear of him under normal circumstances. I was certain that Jared Warwick was a man of honor when he had his wits about him.

Firmly, I pushed aside the knowledge that he could also be a most attractive man. That was none of my affair. It was the child who mattered.

"I promise to think about it," I said, raising my head to look at him squarely.

His black eyes had a hypnotic quality and held me fast. "I want you to come," he said in a low tone. "Very much."

I almost nodded then in acquiescence. But my cautious Scottish nature, this time, held me back. "We'll see. A bit more tea, Mr. Warwick?" I asked sweetly.

"Yes, thank you," he replied. His smile was full of confidence.

Chapter Three

The fog had lifted by the time our maid, Betty Ann, arrived and she was immediately dispatched to hail a cab while I overrode her goggle-eyed surprise.

I offered to accompany Jared Warwick to a doctor, but he refused, saying it was quite unnecessary. "The cabby can take me, and you can seek your greatly needed rest."

He walked to the door beside me unaided, a bit unsteadily. "I can't tell you how much I appreciate all that you have done for me, Miss MacNeil, and I pray that you will do a little more by coming to us at Brendan's Isle."

His black eyes sent their urgent message boring into me and I felt a little weakness in the knees. He took my hand and kissed it solemnly as though it were a seal upon a bargain. For a brief second, his gaze rested on my face, then he swung away and the cabby drove him off.

I watched as they vanished out of sight down the cobblestone street, which was now filled with the noise of horses' hooves and rattling carts and vendors' morning cries.

"Hot cross buns!" "Fresh-caught eels!" "Baked taters, only two a penny!"

I closed the door, then had to endure the excited questions of young Betty Ann, who considered herself one of the family. Where had he come from? How bad was he hurt? A real gentleman, he looked. Rich and handsome, too. Would I be seeing him again? She put a hand up to her mouth and tittered.

Finally, I shooed her to the kitchen, demanding that she start some breakfast.

A few minutes later, Octavia arrived home. Over a cup of tea, I told her about the recent adventure I had experienced (omitting, of course, the laudanum reaction) and then described the amazing offer Jared Warwick had made me to nurse his child at Brendan's Isle.

Octavia's reaction was quite predictable. "You must be out of your mind!" Her teacup rattled in its saucer as she plunked it down. "A perfect stranger asks you to give up everything and travel down the coast to some remote, unknown island. And you say you will 'think about it.'" Octavia's grey curls trembled with her agitation.

"It was reckless enough to take him into your home last night; however, since you are a nurse, the circumstances might be overlooked, but this—to go down to him on an island—" She choked and had to gulp some tea. "Why, child, the man could be anything. A trafficker in white slaves, a rogue of the first water—"

I gave a weary sigh, leaning my head upon my hand. "He promised to furnish references. Really, Octavia, I believe he is a gentleman of wealth and good standing. He said he was a writer."

"What does that signify? Have you ever heard of him?" Octavia demanded. "Well, neither have I. Every week I bring home an armload of books from the Circulating Library, yet never have I heard of an author named Jared Warwick."

"He promised me a very generous salary."

"Ha! That last item is suspicious in itself. How does he know you will be worth it?" Octavia peered over her steel-rimmed spectacles and said in a hollow tone, "There is no telling what you might have to do to earn that money!"

The argument continued until, finally, it was abruptly halted by the clanging of the front door knocker.

"Maybe he's come back," I gasped.

"Or maybe it's the police," my cousin countered darkly.

But it was neither.

To our utter astonishment, a regular procession of delivery men began to unload great baskets at our door of the most luxurious treats: glacéd fruits, imported chocolates, frosted hothouse grapes, a half-dozen bottles of various choice wines, a whole roast goose, and, last, boxes of spring blooms. Lilacs, primroses, tulips, and daffodils all nesting in beds of fern and paper lace.

Just one card accompanied the deliveries. It was addressed to me and merely said: "A small token of my undying gratitude," in a bold, masculine scrawl.

Neither of us made any suggestion of sending the lavish gifts back to the shops. In fact, Octavia's initial amazement soon changed to cautious pleasure. "I never hoped to taste such things, did you, Margaret? I believe Mr. Warwick has shown a certain sensitivity. To offer money would have insulted your kindness. This way, we can accept gracefully. However, as to your working for him, well, we will have to discuss that further."

Though I agreed that he was indeed generous and sensitive, a corner of my mind wondered if perhaps the gifts might also be Jared Warwick's way of urging my cooperation.

A few days later, the treat was followed by a long letter to me, in which he described his home with a writer's fluency. "Brendan's Isle is filled with every sort of flower at this time: daisies, violets, harebells — tiny, sweet-scented things growing wild and plentiful in the sheltered meadows. The beach below is fascinating, alternating between coves of golden sand and places where the waves are wild, green horses flaunting manes of foam. The house stands alone on a high plateau above a little fishing village and has a formal garden and a grove of trees. It is not old as English manors go, having only been built two hundred years ago. Inside, it has been furnished with marble statues, tapestries, and Persian carpets, all dictated by Mrs. Warwick's taste, her knowledge of such things being quite superior to my own."

He included several references in the letter, and, after I had duly checked the local ones, I knew there was no reason for delay. I wrote to Jared Warwick and accepted.

Octavia's objections had been overcome. At least she said no more about them, only wished me well when I set out six days later armed with luggage and a first-class ticket sent to me by Mr. Warwick for the Cornwall train.

I had never traveled on a railway coach before, and, when I was settled in the "Ladies Only" section, I gazed around with unabashed delight. Everything was paneled in rich walnut with gleaming brass fittings. My feet rested on a carpeted foot-warmer, while my head reclined on the back of a stationary armchair tufted in lemon-yellow plush. Fringed shades could be rolled up or down the double windows, and an embroidered canvas handhold was in easy reach for unexpected jerks.

Four other passengers soon entered to complete our compartment's quota: two quiet, elderly ladies traveling together, and a young woman who was soon occupied with entertaining a rather restless little boy.

I had no wish for conversation, I was much too excited by my own thoughts, so, after nodding to each one, I pretended to read *The Ladies' Magazine*, while, in truth, my mind was seeing Jared Warwick's latest letter: "My servant, James, will meet you at the Lingrove station on Tuesday next and conduct you across the bay to Brendan's Isle, where you will be assured of my most eager welcome."

Only one thing had been lacking in the letter and that was any mention of a welcome from his wife and daughter. Perhaps it had just been an oversight. However, I couldn't help wondering uneasily what might await me on the island. Would the child, Harriet, like me? Would she accept my discipline and therapy? I had consulted with a doctor at the hospital on the care of useless limbs, but would the mother let me put the exercises into practice? Somehow into my mind had crept the idea that Mrs. Warwick might be impatient and unsympathetic with her daughter's condition.

I lowered my magazine and gazed out of the window, only vaguely conscious of the passing landscape slipping into southern lushness of green meadows, flowering hedgerows, and young spring lambs disporting on the rolling hills. Here and there, a gothic church spire arrested my attention in the little towns, but, as the day wore on, I had a restless feeling and began to wish the trip would end. The train had begun to seem confining. It rattled and shook and was almost airless. When the window was lowered, cinders blew into the car and it had to be closed at once. Everyone was talking to each other now, the little boy constantly wanting to know when they would reach Cornwall and when the speed would be increased from twenty miles an hour.

Personally, I thought the speed was quite dangerous enough and found myself longing for the old stage-coach stops to stretch my legs and the cozy inns where one could eat a nice hot meal such as I had enjoyed on my trip from Scotland down to London.

However, the two old ladies, evidently seasoned travelers, shared some bags of fruit and biscuits with us, and finally the day moved into late afternoon. When the town of Lingrove was announced, my heart began a rapid tattoo as I gathered up my things and bade goodbye to my erstwhile companions. All I was really conscious of, however, was the thought that soon I would see the darkly fascinating face of Jared Warwick . . . his wife . . . his daughter . . . the unknown island.

The train ground to a swaying halt. My luggage was deposited on a wooden platform, and, in seconds, I was down the steps to stare around with mixed emo-

31

tions at the sudden darkness of the day. Purple clouds like huge, ripe plums, about to burst with rain, surged across the sky. As the train roared out of sight, a few drops began to patter on the cinder path. Unfortunately my umbrella had been packed beneath my clothes and, in a spurt of vanity, I was wearing my best bonnet.

The railway platform had the merest shelter from the elements, just a tiny roof, but I knew someone was due to meet me here. Soon my straining eyes saw a man striding through the thrashing trees that lined the quay. When he stopped in front of me, his black eyes, in a young, red-cheeked face, raked me much more boldly than I liked.

"I'm James from Brendan's Isle. Are you the nurse?"

My nod was cool and dignified. "I am Miss Mac-Neil. Is the boat here?"

"We take the ferry. It's waitin' just beyond." With a strong grip, he gathered up my portmanteau and carryall and strode across the track toward the bay, leaving me to stumble after him.

We were the only passengers when we climbed aboard the ferry. It was a flat, open type, containing several planked seats beneath a fluttering, tattered awning. The grizzled pilot had only a taciturn grunt for us before he steered into the choppy sea.

James went to stand beside him, but soon the rain increased and he returned to take a seat close to me beneath the doubtful shelter of the awning. His bright eyes fastened on me with unconcealed interest and approval, and I moved away, uneasily, from the contact of his bulging thighs and muscled arms. His face had a coarse handsomeness and a constant smirk that probably indicated huge success with scullery maids.

"So you're the new nurse, then," he purred, knowing eyes moving up and down the outlines of my tightly buttoned jacket. "You certainly are a fine-looking figure of a woman, if I may make so bold."

I stared, wooden-faced, across the heaving water. I didn't wish to start any unpleasantness with him, but neither would I allow familiarities.

In a dignified tone, I asked, "Please tell me about the island. Who lives there? How big is it?"

"Five or ten miles long. I dunno." He ran a large hand through his mop of curls. "And who lives there? In the village mebbe fifty souls, I reckon. And up above? Them."

"Them?"

"The master what owns it all, and his missus."

"And the child, of course."

"Aye, her too. Sour as a crabapple since she fell."

My heart sank a little at this description.

James slid closer, with a deep-throated chuckle. "Mebbe you can make her laugh again, eh, nurse? Such sweet, red lips must mean a right warm heart, I'm thinkin'. Nice for kissin', too."

I turned and fixed him with a frosty eye that in the past had quelled many a rebellious patient. "My good man, I am here to do a job. I expect it to take all my energy and time. There is no desire in me for anything but a businesslike relationship with everyone. Do you take my meaning?"

His mouth twisted. "Taken like a dose o' paregoric. Ah, well, we'll see." Suddenly, he jumped up and pointed. "Look, Miss Nurse, there 'tis, Brendan's Isle. Folks say 'twas a pirates' cove in olden times. There's lots o' caves where treasure could be hidden."

I rose and moved to the damp railing, peering through the curtain of spring rain. A large, high-crowned island rose before me, with sharp-edged rocks girdling the bay like warning fingers. Beyond the shore, I could dimly make out the clustering homes of a small village.

"Where is the manor house?" I inquired of James who had come to stand beside me.

"Up on top."

Though I strained my eyes, I couldn't see a sign of it above the tree-clad hill. The high plateau was shrouded in a veil of rain.

When we landed, there was no time for more than a quick glance at the village as James immediately hurried me into a waiting enclosed carriage. He sprang into the driver's seat, whipping up the pair of greys while I perched gingerly on the chilled black leather seat inside. Peering through the blurred glass window, I obtained an impression of twisting cobblestone streets lined with narrow houses, and numerous fishing boats bobbing at anchor in the bay. But nowhere did I see any people on this dark and stormy day.

The road curved sharply upward from the rocky shore and I was forced to cling tightly to the handstrap as we careened along the narrow, twisting road. Great overhanging rocks lined the way, and tree limbs thrashed and scraped the carriage roof in the rising, moaning wind. Distant claps of thunder heightened the impression of threat that was beginning to overwhelm me.

I gave a shudder of relief when we finally rolled into a high, stone-walled enclosure at the top. The carriage, driven at the same breakneck speed, rattled over a graveled courtyard and rocked violently to a halt, almost flinging me from my seat.

James opened the door and swept me out, a grin upon his face. "Did I scare you, then?" he asked hopefully. Evidently he was smarting inwardly from my former rebuff of his advances.

"Not at all." I brushed his arm away and stared at the massive stone facade confronting me. "So, that's the house."

The manor had three stories of multipaned windows set beneath ornate overhangings of carved stone. Four wings spread out from the central hall, unsoftened by tree or vine. Tall brick chimneys rose from various points on the roof amid a hodgepodge of turrets, arches, and balconies in the style known as Gothic.

It was much more elaborate and imposing than I had expected, and I confess that I felt daunted. And just then, as I gazed up at the windows, a face looked down at me, twisted in an expression of utter malice.

Chapter Four

For a moment, I had the most insane desire to turn and run. That face in the window so obviously repulsing me; the cold storm buffeting this remote island; the lack of welcome from the wife and daughter; even the uneasiness that filled me when I encountered James's bold glances . . . all of it was suddenly appalling. *What* was I doing here?

Fearfully, I looked back at the window, and relief washed over me so that I nearly laughed. The nearby carvings were stone images of gargoyles with sneering faces. An errant flash of lightning had reflected them on the glass pane. That was all. I squared my shoulders and followed James into the house.

Inside, I looked around with a swift upsurge of curiosity. We were in a great marble hallway hung with tapestries on paneled walls. Huge glass lamps swung from iron chains in the ceiling, and rows of scantily draped statues stared sightlessly into the gloom.

Since no lights were lit as yet, I barely could make out the austere features of an unsmiling, black-clad woman who glided toward me down the hallway.

"I am the housekeeper, Rachel Grey. You are the new nurse, I presume?" she said in a voice of cool aloofness.

I drew myself erect, knowing I must begin as I would continue, and reflect a certain pride in my profession. "I am Miss MacNeil, the nurse. May I see the master, Jared Warwick?" I hesitated just a fraction. "Or his wife?"

"They will be here presently. James, take the nurse's baggage to the Emerald Room." This was followed by a disapproving sniff, impossible to misinterpret.

James's thick black eyebrows rose and he grinned. "Oh-oh, a fine room for a *nurse*, I'm thinkin' eh, Miss Grey?" He gave a wink. "A right good friend of the master's she must be."

I felt furious that a wave of warmth should sweep my face at his insinuating glance. I spoke to Miss Grey firmly. "Take me to your employers, if you please."

" 'Tis not what I please," the housekeeper muttered, turning aside her head. "A nurse will do no good in this house, I can tell you that. It simply means more work for us, and we are shorthanded as it is."

"I don't intend to burden anyone," I answered. "I will attend to my own wants and those of my patient."

The housekeeper didn't vouchsafe a reply. She flung open a carved oak door and turned up the wick on a rose-shaded globe. By its light, I saw that Miss Grey was middle-aged, with dark hair coiled low on a long, thin neck. Her face seemed pinched into a mold of chronic fretfulness.

"Wait here, nurse," she barked at me and stalked out of the room.

I was glad to be alone for a few minutes and take stock of the room, which was cozy, warm, and beautiful. Shelves of books lined two walls; the other side contained long windows covered from floor to ceiling with damask drapery, looped and swagged with thick gold fringe. Gold tones also appeared in the upholstered sofa and matching chairs drawn to either side of a black marble fireplace. I drew closer to this appealing warmth, holding my chilled hands out to the blazing logs as I watched the light flicker on the elaborate carvings of the mantelpiece and mirror.

Resting in front of the looking glass was a bowl of the strangest flowers I had ever seen. Wide wings of thick-fleshed purple petals flared out from a throat of gold that was shaped like a ruffled trumpet. They were quite the most exquisite flowers I had ever seen, and I thought they must be very rare and valuable.

There was a sudden movement in the mirror's depths, and, quickly, I swung around. A woman entered soundlessly. A woman of astounding beauty. Was this Jared Warwick's wife?

Her face was long and oval, with a thin bow of a mouth and luminous blue eyes. They were fringed with lashes as dark as her hair, in which nestled a purple blossom similar to those above the mantel. Beneath a scarf of golden gauze, her arms and bosom gleamed, as perfect as the marble Venus come to life.

"How do you do, Mrs. Warwick," I ventured. "I am—"

"—the nurse, of course." There was no welcome in the beauty's flat voice as she inspected me with what I saw was blank disinterest. "You're quite wet, I see."

She glided to a tea cart near the sofa and gestured at

the covered dishes and a steaming pot. "My husband thought you might care for some refreshment. Or would you rather just go to your room?"

"I have had no meal since breakfast, madam."

"Well, help yourself, then." Mrs. Warwick shrugged and poured herself a cup of amber fluid. "This plan of Jared's is quite ridiculous, you know."

"No, I don't know that. What do you mean, Mrs. Warwick?" I filled a plate, trying not to bolt down the delicious salmon and cucumber sandwiches as I eyed the other platter containing cake and pastry.

Mrs. Warwick twitched her ruffles across the carpet and put her cup upon the mantelpiece. She stared down at the leaping flames with a cross expression.

"There is nothing wrong with Harriet. No bones were broken, no skin torn. She is just a stubborn, spoiled child who knows she will get more attention as an invalid."

"That opinion is one that I heartily disagree with, Katherine." Jared Warwick's deep, husky voice spoke from the doorway, and hearing those remembered tones, I spun around to greet him.

My eyes widened in surprise. How different he looked! Quite aristocratic in a ruffled shirt and elegant black velvet coat, his thick hair smooth and tamed. As he advanced into the room, his gaze sought mine, and a smile curved the full, firm mouth as he reached out for my hand.

His grip was as compelling and electrifying as before, and my fingers trembled slightly before he released them slowly. "I'm so very glad to see you here, Miss MacNeil. How was the train ride?"

"Exciting, interesting. And very fast. Thank you—

for everything."

"It was nothing."

"Has your wound given you any further trouble, Mr. Warwick?"

"None at all. It has healed very well. The doctor said that your swift and competent care probably saved my life."

All during this exchange, Mrs. Warwick had stood with her back to us, staring at the flames. Her husband looked at her, a little impatiently, I thought. "Katherine, I believe you and Miss MacNeil were discussing Harriet when I entered—"

"It doesn't matter about my views, I guess. The nurse is here, a *fait accompli*." His wife turned slowly, a faint, malicious smile curving the cherry-red bow of her lips.

Jared Warwick halted, heavy brows meeting in a frown. His black eyes fastened on her hair as she preened before him.

"Yes, Jared, I took some precious orchids from your hothouse. You know I can't resist the cattelayas when they are in bloom. Don't you agree that they become me, dearest?" She slid a little closer to him and ran her white hands up the velvet lapels of his jacket until they reached his face. Her red lips parted, inches from his own, with deliberate invitation.

Her husband didn't move or speak. Neither did he smile.

I thought his wife's actions were exceedingly embarrassing and in the poorest taste—stroking hands and proffered lips in the presence of a complete stranger! I moved toward the door and cleared my throat. "Could someone please show me to my room?"

Leisurely, Mr. Warwick pulled down his wife's caressing hands and stepped away, his face as unresponsive as the marble statues in the hallway. "I will show you to your room, Miss MacNeil. I want a word with you about my daughter. A matter that holds little interest for my wife."

As we headed for the door, there was an indrawn, hissing breath behind us. The next instant, something crashed upon the grate. I looked back, startled, as Mrs. Warwick ran across the room and vanished down the hallway.

A teacup lay in fragments on the hearth.

Completely ignoring his wife's peculiar actions, Jared Warwick took my elbow in his palm. "My dear, you are soaked and shivering. Come, I will escort you to your room where you can change."

Mrs. Warwick faded from my thoughts. All I was conscious of was the magnetism of this big, dark man whose fingers seemed to warm my flesh right through the fabric of my sleeve. The coldness had left his face as he looked at me, and his husky voice seemed warmer, deeper, when he spoke. "Your room is next to Harriet's. We moved her downstairs after the accident to make it more accessible for the servants."

"How is your daughter?"

He shrugged. "No better, but no worse. Perhaps your wholesome presence will dispel her apathy. You are young, sensible, and dauntless. Harriet was like that once."

I felt a glow of pleasure. "I sincerely hope that I will be of some help to her. But—" I threw him a hesitant, sidelong glance. "Mr. Warwick, your wife contends that there is no physical reason for your daughter's in-

41

ability to walk. I would like to speak to the physician who attended Harriet. When does he come to see her?"

"Dr. Korman will come tomorrow if the storm lets up. I told him about you and he expressed the greatest approval. I have had a difficult time finding someone suitable for Harriet. Those who were competent did not want to live in such isolation and left after a short time. The others, well, they simply wouldn't do."

He stopped before a door with a brass key protruding from the large, old-fashioned lock. "Here is your room. I hope you will be comfortable. The maid, Annie, sleeps close by. She will attend to your wants as she does Harriet's."

He pushed open the door and I gave an exclamation of delight. It was by far the most luxurious bedroom I had ever seen. Oil lamps shone softly on the black oak furniture resting on a deep, soft rug of patterned leaves and flowers. A draped canopy above the bed and long, fringed curtains repeated the various shades of green. Creamy, gold-flocked paper covered the walls and ended in a frieze of plaster cupids. In the fireplace, apple logs gave out a cheerful crackle; and a bowl of yellow roses added to the sense of welcome.

I bent above the flowers, inhaling their sweet fragrance. "Oh, lovely! How on earth do you raise them in April, Mr. Warwick? And I saw such exotic flowers in the library—" Instantly, I regretted mentioning the strange purple blooms, remembering how they had aroused his anger.

However, he responded mildly enough. "I have a hothouse, Miss MacNeil. It was my grandfather's hobby, and I preserve it in his memory. I can grow roses and orchids all year long by keeping the glass en-

42

closure warm and moist. I will show it to you sometime if you are interested. Now, is there anything else you need? I'll send the maid in with hot water."

"Oh, thank you. The room is quite perfect and so very beautiful."

"I thought its colors would be especially flattering to someone with such lovely auburn hair," he murmured.

His narrowed gaze was slightly disconcerting and I was glad of an interruption at that moment. I could hear a voice raised in the room next door, and although it was impossible to distinguish any words, I imagined that the youthful treble might belong to Harriet.

"Mr. Warwick, when can I meet my patient?"

"Perhaps tonight. I told her that you were coming." He turned toward the door, but then glanced back. "Would you prefer to have your supper here, or do you wish to join us in the dining room?"

"I think that I would like to have a tray here in my room tonight," I answered as a sudden wave of weariness engulfed me. Too late, I remembered the house-keeper's acid remarks about extra work, and I hurried to the door to offer a retraction. But my employer had vanished down the hall.

I closed the door, and, shivering a little, hurried over to stand before the fire. I removed my bonnet, looking regretfully at the fine feathers now hanging limp and rain-soaked like the emerald satin ribbon. I gave a fleeting laugh without much humor in it as I imagined the bedraggled appearance I must have presented to my employers. Mrs. Warwick had been scornful of me, that was obvious. But Mr. Warwick had been all kind-ness and solicitude. I hoped with all my heart that I wouldn't disappoint him.

Drawing off my clammy skirt and jacket, I hung them across a chair to dry, then unpacked my old blue robe. I pulled it tightly around my shivering body, unplaited my hair, and sank down on the rug, holding out my hands to the flames with a wearily expelled breath.

When a loud knock sounded at the door, I thought it must be the maid and called, "Come in," feeling eager at the prospect of hot water.

A young girl in a black uniform and long white apron entered. She had a fresh, country face and well-developed figure. Depositing a can of steaming water on the floor, she gave an awkward curtsey and said her name was Annie. Behind her came James with a zinc hipbath and towels. And a large-toothed grin.

Hastily drawing my robe together, I struggled to my feet, wishing I had not taken down my hair just yet when I saw the brash, young man eying it with bold approval.

"Here's the tub for your bath, Miss Nurse. Right by the fire I'll put it and then fetch more hot water. Make your pretty skin grow warm and rosy." His rolling eyes seemed to be savoring a mental picture of it.

"I'll fetch the water, James," Annie told him sharply. "You should get back to the stables."

I wondered what James's function was? Coachman? Footman? Groom? Probably all three. This remote house might be rather understaffed.

"Ah, Annie, it's so cold out there," James protested. "I thought I might sleep somewheres warm tonight." There was such blatant suggestion in his bold black eyes that Annie grew red, mumbled inarticulately, and fled from the room, leaving me alone with the disturbing James.

He crossed his arms and grinned at me. "I guess I better fetch the water. It's too heavy for poor Annie," he said, not moving.

"I want Annie to bring the water," I snapped. "And *only* Annie, do you understand?"

"Ah, now then, don't you like me? Most girls do. I like you real well." He sidled closer and touched the tumbled hair upon my shoulders.

"Get out!" I hissed, leaping out of his reach. "Or I shall report you to the master."

His eyes grew round. "For what? I've just tried bein' friendly." He took a step toward me, but was halted by a stern voice from the doorway.

"What are you doing up here, my man?" Miss Grey, cold of voice and mien, stepped into the room in her long black gown, the household keys jangling at her waistband from a silver chatelaine.

A smirk of mock servility crossed James's face. "Just helping Annie, if you please, ma'am."

"I don't please." The housekeeper glared at him. "I've seen how Annie looks after you've 'helped' her. One of these days you'll be dismissed without a character from me or Master."

James merely laughed and swaggered toward the door. "Who would do my work, then, eh? Don't try to threaten me, Miss Grey."

"Such insolence!" Watching his retreating figure, the housekeeper whispered balefully, "Watch out for that one. He's a bad lot." Her lip curled slightly as she eyed my robe and unbound hair. "Unless you like attentions from such a common person?"

"Not from him or from anyone else," I cried indignantly. "I'm here to care for Miss Harriet. And nothing

45

else."

Miss Grey didn't answer, but she gave a sweeping glance around the lovely room, then, with pursed lips, she turned away, and the door shut smartly after her.

When the water arrived, Annie was alone.

After that, I thrust the big key into the lock and at last relaxed into my tub. Well, I was here. On Brendan's Isle. With things both good and bad. The house was beautiful, my room was perfect. As for the inmates, I dismissed James as someone I could handle. If necessary, I wouldn't hesitate to report any further familiarity. Miss Grey was just a typical housekeeper, jealous of her authority. We would go our separate ways and I would try to trouble her as little as possible.

As for Mrs. Warwick's cold reception, I couldn't feel surprised. As I'd suspected, she had no sympathy for the project. She also had a strange manner around her husband, as though she cared for him too much and would be angry if anyone usurped his attention from herself. But that was none of my affair.

As for Mr. Warwick . . . I smiled a little dreamily. He was even nicer than I'd remembered. A warm, vital, attractive man. I knew I would enjoy my contacts with him and that I could count on him to give me every assistance.

That left Harriet to be assessed. So far, she was the unknown quantity. Just then, as if in answer to my thoughts, a shriek issued from the adjoining room.

Chapter Five

Without stopping to dress, I toweled quickly, flung on my robe, and sped to the room next door. It was unlocked and I burst in, not bothering to knock.

A young girl about twelve years old lay sprawled upon the carpet beside an overturned wheelchair. A plaid skirt was tangled around her knees, and, above a plain, round-necked collar, a childish, frightened face peered at me between strands of long brown hair.

"Well, aren't you going to help me back into that hateful chair?" the girl shrilled, and two tears slid down her cheeks. "You *are* the nurse, aren't you?"

"Yes, lassie, I am Miss MacNeil." I righted the chair, then grasped the girl and hauled her up. "What happened just now?"

"The stupid chair tipped over."

"Chairs are neither stupid nor smart. What made it tip over?"

"I don't know—oh, I guess I turned the steering bar too fast. Why are you pawing at my legs and arms?"

"I see no bumps or bruises. You're all right, Harriet." I stepped back and surveyed my glowering patient with a smile.

"A lot you know! And my name is *Miss* Harriet."

"Oh, we're going to be formal, are we? That's no fun."

"Fun! What's that?" The girl's lip tried to sneer but trembled instead. Instantly she subdued the weakness by tightening her mouth and glaring defiantly. "You might as well not bother to unpack your bags, nurse. You can't do me any good. No one can."

"Who told you that? The doctor? Your parents?"

Harriet didn't answer.

I noticed that she was trembling. Could she be cold? There was a fire in the black marble grate, and heavy, dark red drapery shut out the storm-filled night. But the furniture was big and somber and too gloomy for a young girl's room. I saw books strewn upon the floor and bed, but there were no dolls, toys, or games of any description. Perhaps Harriet was too old for such distractions. If that was so, how did she amuse herself? No companions, a disinterested mother, and a father busy with his writing. She didn't even seem to have a pet.

The poor child's face was filled with a chilled misery. When I saw a paisley shawl beside the chair, I picked it up. "Do you want this across your lap?"

The girl jerked it from my hands. "So you won't have to look at my sick, wasted legs?"

"My job is looking at wasted limbs—among other things. And yours are in no way wasted. Thin, perhaps, but massage should help that. Can you stand? Or move your legs at all?"

"No," Harriet muttered, hooking a long strand of dark brown hair behind her ear.

Now that I had time to observe her closer, I saw that Harriet's face fell somewhere between her father's square-jawed masculinity and her mother's delicate beauty. The girl had large brown eyes and extremely long lashes. Right now, her mouth looked too large for her face, but she had the same full lips as Jared Warwick. When mature, they probably would have the same sensual appeal that his did.

At this stage, her face still had a childish vulnerability, and I felt my heart go out to her. How difficult for a vital young person to be chained to a wheelchair. And already adopting a hopeless attitude. No wonder her father had become so desperate to help her.

I pulled up a brown upholstered armchair and sat down in it, disregarding Harriet's frown. "Your mother seems to think you don't want to walk. That isn't true, is it?"

The girl's voice rose almost hysterically. "Why should I want something I can never have?"

"I'm not deaf. Talk in a reasonable tone or I shall leave."

"Go then! I don't care."

Immediately, I rose and marched toward the door.

"Wait!"

At the hoarse cry, I turned around and found my patient staring at the closet door, a look of abject terror on her face.

The door was slowly opening.

"S-something's in there! I heard it before—the whispering." Harriet's voice was a mere croak.

There was complete silence in the dark red room as both of us fastened our eyes on the yawning aperture. Nothing emerged. I heard the clock tick on the mantelpiece. A gust of wind belled out the drapes, and, in the distance, waves could be heard crashing on the rock-bound shore.

But neither of us spoke or moved, and I realized that Harriet's fear had become contagious. I had to make a concerted effort to expel my breath and step into the closet. Skirts, blouses, and dresses swayed slightly and a chill air seeped from the ceiling-high enclosure. A narrow crack showed at the back, and when I inserted my fingers I encountered a wall of brick. For some reason, ocean waves could be heard quite clearly. That puzzled me, but I put it down to just a trick of architecture.

At any rate, there was nothing, either natural or supernatural, hiding in the closet. "The wind blew the door open." I stated matter-of-factly. "There seems to be a draft coming through the cracks."

"What about the whispering?" Harriet prodded anxiously.

"I didn't hear anything just now. The closet must have been added over the original walls and doesn't fit too tightly. Voices from another area might be audible. Was that why you screamed just before I came in?"

"Not exactly. The chair turned over. I—I heard the voices and got excited." She looked down, plucking at the shawl. "I hate this room."

"Why don't you take another? There must be many empty bedrooms in a house this size."

"Mama moved me down here after the accident so that I'd be easier to care for. She said we couldn't keep Annie, otherwise. Papa's room is on this floor, but in the other wing. Mama is upstairs, where I used to be."

Mr. and Mrs. Warwick seemed to have odd sleeping

50

arrangements. But it was none of my affair. I turned a determinedly bright smile on my patient. "Well, now there are no stairs for you to bother with and you can get outside more often, can't you?"

"I never go out. Annie's too busy to take me, and I won't be left outside alone. I—I'm afraid."

There was something strange here. The child had some very real fears here to contend with, and I must get to the bottom of them if I intended to help her. But I could see that Harriet was a prickly young person, and I would have to feel my way with her.

"Well, now I'm here you'll never be alone," I said cheerfully. "Do you have a cart and pony? We could go for rides around the island, have picnics, sit upon the beach and watch the waves . . . lots of things. How does that appeal to you?"

"I don't know," Harriet answered dully. Her face was half-covered by the long dark hair as she looked down at her twisting fingers. "Nurse, didn't you hear *anything* just now?"

"No, dear, just the storm."

"This wasn't the storm. Other times I've heard voices whispering, chuckling . . ."

"As I said, sounds might have carried from a room above or underneath."

"There are only cellars below and empty rooms above this one."

Was the child indulging in fantasies just to gain attention, as her mother had suggested? Whether or not that might be true, Harriet seemed to have a very real distress that could be damaging to her recovery.

I stood up briskly. "Suppose we get better acquainted over supper? I'll tell Annie to bring my tray in here

51

while I get dressed. Then we can both eat beside the fire and talk about a lot of things. I've been watching the building of the Crystal Palace. That's the main building of the Great Exhibition opening May First in Hyde Park. Wouldn't you like to hear about that?"

"Why should I? I can never see it."

"Oh, pooh, you don't know that. I read there will be invalid ramps built for handicapped people."

"I don't want to be one of the handicapped people." The girl's voice rose and cracked despairingly.

I looked back over my shoulder, one hand on the china doorknob. "Good for you! Then we must get to work. Exercises and determination can do wonders. You'll see." Nodding briskly, I hurried from the room.

However, while I donned a warm, peacock-blue alpaca and brushed my hair, some of my determined optimism faded. I didn't really know yet if there was any permanent damage to Harriet's limbs, but I had often found that people's attitude had a great influence on their well-being, and that might be part of Harriet's problem. Besides despair over her condition, she was frightened by something else, which puzzled me. A hard road might stretch ahead for both of us.

I decided, however, not to be discouraged at this early stage and pinned a bright smile on my face when I reentered my patient's room.

A little table filled with supper dishes had been placed before the fire, and I was delighted to observe mutton cutlets with sauce piquante, oyster patties, and various side dishes of vegetables and savories, all prepared by some skilled hand. There might be a servant problem on the island, but at least the Warwicks were lucky in their cook.

52

While we ate, I soon discovered that Harriet *did* have an interest in the Crystal Palace. She demanded to know all about it.

"They had to build a fence around the grounds," I told her, "and, like all the other sidewalk spectators, at every opportunity I put my eye to a knothole to observe the progress. It began to bother the workers so they started charging everyone five shillings for a look."

When I paused to sip some golden wine, Harriet prodded me impatiently. "Well, go on, what did you see after paying all that money?"

"Oh, I saw a building three times the size of St. Paul's Cathedral. A fairyland of glass covering nineteen acres. The Crystal Palace even enclosed several giant trees, and a horde of sparrows took up living quarters there. Naturally, they had to be chased out, but how do you suppose they did it?"

Nibbling on a slice of bread, Harriet considered the matter. "They couldn't shoot them because of all the glass. And bird droppings would fall on the expensive exhibits if they were allowed to remain. I give up. What did they do?"

"Well, the queen asked the Duke of Wellington for a solution. After all, he had solved many a crisis during his war career. And in his curt, astute way, he gave his answer: 'Try sparrow-hawks, ma'am.'"

Harriet was round-eyed. "And did that work?"

"Well, it was the strangest thing. Almost as though the birds had received some kind of message, the next day, after the duke's visit, all the sparrows flew out the door and never returned again."

"Is that the truth?"

I chuckled. "That's the story they printed in the

Times. Now, wouldn't you like to see the Great Exhibition? There will be marvelous things from every country in the world. Treasures from the East, an ivory throne from India, jeweled swords, statues made of bronze with colored water bubbling at their feet. Choruses singing and bands playing, and the queen riding by each day. Doesn't it sound exciting?"

Harriet sat up straighter. "Yes," she said imperiously, "I want to go. Nurse, ask my father if there is some way he can take me."

"Why don't you speak to him yourself?"

"I think he might listen better if *you* asked him. He thinks a lot of you. He told us all about the night you saved his life."

"Did he?" I felt a rush of pleasure.

"Yes. It scared me." The light suddenly went out of Harriet's thin face and she slumped back in her chair. Mention of her father's brush with death had made her retreat once more into a frightened shell. She said that she was tired and jerked the bell-pull for her maid, declining any assistance from me with all her former curtness.

Smothering a sigh, I said goodnight, telling myself that Harriet was just a child, spoiled perhaps, and certainly neglected. I would have to feel my way into her confidence and just be patient.

I went back to my room, where the coals were still winking warmly in the grate, the lamplight shedding soft golden radiance around the emerald room. The house was quiet, with only a diminished pattering of the rain. If the next day dawned clear, perhaps I could take my patient for an airing.

The bed looked most inviting as I began my nightly

54

preparations, taking down my hair and undoing the buttons of my dress. In the midst of this, I was startled by a knocking at my door.

"Who's there?" I called, hurrying across the thick green carpet.

"Jared Warwick," came the answer.

What could he want? Quickly, I flung open the door, one hand clutching at the opening of my dress.

For a moment he just stared silently, and I realized his eyes were on my hair. "Too bad you don't always wear it down like that," he murmured. "It's like a copper fire."

He had said something like that once before, winding his strong hand in my tresses so that I couldn't take my mouth from his. The memory sent a wave of crimson heat washing over me, and I shrank back, trembling violently. Why had Jared Warwick come to me this late? Had Octavia been right, after all, in her suspicion about his motives?

But my silly fears were quite short-lived. Mr. Warwick's features were once again cool and his tones businesslike. "I beg your pardon for disturbing you, Miss MacNeil, but I was so anxious to hear your opinion of my daughter. Would it be too much of an imposition for me to ask you to come to the library for a few minutes?"

"No, no, of course not," I managed to stutter as I fumbled with my buttons, feeling like a fool for the ridiculous fancy in which I'd just indulged. "I—I'll be just a moment."

He nodded silently and turned upon his heel.

I shut the door and quickly bundled my hair into a knitted snood. I glanced into the mirror as I buttoned up my dress, relieved to see that I looked once more calm and neat and not like some hoyden with tumbled hair and a gown displaying a bare chest. I had to acknowledge that after that first involuntary remark of Mr. Warwick's, he had reverted to the perfect gentleman he was. At least he was a gentleman in his lucid moments, I amended.

I didn't wish to keep him waiting and sped into the hall so fast I almost collided with Miss Grey, who was evidently making her last rounds.

She looked at me suspiciously. "I thought you would be in bed by this time, nurse."

"Mr. Warwick wishes to have a word with me in the library concerning his daughter."

"Indeed? Well, lock your door when you retire. James is sleeping on a pallet in the kitchen tonight. His room over the stable leaks during storms. Or so he says."

"If he is worrisome, why doesn't Mr. Warwick replace him?"

"You heard what James said. It's hard to get help on this island. Haven't you noticed how shorthanded we are? Two maids, a cook, James, two stable boys, and myself. Fortunately, we acquired a new gardener soon after Miss Harriet's accident. She is quite a lot of extra work these days. And now you're here." The thin brows drew together. "Do you intend to eat in your room from now on as you did tonight?"

"No, I will come to the dining room. Perhaps I can encourage Harriet to join me."

"I think you must be quite adept at *encouragement*, Miss MacNeil," the housekeeper said with peculiar emphasis. She stepped aside and proceeded down the hall.

I watched her with a surge of indignation. Did Miss Grey think I had encouraged James?

Then I had another thought: Perhaps Miss Grey meant Jared Warwick.

Chapter Six

As a result of my encounter with the housekeeper, I felt decidedly uneasy when I entered the library to meet my employer.

But I needn't have worried. Jared Warwick didn't even turn his head when I came in. He stood by the fireplace, his eyes bent upon some evidently perplexing vision as he gazed into the flames. A pipe was clenched between his teeth, and when I spoke his name he merely glanced at me as though his thoughts were far away.

Before our conversation could begin, Mrs. Warwick burst into the room, exclaiming in a high, petulant voice that made me jump. "So here you are, Jared. And the nurse, too. How very cozy! Weren't you about ready to retire, Miss MacNeil?"

It's evident that *you* were, I could have said. Mrs. Warwick's hair had been brushed out of its ringlets and fell in a dark cloud around her shoulders, a purple violet ribbon tied above the perfect oval face. She wore a trailing *robe de nuit* of velvet satin edged with creamy lace, form-fitting and low-necked. She stared at me until I answered her.

"Your husband wished to have a word with me regarding my impression of his daughter."

"That's right," Mr. Warwick said. "Please be seated, nurse. You also, Katherine, since you're here. Now, Miss MacNeil, have you formed any opinions about Harriet's condition?"

I shook my head. "Not yet. Until I speak with the doctor, I can't estimate the damage. Her legs are thin but not as wasted as I expected. However, the child's attitude is poor. She seems depressed and hopeless. If the doctor says there is the slightest chance of her recovery, she must be given every encouragement to walk." I looked directly at the wife. "By all of us."

The great blue eyes took fire as Mrs. Warwick sprang to her feet. "For the love of heaven, nurse, what are you insinuating? I certainly want her to walk. In a few short years, Harriet will be of marriageable age, and, if she remains as she is now, who will want a cranky, wasp-faced invalid? We would be saddled with her for life."

I couldn't speak after this appallingly callous statement. Almost imploringly, I transferred my gaze to Jared Warwick.

Wearily, he rubbed his hand along the back of his neck. "So much of all this is our fault, Miss MacNeil. You see, Harriet overheard my wife and me during an argument. I was saying that I would have liked a son, but now —"

" — now I will have no more children. Once was quite enough. Another time and my figure might be completely ruined." Katherine Warwick drew a deep, proud breath, the violet satin taut across her perfect body.

Her husband eyed her coldly. "So Harriet decided to ride my horse, Black Bob. She was thrown trying to prove that she was as good as any boy." He passed his hand across his eyes. "Poor child . . ."

"Perhaps if you spent more time with her and less time writing in your locked room, Harriet might have accepted and enjoyed her femininity," his wife snapped.

Her husband didn't answer her. Instead he looked at me. "You see the difficulties that lie ahead?"

"The nurse is paid to handle difficulties. That's what she's here for, isn't she?" Mrs. Warwick turned her back on me. "Dearest God, we've been over and over this business of Harriett's *attitude* a dozen times. I'm sick of the subject, Jared."

Suddenly, she sidled closer to him with a taunting glance. "Are you coming upstairs to say goodnight, my *dearest husband*?"

With a cynical, hard smile, he shook his head.

Mrs. Warwick flounced away without another word, her draperies shimmering around her, while Mr. Warwick watched her with an odd expression on his face. After she had gone, violet perfume lingered on the air like a ghostly presence.

From my corner of the brocade couch, I observed my employer with covert curiosity. Tonight the grooves beside his mouth were deep and taut. He and his wife seemed to have a very strange relationship as though they constantly fought some kind of duel. But was it love or hate? Was he resentful of the selfishness she showed toward their only child and of her refusal to have another one? Perhaps that explained the bedrooms on separate floors.

Suddenly, I felt his eyes on me, and when he spoke I realized his thoughts were solely on the child. "It must have been a lonely life for Harriet in many ways," he said slowly, coming to sit beside me on the couch. "Even though I think she enjoyed her boarding school on the mainland, she was left to her own devices here on the island. My wife . . . had other matters on her mind, while my only excuse is that I've been away from home a great deal lately. But now that my research is almost finished, I can stay on Brendan's Isle and complete my book."

I opened my mouth to ask about the nature of his writing, but he went on speaking quickly. "It grows late and you must be tired. Tell me about the evening you just spent with my daughter."

Briefly, I did as he requested. He didn't seem surprised when I mentioned Harriet's terror of the noises in her room. He only shook his head when I told him about the closet door.

"Mr. Warwick, they are very real fears to her," I insisted. "And, although it must have been vibration from the storm, I did see the door swing out."

With a little sigh, he looked down at the gold brocade separating us on the couch. I was very conscious of his nearness. Tonight he wore a dark red smoking jacket over a carelessly unbuttoned white silk shirt that gave a glimpse of black hair curling on his chest. He wore his clothes with a casual indifference, but I could see they were of fine material and perfectly fitted to his strong and virile frame. A little heat rose in my face as I recalled the night when I had bathed his naked back, feeling such compassion for his suffering, even while I noticed the fine-grained skin and the rippling muscles in his well-proportioned body.

I gave a guilty start when I realized how my thoughts had strayed to my employer's masculinity instead of listening to his discussion of Harriet's problem. Which was the only reason I was here.

"My daughter's fears are a part of her suddenly becoming helpless," Mr. Warwick was saying to me now. "She was a very active, lively girl before the accident. Miss MacNeil . . ." He moved a little closer, his black eyes intent on my face. "I'm counting on you to restore that spirit she has lost."

I bit my lip and had to look away. "Mr. Warwick, you — you ask a lot of me."

"Only because I have the greatest faith in you."

"Well . . . I certainly will try my best."

"I know you will. Now, I have another request. I would like you to go horseback riding with me tomorrow morning."

"Tomorrow?" I faltered. "But shouldn't I be with Harriet? Didn't you say the doctor might be coming?"

"Yes, the doctor will be here. There are also some houseguests of my wife's arriving tomorrow to stay for several days. Our time for discussion will henceforth be limited. So, after the doctor's visit, please meet me at the stables. I wish to acquaint you with the island. You do ride, don't you?"

"Yes, but I haven't for a long time. And I'm afraid I didn't bring a riding habit."

He gave an impatient gesture and stood up. "Any sensible skirt and jacket will do fine. We're not going on a steeplechase."

"Very well," I murmured, wishing that all my clothes

weren't "sensible."

He went to stand before the fire, staring silently at the greying ashes. Only an occasional red wink like a tiny star proclaimed the presence of the dying fire.

The room was getting cold, and I was weary. I rose and said, "If there is nothing more, Mr. Warwick . . . ?"

He glanced at me and pointed downward to the grate. "Look, that is you. A red-gold spark burning bravely in the greyness of our lives."

"You are fanciful, Mr. Warwick," I said with a short laugh. "I am neither like a spark nor always brave."

"My dear girl, must you be so literal and practical?"

"I fear my life has made me so. Besides, I am a cautious Scot."

"Except for the night you took me into your home."

I flushed and gave a little smile. "Well, Scots are also known for sponsoring lost causes. There was Bonnie Prince Charlie . . . and Mary, Queen of Scots. . . ."

"And a little girl who cannot walk?"

I nodded, and our eyes clung in a surge of mutual sympathy. He put out his hand and raised my palm up to his lips, giving me not the polite, conventional kiss upon the back of the hand but a deep, warm pressure where my skin was soft and sensitive.

A charge like lightning darted through me, strangely pleasant. I heard him say, "Goodnight, my dear."

I'll still never know whether I answered him or not.

Chapter Seven

When daylight woke me the next day, the night before seemed greatly exaggerated in my mind. I had talked with my employer, and, at the end, he had given me a warm kiss upon the hand — probably to ensure my cooperation. I shoved my own reaction firmly from my thoughts.

Since the day was fine, I knew the doctor would be coming to examine Harriet, so I hurried through my dressing, ate a quick breakfast by myself, and went to join my patient.

I found the doctor already in the room. Benjamin Korman was a nattily dressed man from the mainland. He wore a double-breasted frock coat trimmed with braid, a pleated shirt, and a satin waistcoat striped in blue and mauve. He had an air of self-importance, as though an office full of demanding patients waited impatiently somewhere for his distinctive services.

He greeted me pleasantly enough, however, and then proceeded to examine Harriet, who lay prone upon her back in bed, scowling fiercely, a nightgown covering her body. The doctor poked and prodded, flexed and tugged, while I watched curiously and Harriet muttered underneath her breath.

Finally, Dr. Korman lifted Harriet from the bed and attempted to stand her on her feet. She promptly collapsed into his arms. "I told you I can't walk," she howled. "I never will again!"

Dr. Korman returned his patient to her bed and flung the covers over her. Then he beckoned me to the window out of earshot. "I must admit I'm baffled, nurse. I have informed the parents repeatedly that there is absolutely no visible damage to Miss Harriet's limbs. At no time were there any broken bones or bleeding. She was flung over the horse's head and tumbled to the beach. I believe she was in the water, unconscious, up to her waist for quite some time, but, fortunately, the tide was going out when one of the local fishermen found her."

He fingered his neatly trimmed goatee. "If only we could see beneath the skin of a living person to determine if nerves or muscles received damage. However, such damage probably would have been healed after six months of immobility." He shook his head and sighed, the picture of perplexity.

"Perhaps we could try hot baths, massage, and moderate outdoor excursions?" I suggested carefully. "I received instructions at the hospital in London."

"At least it could do no harm." He nodded slowly. "You have my permission, nurse."

He turned back to his patient, picking up a pearl-grey stovepipe hat, jovial now that he was leaving. "Well, missy, I would say you are no worse, at any rate. Follow Nurse MacNeil's advice, and I will call again next month, when I hope to find you greatly improved. Now, I will just have a word with your father in the library."

After he had departed to collect his fee, I turned back to Harriet and found her gazing stonily at the dark red canopy above her bed. "I told you so. Nothing will do me any good."

"We haven't tried everything yet, my girl. Look what a nice day it is." I stepped to the windows, leaning on the sill, and inhaled the fragrance of green grass, lilacs coming into flower, and the tang of salty sea air. The rear of the house had a large area of cultivated gardens enclosed by a stone wall.

"Wouldn't you like to go for a ride in a pony cart, or your wheelchair? Just smell the flowers and the sea . . . and you can hear the birds." I looked back eagerly at Harriet, then went to stand beside her bed.

She hitched herself up to lean upon her elbow and gazed wistfully at the view of trees and azure sky. "Well . . . maybe we could go out for a little while. But you would have to go with me, nurse. I won't be left alone for a single minute, you know." She looked up at me with the same dark intentness as her father.

"Of course, I'll stay with you," I said. "But there's something I must do first. I promised to go riding with your father after the doctor's visit."

Harriet's face clouded. "Whatever for?"

"He wants to show me the island so I'll know my way around."

"He wants to talk about me in secret, you mean."

"Naturally he's concerned about you."

"He—he just feels bad because—because—" Harriet's lip trembled and she blinked rapidly. "It was all

66

his fault, you know. Wishing he had a boy—"

"Let's not talk about blame or guilt or indulge in any self-pity, lassie. That's a complete waste of time. Now, this is what we'll do. You have a warm bath here and I'll tell Annie how to move your legs. After a short ride with your father, I'll be back, and then it will be time for your own outing. How does that sound?"

"I want you to stay with me, nurse. That's your job. Not gallivanting around with Papa."

"I'm not gallivanting. I'm obeying my employer's orders, that's all." Forestalling any further argument, I swept out the door.

I found Annie, gave her my instructions, then went to my room to change, since I had been wearing a cambric dress and apron for the doctor's visit. How I longed for a regular riding outfit, a fashionably draped black skirt and a top hat sporting a long veil, like the ladies wore cantering on Rotten Row in London. But there was nothing for me but to don my old brown serge and tuck my hair into a snood with a few more hairpins to secure unruly curls.

When I stepped outside, I paused to listen with delight to the gulls calling to each other and the waves dashing on the beach, which had to be right below. The water sounded much less noisy than last night, and I decided the sunny day would do Harriet a world of good. The garden here was sheltered from the wind, with brick paths, trees, and flower beds just coming into bloom.

On closer inspection, however, I saw that the plots were overgrown with weeds and untrimmed growth. Just as I was wondering if the servant problem had affected the outdoors as well, I spied a man working among the plants, albeit in a rather haphazard fashion.

I approached him and inquired the way to the stables. He was thin and sharp-faced, with an accent more likely to be found in London's seedier districts than on this southern coast. He said his name was Bascom, and, though polite enough, something in his intense scrutiny made me as uneasy as James's frankly bold appraisal. He also seemed to know me.

"Coo, so you're the nurse? A young one, eh?" He fingered his pointed chin.

"The stables?" I repeated.

"Right, miss. Easy as one-two-three. Just stay on this 'ere path and you can't miss 'em. Just beyond the greenhouse see?"

I turned my head and glimpsed a flash of light striking on panes of glass beyond the trees. "Is that where the orchids grow?"

"Right you are, and a lot o' ruddy nonsense, I calls it. Growin' jungle flowers in a bubble made o' glass. Blimey, the master could be doin' somethin' better with 'is time, says I."

I felt like saying, "No one asked you," but I held my peace and continued on my way, approaching the greenhouse with great curiosity. I found it to be a beautiful little building made something like the Crystal Palace, with wrought iron bands curving gracefully to hold the panes of glass. The dome was fashioned in the manner of a Turkish mosque.

I stepped closer, shielding my eyes as I peered inside at the dim interior. It seemed to be crowded with thick-fleshed, leafy plants. Trailing ferns covered mossy banks, with little paths of bark winding in and out. From tall, rough-trunked trees hung bunches of tiny orchids in shades of pink and lavender. There was a hushed, steamy atmosphere beyond the glass, unnatural in its parasitic growth. I almost expected to see a vicious jungle snake glide out between the pots of heavy purple flowers drooping on the ground.

It was strange that Katherine Warwick should want to pluck these big, bold blooms, which must be so rare and difficult to grow. Perhaps Katherine was somewhat like the orchids herself. A beautiful, exotic-looking creature, who wanted a pampered, indulgent life untroubled by anything as complicated as an invalid child. She didn't even work among the orchids, probably, but left that for her husband, then she plundered the spoils to feed her vanity.

Abruptly, I reared back from the glass, chiding myself. I was as bad as Bascom, criticizing my employers. I tore my gaze away from the unpleasant, sprawling growth. It was making me too fanciful.

I drew a deep, reviving breath of sea air and headed briskly in the direction of the stables, my spirits rising at the thought of riding out with Jared Warwick.

Chapter Eight

Upon leaving the walled-in garden, I found myself in a completely different terrain. On the cliff side, the land dropped steeply, covered by a dense thicket of bushes almost to the water's edge. The wind blew strongly, whipping my clothes against my body and loosening strands of my hair. Leaning over, I stared at the cove far below, which contained a small, rough beach, a place of jagged rocks where spume was flung like fountains by the blue-green waves. It was a fierce, wild place, reminiscent of the Scottish coasts I'd known, with their crystal-clean, cold strength.

My jacket opened as I stretched my arms and inhaled great lungfuls of the invigorating air. How glad I was that my firm body needed no restriction from a corset, as was the common mode. Those whalebone prisons would make it impossible ever to draw more than a shallow breath of air.

Suddenly, I heard a footfall and a shadow seemed to touch my face. My eyes flew open and I beheld James standing at my side, a few scant feet away.

As usual, he was grinning, his bold eyes devouring me with frank enjoyment as the wind drew my garments taut against my curves. He wagged his head. "Ah, Miss Nurse, what a prime, full-figured lass you are, to be sure. 'Tis plain I would enjoy knowing you much better."

I fell back, jerking my jacket closed and glaring at the cheeky, red-lipped face with its gloss of common handsomeness. "You are impudent, young man," I snapped. "And had better watch your step. I'll not tolerate such remarks about my person!"

"Naw, then, I meant no harm. 'Tis just that I like what I see." Abruptly, the wheedling note vanished from his voice, and he cleared his throat as his head jerked sideways. "Here comes Master with the horses."

Thankfully, I hurried toward my employer. Since Jared was already in the saddle, I could not refuse James's help in mounting a pretty, sorrel mare. However, as he raised my foot, the young devil slyly pressed my leg above the low, half-boot I wore.

Without compunction, I kicked out smartly, catching him on the arm.

"Ow," he cried. "Watch out." He sprang out of the way as I deftly turned the horse.

Jared moved up beside me. "Is everything all right? Are you nervous, Miss MacNeil? I can vouch for Pretty Nell. She is a gentle, good-natured lady."

"More so than some other ladies I could mention," James muttered, though an irrepressible grin tugged at his lips.

Ignoring this, I answered quickly, "I'm quite ready, Mr. Warwick. But I must say your own mount seems a little nervous."

The black stallion was stepping high, like a temperamental dancer, with rolling eyes and tossing head. Jared spoke firmly to the beast and rode him in a tight circle. In a few minutes, the animal seemed slightly calmer.

Jared patted the sleek neck. "This is Black Bob. A rather high strung beast, I'm afraid. "Yes," he said, looking at me levelly. "This is the horse that Harriet tried to ride."

I couldn't help the shocked exclamation that burst from my lips. "How terrible! And the cliff here is so high. It's a wonder the child wasn't killed."

"Oh, the place she fell from wasn't nearly as high as this. Farther on, the path winds down the hill right to the beach. Come, we'll go there so you can see it."

Today Jared wore black breeches and a white, full-sleeved shirt beneath a leather vest. He looked younger and much more relaxed this morning as we started off along the sun-dappled path.

Perfectly at ease, we discussed the doctor's visit, and I told him of my plans for helping Harriet. "I would like to take her on excursions around the island, either in a pony cart or her wheelchair. I think she should stop huddling in her room."

"I agree." Some of the light faded from his face, and he frowned. "She almost seems *afraid* to leave the house."

"Weather like this would be good for her," I pronounced emphatically. "We could have a picnic, perhaps, with a rug for her to sit on and a book to read." I gave a sigh of pleasure as I glanced around. "This would be a delightful spot to bring her."

We were trotting side by side beneath an avenue of

trees with a meadow stretching out beyond, lush and green in its new spring growth. Millions of tiny flowers starred the grass: yellow cat's ear, wild iris in shades of lavender and gold, the purple-pink of foxglove. Around the sides grew leafy bushes, interspersed amid low rocks. The path wandered toward a rise of ground, so that here in the hollow it was warm and protected from sea winds.

"I told you the island would be beautiful this time of year." Jared Warwick turned to smile. But suddenly, Black Bob grew restless, tossing his harness and stepping high again.

I eyed the beast uneasily. "Are we approaching the spot where your horse threw Harriet? Perhaps he remembers—"

"No, we're not there yet. Bob does seem strangely skittish today. He probably doesn't get enough exercise since I've been concentrating on my book. I think I should let him out for a short gallop. Will you be all right if I leave you for a few minutes? Unless you care to join us—"

"No, thank you. I haven't ridden for some time, and I feel a little rusty. I prefer a calmer gait, so I'll wait right here for your return."

Jared nodded and touched the sleek black body with his heels. "Go, Black Bob, go!" It was all the eager animal required. With a great bound, he was off, and Jared waved his hand boyishly above his head. I had a notion he would enjoy the race as much as the horse. They vanished around a curve of trees, and soon all that could be heard was the thudding of receding hooves. Then even that sound faded in the distance.

I slid down from my horse after a few minutes, looping the reins around a limb. Then I crossed to the edge of the cliff, where the ocean stretched to the horizon, sparkling with a million diamond chips of light. A few fishing boats bobbed on the surface, their sails belling in the breeze. I waved to them, not knowing if they could even see me.

Large rocks lined the bluff's edge, and I sank down with my back against a sun-warmed crag. Below was a narrow beach covered with jagged stones thrusting like upraised hands out of the rolling waves. It would be an interesting place to explore — the shoreline of this island. It was just as Jared had described it: a place of peace and beauty side by side with the perilous and rugged.

Thinking of Jared, it suddenly seemed to me that he had been gone a longer time than he had indicated he would be. I rose and stretched, shading my eyes as I gazed back along the road. There was no sign of horse or rider. And no echo of returning hooves.

But then I heard another sound. A scattering of rocks, as though something moved below the cliff. I leaned far over the cliff's edge, but could see no one.

"Hello," I called. "Is anybody there?" No one answered. Only a stone clattered downward, bounding into the sea as it cleared the bushes that screened the hillside.

I turned away, sudden fear engulfing me. Had something happened to Jared? Had Black Bob thrown another rider? Perhaps his master was now lying somewhere, unconscious at the bottom of a cliff.

I was astonished at the rush of pain as my heart began to pound against my ribs. I clenched my hands. Dear heaven, how could I find him? I didn't know the island. But I could follow the direction he had taken, I reasoned, forcing order into my frightened thoughts. Maybe I would just discover him resting his horse somewhere in the shade.

But I still felt apprehensive as I ran back to Nell and scrambled into the saddle as best I could without a block to mount or someone to help me. Immediately, I put the horse into a gallop, speeding along the path that Jared had taken. We were soon going at a terrific pace, and, uneasily, I began to draw back on the reins, still a little unsure of my riding skill. But the horse had got the bit into her teeth, and her pace continued unabated even when I pulled with every ounce of strength at my command. Pretty Nell was riding out of control, a gleeful rebel when she discovered an uncertain rider on her back.

Trees flew past in a dizzy blur. Wind whipped my hair loose from its snood and it streamed across my vision like a copper-colored haze. Now I couldn't even see the road! Abandoning all attempts to halt the excited animal, I leaned forward, twining my fingers in the horse's mane and clinging desperately with all my might.

Finally, I felt the path dip downward, and Nell came to a scrabbling, sliding halt that almost flung me from the saddle, it was so unexpected. My knee was firmly hooked around the pommel, however, and my hands, grown strong from nursing, had a frozen grip that kept me in the seat. A spray of salt came on the breeze, and, with a shuddering gasp, I brushed the hair out of my eyes.

Nell had stopped on the very edge of a cliff.

For a moment, I could only cling, trembling, in the

saddle, trying to regain my breath and wits. Thank goodness, I hadn't been thrown! I climbed down stiffly and noted a rocky path winding downward toward the sea, about fifty feet or so above the beach. Why had Pretty Nell halted instead of plunging down the trail?

Then I heard it.

A low moan came from somewhere on the twisting path ahead. I stumbled forward, past encroaching bushes, dodging beneath overhanging rocks and wind-gnarled trees, until, around a hidden curve, I found him. Sprawled upon the ground, unconscious.

"Jared," I screamed, running to his side and falling upon my knees. Blood trailed down his temple in a thin red line. For an instant, my heart seemed to freeze and stop in its frantic beating.

Hands shaking, I felt his heart. Thank God, he was alive! I pressed exploring fingers down his arms and legs. There were no broken bones and no other bleeding beyond the cut on his head. Springing up, I ran to a tide pool trapped among the rocks and dipped the handkerchief I never was without into the cold salt water.

When I applied it to his temple, Jared's eyes flew open. "Hello, Margaret," he said in normal tones. "Are you rescuing me again?"

He attempted to sit up, but I placed a restraining hand upon his chest. "Wait—do you feel sick or dizzy?" He shook his head. I examined the pupils of each eye. There was no dilation, neither was there any bleeding from ears or nose.

"All right, you don't show any symptoms of concussion." Placing an arm around his shoulders, I drew him into a sitting position, propping myself against a rock so I could hold him.

I dabbed my handkerchief at the cut in his forehead. "What happened? I don't see Black Bob anywhere. Did he throw you and then bolt?"

Jared made no move to leave my supporting arm, and I became very much aware of the heavy shoulder pressing into mine, the rough, black head inches from my own, the masculine aroma of soap and horse and sun-warmed skin.

"Black Bob shied. A stone hit him," Jared answered.

"A—stone? It just fell on him?" I glanced uncomprehendingly at the overhanging rocks.

"Perhaps." His thick-lashed black eyes narrowed at me. "Did you see anyone about?"

"N-no." Before I thought, my arm tightened across his back. "Do you think someone could have thrown a stone on purpose? Dear God, *who*?"

"Don't look so frightened." His voice deepened. "No one will hurt you. I promise that."

"It's you, isn't it?" I whispered as a thought struck me. "Someone is after *you*. Why? *Who is it?*"

He pulled away and struggled to his feet, drawing a deep breath as he stared at the sea. A frown sharpened his rugged features, the momentary warmth completely vanishing. "I don't know the answers," he threw out savagely. "I wish to God I did."

"Has this something to do with your being stabbed? I think you should tell me what is happening here—"

"No, I can't. Sometimes it's safer not to know too much. Besides, it's still not clear to me. Not yet."

He avoided my detaining hand and slithered down the rocky path to the beach, whistling shrilly. "Where can that confounded horse have gone?"

I hurried after him. "Are you sure you are all right, Ja—I mean, Mr. Warwick?"

"Of course, I'm all right," he returned impatiently, looking up and down the shore. "I guess Bob returned to the stables. There's another path farther along the beach, a shortcut that leads back to the stables and the house."

I followed the direction of his gaze, holding back my flying hair and billowing brown skirt. "When I was waiting for you, I heard a sound like sliding rocks. Someone climbing through the shortcut might have made that sound. Or—an animal. I called, but no one answered."

"You didn't see anything?"

I shook my head. "It could have been a villager, I suppose."

"Perhaps." His face looked closed.

Jared, why won't you confide in me? I moaned inwardly. I felt a slight surprise that, in my thoughts, Mr. Warwick had lately become Jared. I noticed that he had called me Margaret when he'd first opened his eyes. It had had a pleasant, almost caressing sound when uttered in his husky voice.

He turned to look at me now with half-shut eyes. "We will have to go back together, on your horse."

My face grew warm at the picture that created, and I turned away with a forced laugh on my lips. "Poor Nell. What a load for her."

"It can't be helped. I don't feel up to walking." He glanced down at his hands. "You may have to hold the reins." His palms were lacerated with long, red streaks and shredded skin where he had fallen heavily on the sharp stones of the path.

"Oh, you've cut them dreadfully," I exclaimed. "Here, put your hands in the tide pool and I'll bathe them with my handkerchief."

He attempted to unbutton his cuffs, but I came swiftly to his aid. Then I rolled the sleeves up to his elbows and we both knelt on the rocks above the pool. He winced at the touch of salt on his sore palms.

"I know it hurts," I said, "but salt will both cleanse and heal."

"I trust your judgment, Margaret. By the way, do you mind my calling you by your first name? It's how I always think of you, and it seems more natural, somehow."

My hand that was holding his above the pool suddenly trembled. "No, I — I don't mind . . . except . . ."

What would Katherine Warwick think of such familiarity? I knew full well that the entire household would disapprove of this sign of favor from my employer.

"Don't worry," he said, reading my thoughts. "In front of others you will still be Miss MacNeil. The very proper Miss MacNeil."

He withdrew his hands and rose. I stood also, alerted by the suddenly grim light in his face. "I want you to be on your guard, Margaret, at all times. I know that I have an enemy, but, truthfully, I do not know his name. More than that I cannot tell you. Now, we must be getting back."

He started up the path. "Let's hope that Pretty Nell hasn't run off like that wretched Bob. I think I'll have to sell that horse. He's getting unpredictable."

We found the mare peacefully cropping grass in the meadow, and she made no protest when I mounted her from a nearby rock and Jared climbed up behind. He settled his tall body rather close to mine, his arms clasping me snugly around the waist. In this manner, we started back to the house, letting the horse set her own pace.

I was aghast at my reaction to Jared's closeness and had to fight to calm my rapid breathing. Our bodies swayed together constantly. His body felt hard and muscled, with a kind of sun-warmed comfort, pressing close against my back and waist. I had never been so conscious of a man's body in my life. It was quite a while before I could steady my voice enough to say, "Harriet will wonder where we are. I told her that I would be gone just a little while."

"Oh, I'm sure our houseguests arrived long ago, and the excitement has undoubtedly distracted Harriet," Jared said. "Lady Sylvia always makes quite a fuss over my daughter — at least, at first."

"Lady Sylvia? Is she one of the guests?"

"Yes, a new friend of Katherine's whom she met last year in London at some affair or other." He gave a short, hard laugh. "If Katherine doesn't have these occasional house parties, she swears her life would be unbearable. She wants to live in London, but I abhor the place. Such a move will only happen when I am dead and buried."

An appalling thought made my body jerk. Could *Katherine Warwick* be responsible for the attempts on her husband's life? Was she that anxious to be free?

I thrust the terrible idea out of my mind. Why, his wife usually acted as though she adored her husband, didn't she? He was the one who seemed unresponsive.

Was that why he was treating me so warmly? I felt a

little riffle of fear that was not untinged with a strange excitement.

At that very moment, he lowered his head so that the curling strands of my red hair blew across his face. "It's like a fire blazing in the sunshine," he murmured, "and smells like clover blossoms."

Alarmed by his words as well as by my own thoughts, I sat up straighter. Jared gave a smothered laugh.

"Don't try to move away from me just now, my dear. You have no place to go."

Chapter Nine

The remainder of the ride progressed in comparative silence until we reentered the manor house from the garden door.

"It sounds as though your houseguests have arrived," I said, hearing several unfamiliar voices, male and female, coming from a room somewhere near the front of the house.

Jared halted abruptly. He looked down at his scraped hands and torn shirt and shrugged. "I must make myself presentable. Have you got something to put on these cuts?"

"Yes, I'll bring bandages and ointment to your room in just a minute." I raised my eyes to his. "You might have been hurt much worse, you know. *Do* you think someone deliberately startled your horse?"

"Who knows?" he answered flatly and turned away toward the other wing. "Oh, by the way, my room is the last one in this corridor." He stopped to point out his door to me so I would know where to find him.

Back in my own room, I washed my hands and face

and rewound my hair up in its chignon. I returned to Jared's room wearing a fresh white blouse and a dark blue linen skirt. His door was ajar, and he was in the process of selecting a clean shirt from a bureau drawer.

"Oh, pardon me." I stepped back, a little flustered by the sight of his large male torso completely bare above the waist.

He faced me calmly, the shirt dangling from his hand. A wicked light stole into his eyes. "I thought a nurse was used to viewing the uncovered human body. You are as red as a peony."

"I nurse women, not men." I forced my glance to meet his own with calmness.

"Do you wish to wait in the hall outside until I am properly covered?" There was laughter in his voice and a disturbing sensuality in his casual, unembarrassed stance.

I cursed my own white skin that flushed so easily, so betrayingly, but I tilted my chin and answered steadily, "I assure you, Mr. Warwick, the sight of your bared chest is not about to make me swoon. I attended you before without your shirt, if you remember. And, as you just reminded me, I am a nurse. Do you need help with the buttons?"

"Yes, please," he answered with deceptive meekness. "Margaret, your reactions are delicious." He chuckled deeply.

I didn't ask him what he meant. I buttoned his shirt and bathed his hands, smoothing on a soothing balm and then fastening clean strips of cloth around the palms.

"The competent nurse has emerged once more, cool and professional." Jared smiled at me, then flexed his fingers. "That should be fine. I can eat and even hold a pen. But before I indulge in either activity, I suppose I must exchange a few pleasantries with my wife's guests."

He folded a black silk cloth around his neck and I helped him pull on a morning coat of pearl-grey broadcloth.

"Thank you, Margaret. If ever you give up nursing, you could be an admirable ladies' maid—or valet." He grinned at me.

I didn't return his smile as I stared up gravely into his face. "I only wish . . ."

He quirked an eyebrow. "What do you wish, Margaret MacNeil?"

"Only that you would be extra careful from now on in everything you do."

"That's good advice," he answered gruffly, giving me a long, strange look. Almost underneath his breath, he muttered, "Trouble is, there is a danger right at my side . . . that I am helpless to combat."

"What do you mean?" I asked, wonderingly.

He didn't answer me, only took my elbow in his hand and steered me down the hall. "Come, I want you to meet the guests."

When we reached the drawing room, it seemed to be crowded with a lot of people all talking at once. There was a blaze of crystal chandeliers, gold-leaf woodwork, and flashing colors of silk and satin attire that to my untutored eye seemed more suitable to evening wear than midday.

Following a trifle uncertainly in Jared's wake, I soon discovered that in reality the guests were only three in number. A young blond woman, not pretty but arresting, was dressed all in black and seemed to be the focal point of Katherine Warwick's attention. The other woman was much older. Sharp of eye, her shrewd, foreign-looking face had a mask of rouge and powder. The third member of the party, who was later introduced as Katherine's cousin, Timothy Banks, had a round, boyish face, flamboyant clothes of green and white checks, and sported a quizzing glass, which he raised to inspect me, rather like a London dandy, or a "swell," as he would have been referred to in my neighborhood of Holborn.

Suddenly, I became aware that all conversation had ceased at our entry and every eye was turned in our direction.

Harriet whirled around in her wheelchair, cutting through the silence with a yelp. "Where on earth have you two been? You were due back hours ago!" Her voice rose shrilly. "Papa! Whatever happened to your hands?"

Katherine, wearing pale mauve silk with a purple orchid at her breast, glided swiftly forward. "Oh, heavens, darling, did you hurt your hands?" She caught them up, and Jared winced. Unseen by anyone but me, Katherine tightened her hold before she dropped them with a cruel smile. "Oh, sorry, dearest. Whatever happened to you?"

"It's nothing. Black Bob threw me, and I cut my hands on some rocks. Nurse MacNeil bandaged them for me."

Katherine's eyes slitted toward me. "Has our kind nurse been attending you all morning? Miss MacNeil, I thought your duties only concerned my daughter."

"I merely happened to be present when your husband needed help." My voice was stiff. "Certainly I could not refuse."

"Oh, dear no," Katherine fluted. "It is just that our guests were getting anxious about Jared's extended absence. How was it that you 'happened to be present'?" There was such venom in the thin, red lips that I felt a stab of fear.

But Jared answered her calmly. "I was showing Nurse MacNeil around the island so she can take Harriet on some excursions. Now if you'll excuse me, my dear wife, I will greet our guests."

He strode across the purple-flowered rug toward the company, who were all watching avidly, undoubtedly digesting every nuance and hidden meaning in our words.

"I beg everyone's forgiveness for being late." Jared sounded remarkably suave and urbane now. "I was detained by a slight accident. But now I welcome all of you to Brendan's Isle."

The older woman extended a jeweled claw over which Jared bowed and pressed his lips. "My dear Vivienne Lelong, enchanting as ever. It's a joy to see you." They spoke a few words in rapid French, then the woman transferred her hawklike gaze to me. In one all-encompassing glance, she seemed to assess with accuracy my face, figure, age, and social status, bringing a flood of color to my cheeks.

So far, I had remained beside Harriet's chair, only bowing when Jared introduced me. I had taken time to observe everyone and everything in the beautiful blue and silver room. I saw the walls were very high, the lower half paneled in silk moire, the upper half a field of plaster scrolls picked out in gold. The long windows were draped and swagged in the same azure brocade as the chairs and sofas, the drapes tied back with ropes of twisted silver cord. Small tables and carved mahogany whatnots rested on a rich Persian carpet of muted blues, and purples.

Glancing in a gilded mirror above the marble fireplace, I saw the occupants of the room reflected as if in a painting. The young woman, who had been introduced as "the countess, Lady Sylvia," was looking provocatively up at Jared. I noticed that Jared glanced with a thoroughly masculine appraisal at her low-necked, jet-trimmed bodice of black taffeta and lace.

"Surely, Sylvia, you are not still in mourning for your husband?" he drawled. "When you came here six months ago, I understood that you had defied convention by attending parties once again."

"Quite true, I'm afraid, dear Jared. I fear I was too lonesome to tolerate the regular period of seclusion. The only reason I am still wearing black is because I have all these gowns left from my mourning period and, alas, no money to buy new clothes." She made a little moue, unfurling a fan of black lace and trailing it across her snowy bosom.

Vivienne Lelong leaned toward her. "Of course, black is most flattering to your white skin, *cherié*, but would not that wealthy uncle of your deceased husband's provide you with some gowns now that you are a lone widow?"

A hard light filled the countess's long, green eyes. "He would not. Everything he gives exacts a price."

"Then the solution would appear to be a new husband. And a rich one, *naturalement*."

"Even that requires money, dear Vivienne. Money

to buy proper clothes, to entertain, to travel. The departed count left only debts. Besides . . ." Her eyes swept Jared, smilingly. "The attractive men with money are already married."

Katherine laughed, a rather defiant sound. "Darling, you may *look* at my dear husband, but that is all, I warn you. Why, Jared is so devoted to me, he can't even bear to have me go visiting in London. Isn't that true, my dearest love?"

"As you say," Jared replied evenly.

I noticed that, around her friends, Katherine Warwick seemed quite different; a kind of hectic gaiety engulfed her. Was her daily life so very boring without the stimulus of company? How could it be — married to such a vital, magnetic man as Jared Warwick?

I couldn't help staring at her as Katherine's great blue eyes glittered and she flung out her slender, gauze-draped arms. "Dear friends, since I cannot leave my island, you all must stay here for a very long, extended visit. That is the solution."

Lady Sylvia laughed lightly. "Katherine, my love, how long do you think we city mice could endure the bucolic life? Even for your sweet sake?"

"Oh, I do wish you could return with us, Cousin Kate," Timothy cried. "Everything's so gay in London, with the Exhibition to open soon." He sprang to his feet and executed a few dance steps, singing in a playful falsetto:

"Dear Bertie and Vickie have put on a show,
And Lunnon's the place every swell wants ter go.
To see the glass palace so mighty and grand,
Crowded with loot from all over the land."

Harriet laughed delightedly. " 'Bertie' is Prince Albert and 'Vickie' is the queen, isn't that right?" She clapped her hands and crowed. "Oh, do some more!"

"Cousin Timmy, perhaps you can perform at my birthday ball this year," Katherine told him gaily.

"Ah, when is this ball?" Sylvia inquired. "I trust we are all invited?"

"Indeed, you are." Katherine clasped her friend's arm. "I am considering a masquerade party. What do you think of that idea?"

Before Sylvia could reply, luncheon was announced, and a general exodus began toward the dining room. But as Jared began to follow his guests, I placed a detaining hand upon his sleeve. "Perhaps Harriet and I should take lunch in her room. With all the people arriving, she's had so much excitement—"

"No, I haven't!" Harriet shrilled, thumping the arm of her chair and glaring at me. "Nurse MacNeil, don't you dare ruin my day. Papa, push me to the table. *Please!*" She caught his hand, giving him a melting look. "I want to talk to Sylvia. Everybody was out all morning wandering around the grounds. I've hardly had a word with her, and she's always so much fun."

Jared's face looked bright and happy, and I wondered if it were because of the presence of the worldly, fascinating countess who seemed so interested in him.

At any rate, he was in a mood to humor his daughter. "I think we could let Harriet join the party today. Perhaps if she took a nap this afternoon?"

"Yes, yes, I promise I'll do that." Harriet's head bobbed vigorously.

I followed them into the dining room with some misgivings, especially when Harriet imperiously insisted on being seated next to Sylvia and Timothy had to give up his own place. The child could easily become quite spoiled. I watched her tug at the countess's arm to distract her from a discusssion with Jared.

Sylvia laughingly disengaged her sleeve. "Wait your turn, my poppet. I am speaking with your father." She leaned across the table and continued. "I have started a few orchids in pots to repay dear Vivienne for her hospitality to me, but London air is so filthy, I fear for their survival. May I see how yours are growing, Jared? Could you conduct me through your greenhouse after lunch? That is, if you can spare the time from your writing. By the way, how is the current book progressing?"

"I never discuss my work while it is in progress, my dear Sylvia. That is why my workroom is locked, even to the maids, so no one else can discuss it either." He smiled at her over the gold rim of his wine glass. "However, I will be pleased to show the greenhouse to anyone who is interested."

Timothy, devouring the light repast of poached fish and pigeon pie accompanied by boiled asparagus and banana fritters, decided he would prefer a nap when lunch was finished. "We all came down on the train, you know. Devilish long ride, by Jove. Had to rise at the crack of dawn."

"Bah, these trains travel at such a ghastly speed—quite dangerous." Vivienne wagged her turbaned head. "Me, I prefer the so-quiet travel of a coach, with its stops to stretch the legs."

"I think that I agree," I burst out, without thinking. It was my first remark during the entire luncheon, and the Frenchwoman looked as though the chair had found a voice.

She sniffed skeptically. "So. Have you actually traveled on the new trains, mademoiselle?"

"When I hired Miss MacNeil, I sent her a first-class railway ticket," Jared drawled.

"Oh, and I enjoyed it, too," I hastened to say, instantly regretting my former tactlessness. "It was just toward the end that I found it somewhat confining."

"*Tiens*, you have a most generous employer, nurse." Madame Lelong's reptilian gaze moved speculatively across my face to Jared's.

Yes, he was generous and warm and quite agreeable to these guests of his wife's, who probably were to him merely an unwelcome distraction from his work. Didn't Katherine appreciate him at all, I wondered indignantly, remembering her sly, angry pressure on his poor hands.

Jared pushed back his chair. "If everyone is finished, I suggest we adjourn to the greenhouse. At least, those of you who wish to see it."

He offered his arm to the older woman, and I heard her say as they walked away, "The nurse is rather pretty, *oui*? If one does not object to hair of that flamboyant shade, of course."

Harriet tugged at my arm. "Come, nurse, wheel me up to Sylvia. Oh, fiddle, now she's taken Papa's other arm and there's no room for me."

Timothy strolled away toward the stairs, already stifling a yawn. And Katherine Warwick, seeing she was deserted, flounced after him. They went up the stairs arm in arm, laughing together, while the rest of us followed Jared through a small side door.

A rush of warm, moist air greeted us. It smelled of mould and earth and damp, green leaves, as well as something cloying and unfamiliar. There were orchids everywhere, lush, thick-fleshed blooms planted in pots of clay or mossy mounds of earth. There were green orchids, brown orchids, striped orchids, as well as the ubiquitous purple. The few plants of yellow roses were overshadowed by the more exotic flowers like timid schoolgirls in a company of courtesans.

Some orchids clung to the bark of banana trees, and Jared pointed to them. "Those are called epiphytes. They are a parasite, as you can see, and feed on air."

We all tilted our heads back to observe the clustering flowers that looked like pink and white clouds of butterflies. High above, the glass dome had louvers to close and open vents located near the top.

"The dampness of the sea gives a nice humidity," Jared explained. "And this trough or brazier is kept fired with coals at all times to warm the air. My grandfather built this conservatory, and I've kept it up in his memory. The orchids really don't require much care once they are growing well. A little fertilizer, plenty of water, and arsenic for the occasional bug."

"One of the flowers has a divine fragrance," Lady Sylvia said, sniffing. "Which is it, pray?"

" 'Lady of the Night.' Most suitable for you in your ebony attire." Jared broke off a blossom of pure white and handed it to her.

The countess tucked it in the cleavage of her bosom, holding Jared's eyes with a slow smile. "Your wife has a passion for the big purple orchids you call cattelayas, but I prefer the creaminess of this variety." Her fingers traced the white skin mounding out of the black gown near the flower.

Vivienne chuckled. "And which do you prefer, *mon* Jared?" She pronounced his name "Ja-reed." Her hooded eyes shifted and fastened on my auburn hair. "Perhaps you like an entirely different color, *hein?*"

Jared looked at me with an inscrutable expression, and for a moment our eyes clung. His were filled with a frightening intensity, and mine, I was sure, with a kind of startled apprehension. The green gloom of the glass house threw an eerie light across his face. He seemed to be a stranger peering at me between his heavy, sensually narrowed lids.

Suddenly, I felt a dizzy, frightening sensation. The heat, the closely packed exotic blooms with their bold, flamboyant petals, the wavering glow coming through the windows . . . it all seemed as unpleasant as the sophisticated game of innuendo and titillation going on all around me.

I stumbled backward, wanting desperately to leave this erotic orchid house. Disregarding Harriet's loud cries of outrage, I firmly grasped the wheelchair in my hands and departed at top speed.

Chapter Ten

As soon as I awoke next morning, I wondered if Jared would need a new dressing on his hands. They had not seemed to bother him the previous evening at supper, but then he was not one to complain. He had only appeared briefly in the evening, in spite of Lady Sylvia's efforts to detain him, and the company had been compelled to get along without his presence.

After dinner, I could hear shrieks of laughter, songs by Timothy, and the tinkling of a piano. The noise was muted in the back wing where Harriet and I slept. But it must have continued very late, for in the morning, when I made my way to Jared's room, everything was still and quiet.

Of course, the servants were about, silently sweeping carpets, polishing grates, dusting furniture, and one of them had left a morning tray by Jared's door. He hadn't touched it yet. The silver pot, the pristine china, the dish of fruit, and little breakfast cakes all looked very tempting and reminded me that I was hungry. Impulsively, I popped a cake into my mouth, and then, swallowing hastily, rapped softly at the door. "Jared, are you awake? It's Margaret MacNeil. Shall I fix your hands?"

There was no answer: I knocked again, then shrugged. Perhaps he was still asleep, or perhaps he was up already enjoying a morning stroll outdoors before the exuberant houseguests took it over for games of lawn tennis and croquet.

I looked once more at the plate of tempting almond cakes but resisted the impulse for another bite. After all, they were intended for Jared's breakfast—not my own.

I turned away intending to seek my own food. But when I passed the hallway leading to the garden, I decided to go outside on the chance that I would find my employer. I should check on Jared's hands first thing.

I saw him almost immediately, striding purposefully along the brick walk, hands thrust in his pockets, the sleeves of an open-necked white shirt billowing beneath a casual, checked waistcoat. He was frowning at the ground beneath his feet and was almost upon me when his head jerked up and a look of pleased surprise softened his grim expression.

"Margaret! You're up with the robins. How fresh and wholesome you look in that blue and white."

His description sounded depressingly dull to my ears, and I suppressed a wistful sigh for satin flounces, flowers in my hair, and gauzy shawls. Ah, well. I was the blue-and-white-chambray type, and there was just no help for it.

"I wondered if you needed a new dressing on your hands," I said. "How are they?"

He withdrew them from his pocket. "I removed the

bandages. See, they're healing well." He extended the red-streaked palms and I touched them gently.

"Yes, they will do fine now without a covering. The skin is hardening on the cuts. Nature's own bandage," I added with a little smile.

We turned our footsteps toward the house and he slanted an inquiring glance at me. "Now that you have met the guests, what do you think of them?"

How should I answer? It was not my place to say: Timothy Banks seems frivolous and immature. Vivienne Lelong has a malicious streak, and Lady Sylvia seems . . . immoral.

Instead, I said aloud. "Well, Mr. Banks certainly has a gay, amusing manner. Madame Lelong is cynical, perhaps, but she seems fond of Lady Sylvia and your wife." I hesitated.

"Go on. What *about* the countess, oh wise and practical Nurse MacNeil?"

"She admires you," I said carefully. "She's very sophisticated, very attractive. And likes orchids, doesn't she?"

When Jared didn't reply, I glanced at him. He was frowning. "Speaking of orchids, Margaret, did you notice a green bottle in the glass house yesterday? On a shelf beside some tools?"

"I don't remember anything but orchids, overwhelmingly large and very purple. What was in this bottle?"

"Arsenic that we use to kill bugs and rats. Bascom said he couldn't find it last night. Then this morning it was back, but not exactly where it had been. I guess he just didn't look very hard."

Arsenic . . . a deadly poison . . . completely tasteless and colorless. Any other flavoring would cover it completely. I recalled several cases in the hospital where a child had accidentally received a dose. Usually it was fatal unless caught in time.

And somebody was trying to harm Jared. . . .

"Probably Bascom misplaced the bottle and forgot," I heard Jared say. "Just the same, I must alert the kitchen. Be sure you only eat what everyone else is eating today." He pushed open the rear door. "I usually have a tray in my room, but today I want a substantial breakfast. Oh, there's Miss Grey, I'll go and speak to her."

He strode down the hallway toward the black-gowned housekeeper while my thoughts began to spin. That food before his door . . . that cake I'd eaten . . . I flew down the hall and found the tray was gone!

A darkness seemed to swim before my vision. Was I imagining this sudden nausea and dizzy feeling? I broke out in a sweat and leaned, trembling, against the wall. Had I taken a poisoned cake intended just for Jared? I could take no chances. Stumbling and running, I gained my room just as Annie appeared with the morning jug of hot water.

"Oh, miss, what ails you? You look so green!"

"Get me the powdered mustard from the kitchen," I gasped. "And don't let anyone eat those almond cakes. No questions! Hurry!" My stomach was already heaving and I emptied its meager contents promptly in the basin.

When Annie returned, Miss Grey accompanied her. In order to achieve a thorough cleansing, I grabbed the mustard and mixed it with the water, pouring glass after glass of the nauseating stuff down my burning throat. Finally, I lay upon the bed, spent, depleted, and chilled. But still alive.

Miss Grey drew a blanket across my body. She had been curtly efficient during the entire operation, but now she asked some questions. "You think the cakes were poisoned, nurse?"

I rolled my head from side to side and answered weakly. "I don't know. Arsenic perhaps. Did anybody else eat them? Who made them?"

"They were thrown out as soon as Annie told us, and no one else eats as early as the master. However, Cook is above suspicion. She's been here over twenty years." Miss Grey's eye grew frosty. "I have been here ten. No one working in the manor would do such a thing as put arsenic in a cake. Why should they? The family is well-liked, and the wages are extremely generous."

"How do you explain it, then?" I wheezed.

"I don't."

The housekeeper left the room. Soon after that, Jared arrived, accompanied by Harriet in her wheel-chair. They both looked anxious.

Jared came directly to the bed and sought my hand. "I heard that something made you ill, my dear. How are you feeling now?"

"Much better." I forced a smile. "I ate one of those almond cakes intended for your breakfast, and per-haps—"

"Miss Grey told me," he interrupted. "You said there might have been arsenic in them. But Bascom says he doesn't see any less arsenic in the bottle, so perhaps you are mistaken."

"Perhaps." I sighed. "It might have been just an upset stomach combined with nervousness. You said the arsenic had been misplaced, and I was immediately afraid a drop of poison might have been added to the icing while they sat in the hall."

Harriet looked frightened and cried shrilly, "Who would do such a thing? Who?"

I didn't answer, but I thought: *anyone*. Sylvia, Timothy, Madame Lelong, Katherine . . . the cakes had been accessible to anyone who passed.

"I'll question everyone, never fear." Jared still held my hand and rubbed the fingers absently with his thumb while he gazed across the room. His face, unlike the gentle pressure of his hand, looked hard as flint and just as unyielding. "I'll send Annie in with toast and tea. That should go down well." He gave me one last smile, forced out with difficulty, then he left.

Perhaps Jared was right and I was mistaken in my diagnosis. It could have been just my imagination, which had stimulated a nervous reaction. That could happen easily enough and make a person thoroughly ill, as I knew well from my nursing experience.

When the door closed behind her father, Harriet wheeled herself up closer to the bed and said in a low, quivering voice, "I think they're trying to kill my papa. There's something awful going on. Someone stabbed him, and then those poisoned cakes were meant for *him*. And so was that burr under Black Bob's saddle."

"I didn't know there had been a burr," I said slowly, turning my head on the pillow to stare at her. "Where did you hear this?"

"James told Annie and she told me. James was worried that he would be fired and didn't want Papa to find out. But Annie wanted me to know. She has worked here since she was my age, and we're good friends."

99

"Could James himself have put the burr beneath the saddle?"

"Why should he? He has a good job here. But *something's* going on." Harriet bit her lip and hooked a strand of dark hair behind her ear. "There's that whispering and movement in my closet, you know. That must mean something."

"Probably the water, dear. The tides coming and going."

"Perhaps." Doubt was written clearly on the young, thin face. "It's true there are lots of caves beneath the ground around here. Papa always said I was too little to explore them and might get lost. And now I—I—can't."

"Listen, Harriet—" I paused to cough. "As soon as I am well—tomorrow, maybe—I'll do some investigating."

"You promise?" Harriet looked comforted. "Well, I better go now. It hurts your throat to talk, doesn't it?" She patted the blanket awkwardly. "I'm awfully glad you're not . . . you know."

So am I, was my inward groan. For a while there, I had felt sick enough to die.

In a few minutes after Harriet's departure, Annie entered with a tray. The crisp buttered toast, soft-cooked egg, and strong, hot, sugared tea set very well. After that, I slept for nearly the whole day, and when I awakened, I felt renewed in mind and limb, with only a trace of weakness to remind me of the wretched business.

I rose and washed, brushed my hair, then went in search of Harriet. To my surprise, Annie told me she had left Harriet in the garden, enjoying the last of the sunny day. Annie had gone to fetch a shawl, but I told

100

her I would take it to my patient.

Outdoors, there was a sweet scent of lilac buds and grass. Seagulls dipped across the sky above the cove, and brown wrens twittered sleepily in the swaying trees beneath which Harriet was sitting.

She greeted me with surprise and pleasure, but it was Bascom who claimed her attention. She gave a disgusted snort, pointing toward him a short way off. "Look at that lazy fellow, squatting on his heels chewing on a blade of grass. Why is he staring at my windows? Wheel me over there, I'll just have a word with him."

Bascom certainly was an unsavory-looking character, I mused, taking in his gap-toothed grin and narrow, ferret face. He looked like those weasels in the slums who "glomed the swag" with nimble fingers from anyone foolish enough to be nearby with money in his pocket.

When Bascom heard the wheelchair approaching, he rose lithely to his feet. " 'Allo, ladies. Fine day, to be sure. Flowers and such-like bustin' out everywhere." His beady eyes sharpened on my face. " 'Eard you was took real bad, miss. All right now, eh?"

"Yes, thank you." Bascom certainly had access to the arsenic bottle, I reflected grimly. And he had only been here about six months, Miss Grey had said. Just about the time of Harriet's accident . . .

"Why aren't you working, my good man?" Harriet now demanded. "Look at all those weeds."

"Aye, just look at 'em." His lips twitched, but, seeing the expression in Harriet's eye, he added hastily, "Right-o, miss, weedin' it is, then." He sauntered off toward a pair of shears lying abandoned on the grass.

101

"I don't trust that man," Harriet hissed to me. "He slips around so — so stealthily. I wouldn't be surprised if he's planning to rob us. Or maybe kidnap me."

"Really, Harriet, that's nonsense and you know it. Your father must have investigated the man."

"Letters of character can be forged," Harriet muttered darkly.

I forced a laugh. "I'm afraid you've been reading too many gothic novels by Mrs. Radcliffe."

Harriet didn't answer, but suddenly, a smile replaced her frown and she began to wave her hands. "Tim, Timmy, over here!"

Her cousin trotted toward us, carrying a bouquet of white and purple orchids. "Greetings, ladies. Prime sort of weather we had today, what?" he gave me a little bow. "Glad to see you are up and about, nurse. Have a posy, you deserve one, although I picked these blossoms in the greenhouse for Cousin Kate. She fancies them upon the dinner table tonight."

I declined the posy with a little laugh, and Harriet looked doubtfully at the big bouquet. "Papa doesn't like to have his greenhouse raided."

"Ah, well, they'll grow back again." He grinned engagingly, looking quite dapper in a pea-green coat and trousers sporting checks of black and white. "I believe it's time for tea. Will you join me, ladies?"

"If you wheel me in I'll give you a nice kiss," Harriet told him with a coquettish glance that reminded me unpleasantly of Lady Sylvia's coy mannerisms.

I began to follow them, but halted abruptly before I reached the house. James was advancing through the little grove of trees, and when he saw me he stopped, then folded his arms and leaned back against a trunk.

His smirk increased when he saw that I was heading in his direction. He fell back into the leafy enclosure and I was forced to follow.

"Just a minute, my good man. I would like a word with you." I kept my tones both cool and distant.

He surveyed me cheekily. "Oh, aye? Guess you want to apologize for kickin' me, eh? Well, it was worth it. A fair, trim ankle like that in my hand—"

I had to grit my teeth. "Will you listen to me? Harriet told me there was a burr placed under Black Rob's saddle when he threw her. I want to know if this is true."

The grin vanished. He looked down sullenly, kicking at the ground. "I didn't put no burr there."

"No one said you did. But did you see one?"

"Mebbe. Yes, since it's you that's askin' . . . I did see one." He raised his eyes. "I don't hold with harmin' little gals."

So. It was true. I drew in my breath and tried to think. The wind stirred in the trees with the salty chill of coming night, causing the boughs to creak and groan. Far below, a gull cried above the crashing, heedless surf.

"Who could have done it?" I whispered.

"Lots of people. All the ones here now was here before."

"Why didn't you tell the master about the burr?"

He gave a grunt. "And mebbe lose m'job? Y'must be daft."

There was nothing more to say. Drawing a deep breath, I turned away, but before I could move James sprang close and gripped my waist. The familiar light was back in his sharp, black eyes. "Now I've told you

103

what you wanted, how's about a reward, then?"

His red-cheeked face drew closer and he ran his tongue across his lips. I twisted furiously. "Let me go, you fool! Do you want me to tell the master?" My voice rose angrily.

"Blimey, laddie-o, ain't you got no work to do?" Bascom stood grinning, a few feet away. "Nurse, they're lookin' for you in the house."

With a disgruntled mutter, James dropped his hands and swung away while I glared after him, rubbing at the place that he had grabbed.

"I'm glad you came along just now—" I began, turning back to Bascom.

But the gardener had disappeared as silently and mysteriously as he had come.

Chapter Eleven

"I heard the whispering again last night," Harriet said a few days later, staring across the sea wall. Her hands were clenched together on her blue muslin pinafore, and, beneath the shadow of her garden hat, the childish face looked pale.

I had been aware all morning that something was troubling the girl and I was glad that she had spoken of her own accord. Since it was only the whispering that bothered her, I was able to speak in a teasing voice of mock-severity. "What book are you reading, now my girl?"

"*The Secrets of Udolfo*," Harriet admitted, "but—"

"Ah-ha, all clanking chains at midnight and ghostly laughter in the subterranean chambers?"

Harriet's lip trembled. "I really *did* hear voices! I'm not imagining things. Remember, you said that you would investigate, Nurse Margaret?"

The friendlier salutation did it. For some time now, the "miss" had been dropped before Harriet's name and its passing had drawn no comment. Now I was "Nurse

Margaret," This, indeed, was progress.

"Very well," I said, "let's talk about it. You hear voices laughing, whispering. At what time?"

"After everyone's asleep. Sometimes I wake up. I used to have a hard time sleeping all night through."

"That was due to lack of exercise."

Harriet nodded. "It's getting better since you started my exercises. But last night I was restless and—I heard it. Like whispers from a grave," she added hollowly.

In spite of the sun-dappled leaves and warm sea breeze, I felt a chill ripple down my spine. "I don't believe in ghosts, lassie," I said lightly. "There is always a logical explanation. Once, I was employed in a great, old house supposedly inhabitated by a spirit. Chairs slid about, tables rocked, doors swung open, things tumbled down from shelves. Well, the new owners didn't like it one bit, so they hired a man called a 'ghost breaker' to come and investigate. And what do you think? He found that canals of water ran beneath the house and were responsible for all the movements and creaking. Whenever he watched for the high tides, things would start to happen. England is honeycombed with underground waterways, so perhaps that's why there are so many 'haunted houses.' "

"Hmmm," was Harriet's only response to this piece of logic. She continued to stare glumly at the ocean.

After a few minutes, an idea suddenly came to me, and, springing to my feet, I clapped my hands. "Harriet, I know what we should do today—let's go for a picnic on the beach."

While I beamed at her, Harriet regarded me warily. "How would I get down there?"

"There must be a path . . ."

"Yes, over there past the trees." The girl's dark eyes began to brighten. "Maybe someone could carry me." She looked about the garden. "Bascom . . . or James . . ."

"We'll see." I didn't like the idea of asking either one, but, when I returned a little later with our lunch packed in a wicker basket, the problem of Harriet's transportation had been solved.

"Timothy has gone to get some rugs and pillows for us," Harriet informed me joyously. "He's going to carry me down to the beach and join our picnic."

I made a quick assessment of the basket's contents. Yes, there should be ample. The pleasant cook had been most generous. Hearing a call just then, I turned to see Timothy hurrying toward us, his arms filled with pillows and soft rugs.

"Ahoy, mates. We're off for the bounding main today, eh?" Above bright yellow trousers and a houndstooth coat, his brown eyes twinkled merrily. A wine bottle protruded from his pocket and he patted it lovingly. "I'll carry this old friend as well as my young coz, if you'll absorb the rugs, dear nurse."

"Are you sure that you can manage Harriet?" I asked, peering down apprehensively at a series of wooden steps set into the cliff, making a steep, zigzagged descent.

"Of course, I can. Easy as kiss your hand." And Timothy proceeded to put his boast into effect. However, when we reached the sandy shore, his face was red and he was panting. He lowered Harriet carefully to the rug that I quickly spread for her.

"By Jupiter, you've gained a few pounds since I used to tote you piggyback around the place," he said, mopping his face and grinning.

Harriet looked up pertly. "I'm growing up, Tim. Soon I'll be thirteen. Are you still going to marry me someday, as you promised when I was little?"

"You'll have far better lads to choose from than your poor old cousin." He leaned back against a boulder, expelling his breath with a grunt.

"Silly! You aren't old, only twenty-nine," Harriet protested.

"But *poor*, I am."

"You certainly don't look it. You have ever so many new clothes."

"Well, you see, all my annual fund from dear, departed Papa's estate goes toward keeping up a front, my love. In that way, I can make a good appearance on the visits extended to me up and down this fair land of ours. Without those invitations from kind friends, I fear that I might starve."

Privately, I wondered why such an able-bodied youth didn't find a job.

But Harriet had other ideas. "Why don't you marry someone rich, Cousin Tim? You're a good-looking and good-natured—"

"I might have married your dear mama once upon a time," he said. "But neither of us had a feather to fly with. And when Jared Warwick came along with all that lovely brass . . ." He shrugged and his voice trailed off a little sadly.

"Mama?" Harriet shrieked. "You were in love with *my mama*? But she's so much older."

"Not really. She only has a five years gain on me." He sighed and stared rather blindly at the sunlit sea, while Harriet continued to regard him with surprise and indignation.

But finally she had to giggle. "And all this time I believed you were waiting just for me."

Timothy collected himself and responded in his usual bantering tones. "Well, I might fancy the delectable Lady Sylvia, but, alas and alack, the lady is as poor as I am. So, young coz, I guess I'll wait for you as planned."

"Well, I just guess you better." Harriet looked gratified and brushed back her hair, giving Timothy an age-old taunt beneath her rather extraordinary lashes.

In my opinion, this line of conversation had gone on far enough, and I stood up briskly, shaking the sand from my chambray skirt. "When I was your age, Harriet, my papa took me to the seashore to build sand castles. If I do say so myself, I became quite an expert. I would, therefore, like to challenge both of you to a contest. Let us see who can build the best castle in a certain length of time. Mr. Banks, you have a watch in your waistcoat pocket. Shall we set the limit at one hour?"

"Splendid idea, Nurse MacNeil." Timothy sprang to his feet, ever the agreeable guest. "I'll just move Harriet closer to the damp sand and accumulate a few things that we'll need: big shells for digging, driftwood, seaweed, and pebbles for decoration. . . ." After a few industrious minutes, he shed his coat, rolled up his shirt sleeves, and consulted his gold watch. "Now then, mates, have at it. May the best one win!"

Amid laughter and banter, we molded cones of sand, patted walls in place, erected gardens with seaweed and twigs, trimmed doorways with pebbles, and so forth. The sun shone warmly as we worked, but the salt air was fresh and cool against our skin, and the cries of gulls and dashing waves made a background of music among the rocks.

When the time was up, Harriet's castle was voted the prettiest, with its gardens and winding paths. Timothy's two-foot mound was voted biggest. And mine was the most ingenious, they all agreed, because I had made a rocky wall and coaxed the waves to enter and surround a castle, making a most convincing moat.

After that, everyone was hungry, and we fell eagerly on the piles of sandwiches containing sweet pink ham, the pickles, stewed plums, tarts, and cakes. Harriet and I drank lemonade and Timothy consumed the wine.

It evidently made him sleepy. After lunch, he stretched out full length, his head upon a pillow. "Will you excuse me, ladies? I believe all that endeavor has earned me a short rest." Soon his chest was rising and falling rhythmically.

Harriet regarded him fondly. "Dear Timmy! Sometimes I'm glad I'm not a boy, after all, so I can tease him about things like getting married. I'm also glad when I look at Lady Sylvia and know that someday I can wear silk and satin, too, and flirt the way she does. It's the strangest thing, I wanted to be a boy so Papa would appreciate me. But now . . ." She threw me a perplexed glance. "Do you know what I mean? I'm not sure that *I* do!"

"I know exactly how you feel, my dear. For me, it came a little later." I began to pack away the plates and cups, then I removed my hat and ran my fingers through my hair. "No one longed to be a boy more than I did. It seemed so unfair that only men could enter the world of medicine."

"But you did become a nurse."

"Yes, but that was only because of my father, his training and encouragement. London only got its first school for nurses in 1848, just three years ago, and there is still a lot of prejudice against women working in the hospitals."

Harriet nodded. "But when did you decide that you were glad to be a girl?"

"Oh, when I met a certain young man." I smiled a little sadly and explained about David and his untimely death. Harriet instantly was all sympathy.

"Then," I continued, "I also came to realize that I could give feminine understanding to the women patients. They seem to like having a woman to confide in and care for them during their confinement."

I couldn't tell Harriet about the other times when I was glad to be a woman, but I could admit it to myself. It was when Jared Warwick was nearby. Never before had I been made so aware of my own femininity. Perhaps it was because he seemed so conscious of it, too. Sometimes he would look at me with wry amusement, sometimes he would listen with the keenest interest to my ramblings. And sometimes . . . a smoldering fire would light his midnight eyes and start my senses clamoring in a way they never had before with quiet, undemanding David.

Jared had given me that feeling just the night before, and now my mind went backward to recall it. . . .

There had been the usual dancing in the hall, and, while Harriet watched the gaiety from her chair, I also sat nearby where I could see the whirling skirts and slippered feet moving on the marble flooring that made a very satisfactory surface for their dancing.

Madame Lelong drew notes of tinkling brilliance from the piano while Jared partnered Lady Sylvia and Timothy danced with Katherine. The ladies' gowns were especially beautiful that night. Katherine's was creamy satin embroidered with purple violets, the flounced skirt caught up with green and lavender ribbon bows. Sylvia had added a scarf of golden gauze to relieve the somberness of her black lace dress, and she wore a cluster of yellow roses to match those in her hair. She was laughing and talking to Jared while they danced. When it ended, she seemed vexed that Timothy came to claim her.

Jared bowed and left her. He had danced once with each of the ladies, as he did every night before withdrawing to his room. I had caught him looking at me sometimes as though about to ask me, too. I couldn't have accepted, of course, but still. . . .

When the music started up again, Jared suddenly loomed up before me. My eyes flew upward with a start to the heavy shoulders in the velvet coat, the white silk ruffles foaming underneath his firm cleft chin. I caught my breath. Was he going to defy convention and ask the *nurse* to dance?

No. All he said was: "I would like you to walk down the hallway with me for a moment."

My foolish hopes were dashed, but I kept my face an unrevealing blank as I rose obediently.

"Are you two going to dance?" Harriet's fluting voice came after us.

"Of course not," her mother answered angrily.

Jared Warwick didn't speak until we were almost at the end of the hall. "Do you care for dancing, Marga-

112

ret? I find it very boring in a short while. But then, I'm not a very good performer."

"It seemed to me you were. As for myself, I've not had much opportunity to dance lately. It was a long time ago."

"Scottish reels, I suppose, with wailing bagpipes and all that sort of thing?"

"Yes, that was fun," I admitted with a little smile.

"Do you think my daughter will ever dance?" He frowned at the cold, white marble floor, his hair blue-black in the flickering wall sconces. A heavy lock fell across his forehead, but he didn't seem to notice.

"Harriet is getting stronger every day," I told him. "I think the time will surely come when mind and body will unite to say: 'Stand up, my girl, stand up and walk.' "

His mouth quirked at my emphatic tone, but he didn't reply. We turned the corner of the hall, but still he continued walking silently, hands folded behind his back.

I knew I should be with my patient. It was getting close to Harriet's bedtime. "If that is all, then—" I began.

He halted abruptly. "Just one more thing. I want to impress on you not to pay attention to anyone else's opinion regarding the wisdom of hiring a nurse for my daughter."

Had Katherine Warwick been questioning his actions? Was she asking for my dismissal? A pang went through my mind.

Suddenly, Jared swung and faced me, reaching out to grip my arms so savagely that I nearly cried out. "Remember, Margaret, I brought you here, and you are answerable only to me. Don't listen to any complaints or criticism you may hear."

"Very well, Mr. Warwick," I quavered faintly.

His hands slid down to clasp my wrists, the pressure in his fingers feeling very firm and masculine and warm. His black eyes traveled urgently across my features. "Do you like it here, Margaret? Are you contented? Is there anything you want that I can get for you?"

I smiled into his dark, compelling face and spoke a little breathlessly. "Don't worry about me. I like Brendan's Isle. I'm very fond of your daughter, and I think we're making progress. And, thank you, there is nothing that I need. Except my hands—" I gave a smothered laugh and tugged. "I should get back to Harriet."

Before complying, he lifted one of my hands and pressed it against his lips, his eyes on mine, so deeply searching. What did he seek? My feminine response to his overpowering masculinity? How easy that would be to give!

I jumped when Katherine Warwick's voice intruded on the intimate moment. "Jared, our guests are waiting for you to dance with them. What are you doing out here in the back hall?"

"Speaking with the nurse about our daughter's progress," he answered silkily. "And I can't dance any more tonight, so please make my apologies to your guests. I have more important work to do. Good evening, ladies." He turned and left. After a venomous glance in his direction, Katherine vanished also.

Alone, I looked down at my hand, still feeling the pressure of his warm, firm mouth upon my trembling palm.

The vision faded. I was back at the beach with Harriet and Timothy, reliving last night like a moonstruck chit. I pushed the errant thoughts away and sat up straighter, drawing a rather quavering, deep breath.

"Are you all right, Nurse Margaret?" Harriet inquired. "Your face is red and you look disturbed. Have you had too much sun? I hate to leave the beach so soon, but if you want to go . . ." She gave a wistful glance at her sleeping cousin. "Shall I wake him?"

"We can stay a little longer," I replied. "I think I will stroll along the shore, just around that point of land. Will you be all right? If you need me, you can shout."

Harriet nodded, leaning back against her pillows. "I'll be fine. I feel so safe and happy here. Maybe I'll catch up on my sleep. There are caves beyond the point, if you want to go exploring." She yawned and shut her eyes, tipping her wide straw hat to shield her from the sun's bright rays.

Nothing could happen to my charge while I was gone, so I set off briskly, welcoming the exercise to clear away the teasing memories of that perplexing, fascinating person—Jared Warwick.

Chapter Twelve

As I trudged along the sandy shore, however, my mind soon reverted to the trouble on this island. Jared Warwick certainly seemed to be in some kind of danger. Why did he refuse to discuss it? Perhaps he didn't want to frighten me away. Or perhaps he didn't trust me absolutely. . . .

The other things, the compliments, the warm expression in his eyes, perhaps they were just designed to keep me happy in my work. I couldn't help remembering his words, like precious beads strung on a chain: "Of course you're beautiful . . . you are intelligent, compassionate, and ready to tread new paths . . . I'm so very glad you're here . . . Margaret, your reactions are delicious. . . ."

Did he mean any of those things? Heaven help me, I wanted to believe him. I was forced, in all honesty, to admit that I found the man exciting. I had never met anyone with such a magnetic personality. Of course, the unusual circumstances of our first meeting undoubtedly contributed to his appeal. I had saved his life

. . . taken care of him alone all night . . . and he had kissed me passionately during his delirium. My face burned at the memory. Could I have tried harder to prevent those kisses? I didn't know.

Fiercely, I exhaled a taut, shaken breath. What was the matter with me? I was acting like a schoolgirl. This would never do — mooning over my employer! I was here to help Harriet, and that was all that should concern me.

With that all settled, I stepped out briskly on the hard-packed shingle, drawing in the cleansing, salt-tinged air. In a short time, I reached the point of the land, and it immediately claimed my interest. From the rocky hillside, great boulders had broken loose and tumbled to the beach. Some of them were worn to pebbles by the action of the waves, others still reared giant heads above the crashing breakers, expending their energy in a hiss of foam along the shore. Tide pools glistened among the rocks and piles of seaweed attracted buzzing gnats. A little farther on, I saw a wide, dark fissure in the side of the cliff. It must be the cave that Harriet had mentioned. Filled with a great surge of curiosity, I started toward it.

Carefully, I climbed over the slippery, wet crags, clutching at projecting corners to prevent a misstep, for the points were very sharp. Once I was on the sand beyond, I found it wet and sparkling with some strange element, like diamonds. It sucked at my low-heeled slippers with invisible hands that tried to impede my progress.

At the low entrance to the cave, I bent and peered inside. At first, it appeared to be a deep, black hole. Though I strained and blinked, I had to go in farther so that my eyes could become adjusted to the lack of light. Then I saw that the cave extended dramatically beyond the opening, with a high roof of projecting limestone spears and an inky pool that stretched into the shadows.

Dare I venture in a little more? I glanced back at the beach. Was the tide coming in or going out? I couldn't tell, but at any rate, the waves still broke a good distance from the cave. Surely it would be safe for a little while, long enough for me to discover if it had tunnels that might extend beneath the house. Thus, I might find the answer to Harriet's fears.

Extremely cautious, but filled with great determination, I crept forward. I now could make out colors on the rough walls where seaweed had stained it pink and purple and green. With surprise, I noted the high-water mark. The entrance must be completely submerged at times. Rocks were piled around the sides as though the ocean had cleared a pathway for the pool. Bending down to peer beneath its glassy surface, I saw living forms: star fish, sea urchins, and anemones with waving, hungry tentacles. Other tiny creatures moved blindly, sluggishly, when I stirred the water with my finger. I found this strange, unfamiliar world completely fascinating.

I now began to see quite well and realized that a faint light filtered down from somewhere up above. There must be a crack leading to outdoors. It shed a glow that seemed to swim and waver, making me feel as though I were a mermaid at the bottom of the sea in a silent, peaceful world. I chuckled at my own whimsy and heard the sound bounce back, reverberating from wall to wall, a ghostly echo that caused my scalp to tingle and halted all my merriment.

Following the pool deeper into the cavern, I soon saw that it narrowed, vanishing through an arched opening in a limestone wall directly facing me. About three feet of space separated rock from water. By bending down, I could see past the arch into another smaller cavern whose walls glowed with sparkling phosphorescence. In the absolute stillness, water dripped as it had for ages, wearing away the stone. Or adding to it.

Then in the tomblike atmosphere, I heard it.

Sounds were coming from directly overhead. Footsteps, doors opening, voices. My breath exploded in a startled gasp. Was I underneath the house? Could this be the source of Harriet's mysterious voices? I must find out!

My eye measured the opening below the arch. Yes, I could get through easily. I was a competent swimmer. Quickly, I unbuckled shoes, drew off cotton hose and garters. On top of them, I laid my long white nurse's apron, and both petticoats. Then I bunched up my skirt and stepped into the stream. Immediately, I sank to my knees in coal-black water. After the initial shock, I proceeded easily by bending over and simply wading through the archway.

On the other side, the water deepened when I straightened up. I didn't venture any farther but stood still in the pool, ears straining, every muscle taut.

From above came the sound of wheels rattling over a stone floor, the clink of bottles, laughter, and the mingling of two voices, male and female. I must be right beneath the house cellars in this part of the cave.

Suddenly, I heard a voice say clearly, "Can you smuggle out a bit of wine for us, love? To have tonight?"

It was James!

A girl's voice giggled, filled with choked excitement. "Stop that, Jamie. Ooo, you're such a naughty boy—"

The rest was cut off by the noise of scuffling and laughter. Then silence. After a moment, the girl—it must be Annie—moaned. "Ah, give over, Jamie, do."

"Just one more kiss." After another silence, he said thickly, "Tonight then, love, in the room above Miss Harriet's?"

"All right, all right. But leave me be now. Just look how you've mussed my dress. . . ."

There were broken, disjointed sentences fading away: "door unlocked . . . midnight . . ." Then the sounds of cart and bottles and voices ceased.

I was so engrossed, I hadn't dared to move, or hardly to breathe. But now I gave a sigh of satisfaction as I realized what had been taking place. Annie was letting James into a room at night, evidently in the wing right over Harriet. Well, a word in Miss Grey's ear would soon end *that*. And Harriet's fears would end, too. The riddle was solved. No more chuckling and whispering "in the room above."

I must go and tell her right away. As I turned to go, something brushed against my bare leg in the water. To my shame, I gave a shriek, jumping uncontrollably. Immediately, the water splashed up to my thighs.

Something had changed inside the cave—and in the pool. I noticed a faint roaring sound and observed that there was a chilled deepening of the black depths. *The life within the water was moving, too.* I gave a gasp of horror. Even as I watched, the rippling, wet darkness rose with a rush and gurgle and closed the opening beneath

120

the arch.

The tide had turned and filled the gap!

Wait now—tides both rose and fell, didn't they? Yes, the level now dropped a little. But there was no time to be lost. With a tightening of my throat, I remembered the high-water marks upon the walls. I must get out at once!

Taking a deep breath, I shut my eyes, ducked my head, and forced my way into the arch. My shaking hands slid around the rough edges of the rock—it seemed an endless time as I groped blindly forward. Then I felt it flatten out and knew I was on the other side. Gasping and coughing, I staggered upright, shaking the cold, stinging water from my eyes.

Plowing through the swollen stream that sucked and surged around my dragging skirts, it wasn't until I could see the entrance that the full force of my predicament struck me. The sea had reached the mouth of the cave, and it was filled with dashing breakers!

My heart was beating frantically as I struggled forward. How could I make it through the tremendous force of that crashing surf? The tide still rose and fell, but the backwash had an amazing strength. If I lost my footing, I knew I would be dashed senseless on the rocks and probably killed.

My breath rasped through my laboring lungs, and I realized that I was on the slender edge of panic, when reason, will, and wits would all desert me. Forcing myself to stop, I pressed my hands against my heaving chest until I grew a little calmer.

The next time that the tide receded, I let it carry me along to the entrance, where I clung with stiff and icy fingers. Then I stared in horror. The beach was gone completely, submerged by water. There was absolutely no escape that way at all.

Suddenly, a figure appeared on the point of the land. It was Jared! He cupped his mouth, but I couldn't hear him, and, though I screamed his name till' I was hoarse, the waves drowned out the sound. He didn't see or hear me. He stared up and down the shore for a long moment, the wind whipping at his hair and shirt, and then he disappeared.

I felt worse than before and began a futile, useless sobbing, repeating Jared's name over and over like a hopeless prayer. My eyes were squeezed shut when the wave took me. It broke over my head in a suffocating, freezing deluge, cutting off my breath like a monstrous hand. Over and over I turned in the roaring darkness, swept back into the cave as helpless as a leaf blown from a tree.

When I felt a rock strike my side, I flung my arms around it automatically, and, when the water drained away, my head and shoulders were above the surface.

I felt as though I had survived by a miracle.

With a strength born of desperation, I dragged myself up higher, retching and coughing out the water I had swallowed. Rocks were all around me, but when I tried to climb, my dress encumbered me with a leaden weight. I tore it down the front and ripped it off. Now I only wore a thin chemise and knee-length drawers. Now I might be able to climb.

I gritted my chattering teeth, clutching the jagged, slippery surfaces until my hands were cut and bleeding, my breath a fiery torment in my lungs. But when the tide surged back again, I was perched several feet above it, clinging to a limestone column with aching arms and shivering, freezing limbs.

I knew I couldn't stay where I was. Eventually the tide would reach me. Was there any other way out of the caves? An opening somewhere in the cliff? A crack in the ceiling?

Then I remembered the light that filtered into the caves, the greenish glow that wasn't phosphorescence. Perhaps the light came from a crevice large enough to permit me to squeeze through. Or at least to be heard when I shouted. I had to try to find it.

Once again I started climbing, going deeper into the caverns, although every instinct screamed for flight in the opposite direction. Grimly, I made myself go on, carefully, gripping tightly, concentrating on firm footholds, never looking downward to where the murderous, black water waited . . .

I blinked. The light . . . wasn't it getting brighter? My weary heart gave a burst of hope. Yes, yes, a fissure! It widened into a natural chimney about three feet wide. It was straight-sided . . . and about twenty feet high. *How on earth could I climb that far?*

I shut my eyes and put my trembling hands over the despairing cry I wasn't able to suppress.

A chimney? My eyes flew open. What about chimney sweeps? Why couldn't I follow their technique? I forced myself to stand upright in the narrow, claustrophobic opening. Suppose I got stuck? I looked up at the patch of sky so high above, suddenly so beautiful. I had to try. It was my only chance.

I pressed my back against one wall, my feet against the other, using my elbows for leverage. I felt my skin scrape raw, saw bloody trickles down my wrists. Jabs of pain shot through my nerves. No matter. Still I climbed. Up and up. Toward that blessed bit of sky.

Almost at the top, I heard someone call my name, and, collecting all my waning strength, I shouted back. The next moment, Jared's arms reached down and drew me to the surface. He felt so warm, so strong! I sobbed his name over and over, pressing my face against his chest. He spoke to me, but I couldn't hear the words. I only heard the pounding of his heart, beating with the same wild clamor as my own.

The hillside seemed to swarm with people who all ran toward me, shouting and calling. But I couldn't speak. I was too exhausted and cold even to think. I sank into a blissful pit of darkness and let my troubles all be whirled away.

Chapter Thirteen

I was only aware of fleeting images after Jared carried me from the cliff: a tub of steaming water; wet garments stripped away by Annie (how glad I was to shed the slimy, sandy things!); someone washing and toweling my hair. . . .

I heard Harriet's shrill, anxious voice, Jared's sounding strangely angry and upset. But not with me . . . wasn't he the person who gently stroked the soothing ointment on my cuts and bruises? There were other voices . . . other faces. . . . At last I felt the feather bed beneath me, a down-filled quilt on top, a warmed brick wrapped in flannel for my feet. And then came sleep, deep and blissfully secure.

Full awareness came much later when long, dark shadows slanted through the emerald curtains. I ached in every muscle, but the pain in hands and limbs was almost gone. And I felt ravenously hungry.

125

Struggling upright on my pillows, I gave a startled gasp. Jared Warwick was ensconced in an armchair by my window. His tousled head rested on his hand, his shirt was open at the neck, one foot rested on his knee.

"So you're awake," he drawled, his deep tones huskier than ever. His eyes looked red and his face seemed drawn and weary. Had he been sitting there since early afternoon? My heart went out to him in gratitude. I smiled and stretched, then sat up and wtrapped my arms around my knees.

"How do you feel, Margaret?" He rose stiffly and walked toward me.

"I feel hungry and I ache." I rubbed my bare arms and winced. "But I'm very glad to be alive."

Wordlessly, he picked up my shawl and draped it across my shoulders. I glanced down in dismay. Good heavens, here I was, sitting up in bed before a man, clothed only in a thin, muslin nightshirt that was slipping down my arms. I drew the shawl together quickly and sank back on the pillows.

"I won't trouble you with questions now, Margaret," he said, "about how you came to get trapped in that cave. It can wait until you're better. I don't need to tell you how glad I — everyone — we're all so relieved that you were found." His voice choked and he turned away, calling back over his shoulder, "I'll send Annie with a tray of supper for you since you're hungry." The door closed softly.

He had been worried, I thought, a little smugly. Very worried! He had carried me into the house, put salve on my bruises, then watched over me until I wakened. I wondered what his wife thought of such concern for a mere nurse?

My contemplation was interrupted by the arrival of Annie with a tray containing a bowl of chicken broth, a slice of turbot, croquettes with peas, and a dish of soft blancmange, which I usually detested, but this time devoured ravenously.

When Annie returned for the tray, I was nearly asleep, but something roused in my mind when I saw the young, full-figured maid with her good-natured, pretty face. Annie . . . and James . . . I should have told Jared about them. Oh, it would have to wait . . . a little longer. . . . It would make no difference now . . .

The next time I woke up, it was morning. Someone had recently put a pot of tea beside my bed, and, while I was drinking the comforting hot beverage, Jared knocked and entered. This time, the shawl was on the bed near at hand, and I flung it quickly around my shoulders.

He looked at me with satisfaction. "No need to ask how you are feeling. The sparkle of health is back in those clear, grey eyes, and there's a pink glow in your cheeks."

"I can get up today," I said, setting the cup down on the bedside table. "I feel quite all right."

"Very well, in a few minutes, my dear. First, I want to hear what happened." He seated himself in a chair and crossed his legs. "How did you get yourself into such a dangerous predicament?"

Feeling a little defensive, I didn't look at him as I answered. "Well, as you know, Harriet claimed to hear voices in her room, murmuring, chuckling, late at night when no one was around. Sometimes the door to her closet moves back and forth."

He regarded me without a word.

"I wanted to set her mind at rest, if I could. I felt certain there must be a perfectly natural explanation. The stormy sea or a full tide sweeping through an underground channel seemed the obvious answer."

"All very well," Jared interrupted, "but why did you go inside the caves alone without a word to anybody?"

"I didn't mean to. It happened on the spur of the moment. But when I stood at the entrance, something seemed to draw me in. And the tide was far out then, truly it was."

"But it comes up very fast at certain times of the year. If you had only discussed this with me first—"

"I'm sorry."

"Well, go on. 'Something drew you in'?" he prompted sardonically.

I tilted my chin. "All right, it was my own curiosity. That, and the necessity of finding an explanation for Harriet."

"And did you succeed?"

"I think so. I waded to the back of the caverns and found that I was directly underneath a portion of the cellars. I could hear something like a cart rattling across a stone floor and the clink of glass. Then I heard the sound of voices. James was there with a girl. I think it must have been Annie. They seemed to be . . . carrying on."

"And the proper Miss MacNeil was shocked?"

"No," I answered calmly. "I know what James is like."

"And what is that?"

"You don't know?"

"I suppose he 'carries on' with any girl who will let

128

him. Miss Grey has complained to me about his pursuit of the maids—though I seriously doubt if they give him too much resistance. He's a handsome rogue. I would get rid of him if help were not so hard to come by on the island—James is skilled with horses." Suddenly, his dark brows drew together. "He hasn't bothered *you*, by any chance?"

"Nothing to worry about. Bascom sent him about his business one night before James could do more than make a few insinuating remarks to me."

Jared's lips tightened. "Soon there will be a hiring fair on the mainland. I think I should attend it. But we have gotten off the subject of your adventure in the caves. Pray continue."

"Well, as I stood there listening, I heard Annie agree to let James into the house at midnight. They mentioned meeting in 'the room above Miss Harriet's.' "

Jared swore without apology. "They are using the empty room upstairs! Annie sleeps down here next to Harriet—but evidently not all night. That settles it," he ground out. "They both must go. Annie even fooled Miss Grey."

Biting my lip, I looked down, smoothing my fingers over the counterpane. "I hate to see Annie leave. She is a big help to me—and Harriet likes her. Is there no other way?"

Jared stared out of the window. After a moment, he said grudgingly, "Perhaps a chastisement will suffice for Annie, and she will behave if James is gone. I'll have a word with both of them tonight, believe me."

He sighed gustily and rubbed the back of his neck. "I have been remiss in straightening out my household, haven't I? First, I neglect my wife and child. Now this

129

problem with the servants goes on right beneath my roof. My only excuse is that I am away so much and so involved with my writing."

I could only stare at him dumbly, amazed at this confidence. Did he regret neglecting Katherine? Did he really care for her? Oddly enough, I didn't find the thought particularly pleasant.

Jared rose and came to stand beside the bed, and, suddenly, his bleak expression lessened. "Women are such frail creatures," he said softly. "A prey to the lusts of men and sometimes helpless before their own emotions. Ah, yes, I know that women can feel desire — even the so-called good women."

I steeled my face to hide the sudden surge of feeling within me. All too well I knew the meaning of the reactions I felt whenever Jared Warwick focused his charm in my direction. He was increasingly attractive to me — yet inwardly I cringed from this unmaidenly admission.

Thank heaven, Jared had no inkling of my thoughts, as evidenced by his next words, which he spoke in a much cooler tone than heretofore.

"You do not lose control very often, do you, Margaret? You are a strong, determined young woman who fought her way out of a flooded cave. I would like to know how you accomplished such a fantastic feat."

To my consternation, he now sat down on the foot of the bed and folded his arms across his chest. Carefully, I slid my legs farther away beneath the covers and saw him smile a little, knowingly. He certainly had no right to be alone with me in my room, especially sitting on the bed! His manners were sometimes unorthodox, to say the least. Hardly those of a true gentleman. And yet . . . did I really mind?

"I'm waiting," Jared said.

Nervously, I cleared my throat and looked away. "Well, I went into the cave and stayed too long. Before I knew what was happening, the tide had come up. The waves were dashing in the entrance, almost covering it. When I looked out, I saw you on the point and tried to call, but you didn't hear me, did you?"

I looked at him inquiringly and saw him shake his head.

My thoughts turned inward, remembering the terror of those moments, and I shuddered. "For a while, I thought that I might drown. I couldn't fight my way through the waves; they were too strong. So I turned back and managed to climb the rocks inside the cave. I could see light coming in from somewhere, and, by following it, I discovered a chimney of rock leading to the outside of the cliff. I climbed it just like those poor little chimney sweeps do."

"Oh, my dear, what a dauntless creature you are," he murmured, and a thread of laughter shook his voice.

I threw him a suspicious glance and then continued. "I only did what had to be done to survive. Otherwise, I would have died. I almost gave up near the end, but I called to you when I was nearly at the top of the chimney. You heard. And lifted me out, thank God." My voice shook, and, for a moment, our sober glances clung, both of us aware of the terrible danger I had been in. His glance was tempered by a slight reproof for my foolhardy conduct, mine by a sheepish acknowledgment of that fact.

Then another memory suffused my face with scarlet heat. "My-My dress," I stammered. "I had to take it off

131

so I could climb the rocks. Those men—did anyone—see—"

"—anything they shouldn't? No, no," he said soothingly. "Believe me, Margaret, everyone was so worried and concerned, all we could think about was that you had been found and were alive and safe. You can't imagine the consternation after Timothy reported you had disappeared. I didn't dream you could be inside the cave, because I saw the tide was clear up to the entrance. Incidentally, when we rescued you, Tim covered you with his jacket, and I carried you inside."

In a surge of embarrassment, I remembered the closeness of our bodies when he held me, his heart pounding against my breast. The wet cloth of my inadequate chemise must have been clinging like a second skin. Of course, he had looked at me. A sensual man like Jared? Even in that time of stress, he would have looked. I felt an odd stab of almost physical excitement.

Luckily, a knock sounded at the door just then, and Jared rose leisurely from the bed and admitted Mollie, the underhousemaid, carrying a silver tray of covered dishes, which she placed across my knees.

"You're spoiling me," I murmured, glancing up at Jared.

"Not at all," he answered. "And when I go to Lingrove, you must come with me, and I will buy you a pair of shoes, or a length of dress material, or anything else that needs replacing."

"Oh, that won't be necessary," I protested.

"I insist that it is. You lost a dress and other things in the performance of your duty—as you saw it." His lips twitched.

132

Mollie was nearly out the door, when he added, "Do you want the maid to brush your hair?"

His eyes were on the tangled, red curls tumbling about my shoulders. "I'll take care of it," I muttered, putting up my hand. "I know it is a mess."

"Not at all. It's very appealing. Now I know how you look in bed."

He left, then, and I certainly was relieved that Mollie had gone, also, so that she didn't hear his last remark. I should reprove him for such suggestive words to me. Did he think a mere nurse was an easy prey, I wondered, with a little wave of indignation.

But my mind was soon diverted by the food, and I ate my breakfast hungrily, devouring two boiled eggs, a kippered herring, soft, white muffins covered with marmalade, and making deep inroads into the pot of tea with milk.

I was barely finished when Harriet entered, eagerly propelling herself up to the bed in her wheelchair. "Margaret, are you all right? Papa said you were. Oh, I'm so glad you weren't hurt. I knew something was wrong when you didn't come back after such a long time. I woke Timmy and he looked all over for you. Soon everyone was searching for you: Papa, James, everyone. How I hated waiting in my room! I know you went in the cave just to help me, didn't you? I felt so guilty. Am I to blame?" she asked, in a tone unusually humble.

"Of course, you're not." I touched her hand.

She smiled and sat up straighter. "Now, tell me everything that happened." Her dark-eyed gaze was as insistent as her father's.

As I began relating the adventure in the cave, I tried

to diminish the horror as much as possible, but, in spite of myself, my voice shook, and I knew my face must reflect the awful memory of that time when my life hung in the balance and I battled elements and surroundings I had never dreamed of heretofore. I had been foolishly daring—so contrary to my cautious nature—but I also had been driven by the determination to set Harriet's mind at rest. And in that I had been successful.

"I don't know how you dared wade through that arch into such black water," Harriet breathed. "Weren't you afraid of the creatures in it? Ugh, I would have died," she shuddered.

"I just didn't stop to think, Harriet. But when something did brush against my leg, I must have jumped a foot into the air."

Her eyes were huge. "You're brave, Nurse Margaret. You really are. And you did it all for me."

I nodded. "Now we know what caused those voices that frightened you. It was Annie and James in the room above yours. I noticed a space behind your wardrobe and the original wall. It must have acted like an air vent to conduct the sound of their voices. As for the movement of the door, that was from the tide coming and going beneath the cellars."

"Just as you thought," Harriet exclaimed. She was silent for a moment. "Well, you've cleared up that mystery. But there are other things. Like Black Bob throwing me—"

"That burr under his saddle might have dropped out of a tree or been blown there by the wind."

Harriet looked skeptical. "What about that knifing of Papa at your door in London? And the food you ate from Papa's tray that nearly poisoned you? That was meant for *him*. Oh, why are these things happening?" she wailed, pounding her fist on the arm of her wheelchair. Her voice dropped to a whisper. "I wonder if Papa has made an enemy . . ."

A sudden thought struck me. "Harriet, these books that your father writes, do you know what they're about?"

"Nobody knows. He keeps the door locked all the time."

"Does he use a pen name?" I asked, remembering that Octavia had said she'd heard of a writer named Jared Warwick. And she was an avid patron of the circulating library, which carried a big line of books.

"What's a 'pen name'?" Harriet's brow quirked. "Oh, I know what you mean. I heard Mama talking to Sylvia one day. She said she didn't want to know anything about his work as long as the books made money and Papa continued using a—a pen name so we wouldn't be embarrassed." She stared at me with a puzzled frown. "Why should we be embarrassed?"

"I don't know . . . Your father told me that he does a lot of research on the mainland. London, I suppose?"

"Yes, and he usually comes back looking like a black devil after digging into things. This time he didn't look like that. Even though it took him a little while to recover from his wound, he seemed—happy. I think he's glad you're here." She added shyly, "And so am I.

I felt a rush of pleasure and a determination to justify such trust. A plan of action should be established. But how? In what direction?

"Harriet, is everyone here above reproach? Miss

135

Grey? Annie? Timothy?"

The girl looked bleak. "I've known them all my life, but sometimes people change and do bad things for money. In *Lady Pamela's Fortune*, she was abducted by her old childhood friend who needed her ransom to cover gambling debts. Maybe Timmy will abduct me for money and I'll be just like a heroine in a novel." She put up her hand to hide a sudden fit of giggles.

I shook my head at her. "This is not a novel, dear. This is serious. We must keep our wits about us always. Too many things are happening." I thought a minute. "Cool and canny — those should be our watchwords."

" 'Cool and Canny,' I like that." I saw her whisper to herself in swift delight, "A secret watchword!" She nodded at me with shining eyes. "I don't think I'll be afraid any more, as long as you are here."

"That's my girl."

After Harriet had gone, I rose and dressed, then sat by the window for a while, thinking, chin upon my hand. I had solved one problem regarding the voices, it was true, but the main question still remained unanswered. I was sure that Jared had an enemy. But why? And who was it?

Katherine Warwick seemed to be the only one who would benefit by his death. She hated her country existence, and, if Jared died, she would be a wealthy woman, free to lead her own life and marry whom she pleased.

Madam Lelong appeared to have no motive whatsoever.

Did Timothy? Perhaps he still loved Katherine and was determined to set her free.

And Sylvia? She might be intrigued by Jared, but what reason would she have for killing him? Unless her love had been spurned and had turned to hate, well-concealed by her flirtatious manner toward him.

There even was a possibility that Jared might have angered someone with his books. Perhaps he had a secret enemy who had penetrated the island.

I gave a groan and shut my eyes. There simply were no answers for me. Yet the time was running out, and the next attempt might very well be fatal.

Chapter Fourteen

That afternoon, at a time when everybody was usually resting, two visitors came to my door. And two very disturbing visitors they proved to be.

The first person to arrive was Katherine Warwick. She was dressed in hyacinth-blue muslin with a berthe of embroidered organdy. Rather casual attire for her, as she usually leaned toward theatrical draperies, but still it was effective and becoming—as was everything she wore.

As she looked at me, however, the beauty of her features was marred by a look of peevish irritation. "Well, nurse, I see that you've recovered," she said. "I heard about your escapade, of course. I can't imagine how you could have been so foolish as to go into those caves alone and upset the entire household."

I had to temper my voice and mien to the obsequiousness proper to a nurse. "I'm sorry, madam. It wasn't my intention to upset the household, I assure you. I only—"

"But still, that's what you did," Mrs. Warwick interrupted. "And well you know it. It wouldn't surprise me if you had planned the act deliberately to attract attention, and then it backfired on you."

While I sputtered a denial, she continued, overriding my words as her face hardened. "You are constantly making excuses to be with my husband. Don't think you fool me. Jared spends as much time 'conferring' with you—" her thin red lips curled scornfully, "—as he does writing in his room these days. One would almost think—"

She broke off, her blue skirts whirling as she spun closer to me. "Has he invited you into his room yet? Has he shown you his secret manuscript? Or doesn't he waste time on such obvious ploys? Does he go straight into . . . other matters? *You know what I mean.*"

I had never been so insulted in my life! I fell back from the proximity of her violet perfume, feeling as though my face had turned to chalk. "Indeed, I don't know what you mean! What are you insinuating?" My own voice grew hard, now—and accusing. "Tell me plainly what you mean, Mrs. Warwick."

My manner seemed to blunt her attack. Suddenly, there was a change of tactics. Mrs. Warwick shrugged, murmuring airily, "Oh, nothing. I merely wondered what you talk about."

She began to stroll around the room, languidly fingering a golden tassel here, a green brocade drape there, her eyes and hands exploring, assessing. I hated the possessive touch she placed on everything. But then the room was really hers—not mine.

I realized that her anger was now held in check by a tremendous willpower as she said blandly, "Jared ordered these furnishings put in here. It must be quite a new experience for you, living in such luxury."

When I didn't answer right away, she quirked an eyebrow at me, staring until I was forced to reply. "Your husband is a very generous man. Because I attended him when he was stabbed, he seemed to feel an obligation to me. I have told him repeatedly that there was no necessity for that."

"Did you really?" Katherine shrugged. "I told him the same thing, but you know how stubborn he can be. Just yesterday, when you disappeared, he was so distraught not a soul could reason with him. I suggested that you might have slipped away to dally with someone in the village, and he roared, 'Miss MacNeil would never *dally* on the job. Or leave her charge waiting on the beach.' I must admit, I didn't share his high opinion of you. We've had too many flighty people in attendance on my daughter."

She delicately smoothed my satin coverlet, but her eyes lifted to pierce my face and mind. "I would advise you, Miss MacNeil, not to go flitting into other dangerous situations, or even my tolerant husband's patience will wear thin."

"I assure you I had a very good reason for going into the caves—" I began stiffly.

"Oh, I'm sure you gave my husband some good explanation for your heedless conduct. He certainly was in your room long enough to hear a dozen such excuses."

I didn't answer. I tried to keep my eyes steady and my face aloof, revealing nothing.

This seemed only to irritate her further. She crossed the room and gripped my arm. Her hand was white

140

and slender, but it had the force of steel. It bit into the soft flesh of my arm, which was still sore from clinging to the rocky cave. An anguished cry escaped me, which Katherine completely disregarded.

"I'm warning you, Miss MacNeil, stick to your duties in the future, and stop trying to insinuate yourself into my husband's presence and good graces."

"I do not—I never—"

Her voice rose shrilly, blotting out my wild denials. "I think by now you may realize that my husband has certain strong, male appetites where women are concerned. Sensing this, the former nurses chased him, and, believe me, he didn't fight them off. Especially that little bit of fluff, Rosie Mason."

My whole body shook with indignation. "Madam, surely you exaggerate. Mr. Warwick has always been the picture of a perfect gentleman. It's absolutely ridiculous to tell me these things about him—to warn me—to suggest that he—that he might—"

My voice gagged and my fingers tightened on the folds of my brown skirt. I felt like tightening my fingers around her throat to halt her silly, vicious utterances.

Why was she lying? Not for a second did I believe that Jared was some kind of a ravening beast lusting after every female near him. Hadn't I seen his reactions to Lady Sylvia's blatant invitations? Wasn't he always kind, considerate, and courteous to me? Of course, I had received a few overly warm remarks from him, but that was nothing, I told myself. Just his gratitude toward someone who had saved his life and now was caring conscientiously for his daughter.

Mrs. Warwick placed her hands on her waist and surveyed me scornfully. "So you don't believe me? Have you really never felt yourself respond to any of his blandishments? Ah, I see your face is changing color. Yes, nurse, even *I* must seek a room not too close to his. If you take my meaning."

Then why was she always taunting and teasing her husband with suggestive invitations in the presence of other people? Playing the adoring wife? Wouldn't a cool manner have been more likely to repulse a too-ardent spouse?

I didn't speak, but I am certain that my face showed absolute rejection of her ridiculous remarks.

"Very well, I've warned you," she hissed angrily. "It will be on your own head if you find yourself mistaken."

She crossed her arms, and a more thoughtful expression filled her face. "Do you want proof? Ask Rosie Mason on the mainland. She has recently rejected nursing, with its attendant annoyance from pursuing husbands and sons in the homes where she was employed. Now she runs a shop of sorts in Lingrove. Selling toys and knick-knacks, I believe. Anyone can point it out."

For the first time, my disbelief wavered. She was offering me *proof*. Ah, well, the Mason woman might have deluded herself that the fascinating Jared Warwick had found her attractive. Perhaps she had made the overtures herself, and had, for this reason, been dismissed by him. I still could not see such an intelligent, kind, thoughtful man as Jared chasing after all the nurses who came into his home. I almost felt like laughing.

Mrs. Warwick's eyes narrowed with suspicion. "Hmmm, perhaps you favor such advances? Perhaps that's why you want no warning from me?"

"Mrs. Warwick," I gasped, "I will not be accused unjustly of improper conduct, or I shall leave this house at once. I have done nothing to be ashamed of. Neither has your husband." I drew myself tall. "Is it your intention to ask for my dismissal? I don't think either Harriet or her father is ready for me to leave. If you have such a hard time finding help, you might find Harriet a problem for some time to come."

Katherine fell back, looking somewhat confused. She really wasn't a very sharp-witted woman, I thought scornfully.

I pressed my advantage. "Your husband told me that I would be treated with every consideration when I came here — not chastised for some imagined wrong like an erring servant. I was to be a companion to your daughter, as well as her nurse."

The woman before me made a final bluff. "Well, what are you complaining about? Your duties are light, you are well paid, you have a lovely room. What more do you want?"

I replied with cold deliberation, telling myself fiercely that I spoke the truth: "*I do not want your husband, Mrs. Warwick.*"

"Just see that you remember that," was Katherine's parting shot. And then she whirled out of the room.

Weak in the knees, I fell into a chair and groaned aloud. I didn't know whether to laugh, sob, or pound the armchair. The stupid, ridiculous woman! What had been her purpose behind all that rigamarole? A child could see her threats were idle. She couldn't force my resignation. Jared was in charge here.

As for the aspersions she had cast on his character — were they supposed to make me shun his company with terror and loathing? I chuckled, then, dry humor coming to my rescue. Jared had called me sensible and practical, had he not? And this I would be, outwardly, at least. I would submerge the attraction I had sometimes felt for him.

I would be especially careful after this talk with his wife. Unfounded though her suspicions were, it was enough that I must have aroused her jealousy. How or why I really couldn't fathom. I stared at my familiar face in the pier glass opposite. Sober grey eyes, controlled, full lips — only the thick red curls gave me the slightest appearance of seduction. No, it was not a face to set men wild. And yet . . . Jared seemed to stare at it quite a bit . . .

A sudden state of bemused speculation crept upon me, but alas, it was rudely shattered the next instant by a pounding on my door.

Before I could even rise or call out an inquiry, the door burst open and my second caller stepped into the room.

It was Lady Sylvia, clad today in ruffles of black organdy. She wore no adornment; *that* was saved for the evening hours, when masculine eyes could view her. Now only her white skin caught my eye, as well as her own green orbs, glittering like emeralds beneath her casually arranged gold ringlets.

Without waiting for an invitation, she crossed the carpet soundlessly and dropped into a chair, pulling it around to face me squarely.

"I hear you had a bad experience in the caves." There was not the slightest trace of sympathy in her voice. "Rather a thoughtless junket, I would say, for someone entrusted with the care of an invalid child."

My former defiance drooped. Unlike Mrs. Warwick's unjust accusation of throwing myself at Jared and seeking to become important in his eyes, this charge from the countess was completely justified.

"You are right, my lady," I sighed. "I was foolhardy, I admit. But you see, there was a valid reason why I went into the cave."

Lady Sylvia arched thin, skillfully darkened eyebrows. "And what was that, pray tell?"

Evidently Jared had not told her what I had discovered.

"Harriet has been frightened by her closet door mysteriously swinging open from time to time," I said. "And the sound of voices coming from some unexplained source."

The countess shifted impatiently. "There is altogether too much attention paid to that child and her foolish fancies."

I ignored this and continued. "I told Harriet I thought the movement of her door might be caused by the tides flooding the caves beneath the house. Yesterday, when Timothy, Harriet, and I went to the beach for a picnic, I decided it was a good opportunity to investigate."

The countess sounded bored. "And you discovered you were right, of course."

"That wasn't all I discovered. By wading through an underground pool in the cave, I found it extended beneath the cellars of this house. I heard two voices speaking. They were discussing a rendezvous at midnight in the empty room above Harriet's. It was their voices she would hear, whispering and chuckling."

"It was James and Annie, I suppose?"

My eyes widened. "How did you know?"

"Oh, I've seen them in the corridor a few times, giggling, squirming, and kissing. He's a good-looking rascal, isn't he?" The countess looked away with a slight smile.

"Why didn't you tell Mr. Warwick?"

"Why should I? I'm not mistress here. The romantic romps of the servants do not interest me in the slightest." Her green gaze sharpened. "But—you do. I've never seen Jared so upset as he was when you disappeared. And there are other marks of his—um—appreciation. This splendid room, for one, furnished by his own hand, I've heard. An emerald nest to complement a pretty redhead. Just how long have you and Jared known each other?" The curious glance she bent on me was slightly tinged with a cynical amusement.

Somehow I didn't resent her questions as much as I had Mrs. Warwick's, and I answered frankly. "We met once in London when he had an accident near my home and I cared for him. After that, he asked me to come here and see what I could do for Harriet. How long have *you* known Mr. Warwick?" I asked, turning the tables boldly. *And how well*? I longed to add. But I was not that bold.

The countess answered as readily as I had. "I met Mrs. Warwick at Vivienne Lelong's salon in London a little over six months ago. We became friends, and soon she started inviting me down here on visits. That's when I met Jared."

"Were you here when Harriet had her accident?"

"Yes, and so were Vivienne and Timothy. The child was home from boarding school recuperating from *la grippe*. She was bored and in a bad mood, as I recall.

146

Jealous because her father was so busy with his book and because I took up her mother's time. Anyway, to gain attention, Harriet tried to ride a horse much too big for her. You know the outcome."

Lady Sylvia had a cynical version of the accident, probably from the tongue of Mrs. Warwick. I didn't comment. The real story was too involved.

The countess left soon after, swishing from the room as imperiously as she had entered, with never a word about my condition. Like the servant's problems, it didn't interest her.

Why had she come? My experience in the caves and Jared's reaction to it had triggered some strange behavior on the parts of the two women who had visited me this afternoon. If it wasn't so ridiculous, I would suspect that they were jealous of me.

And if they had known about the note that night from Jared and my prompt response, they would have had fresh fuel for their speculations.

Chapter Fifteen

I spent the evening resting in my room without any further visitors, except for Mollie who brought my supper on a tray. I made no more objections regarding this indulgence, but sat up eagerly in a chair to consume the victuals placed on a small table across my knees.

The fare consisted of stronger, tastier morsels than before, and I was pleased to be considered past the stage of requiring clear broth and blancmange. Tonight I was served game soup, a slice of turbot with lobster sauce, potato sprouts with new creamed peas, a compote of spiced apples, currant jelly tart, and a glass of very nice madeira. It was all served on gold-rimmed plates. The tray cloth had pansies embroidered on a snowy linen. Quite the finest attention I had received thus far.

Could Jared have had a hand in the direction of my meal? Miss Grey would not have been likely to so favor a mere nurse; especially one whose place in the house she already questioned as not being the innocent nursing assignment it claimed to be. I was sure she believed that I was some former light o' love of the master's brought here for his own illicit pleasure. The idea made me chuckle, even while a thread of speculation trickled through my mind. Did Jared have light o' loves? After a minute, I chided myself sternly. Why would I even *think* about such a matter? It certainly was no concern of mine.

No, Jared, acting merely as a thoughtful employer, must have instructed Cook to prepare my meal quite carefully and serve it as though I were a favored guest. I tried to quell the rush of pleasure this idea gave me by reminding myself that it was only Jared's kindness and concern for someone ably caring for his daughter. He knew that my unfortunate experience in the cave had been the result of my desire to discover the source of the frightening noises in her room.

Yes, and I had accomplished something there. One mystery had been solved. But a greater one remained. *Who was trying to harm Jared?*

Absently, I chewed a sauce-coated bite of fish, but, since no ideas came to me, I pushed back the lace curtain from the pane and stared out of the window, hoping to extract a little calmness from the scene. It was almost the season of our longest English twilights, and the garden was still visible, with its rustling trees, low, fragrant bushes by the sea wall, and, far away, the distant band of darkening, blue water. It all was so peaceful . . . so lovely . . .

But something evil lay concealed on this bit of land called Brendan's Isle. Something had struck several times, with a malice aimed at Jared. Once it had erred and struck his daughter. Once I had absorbed the wickedness when I ate the cake containing poison.

I sipped my wine and frowned. Malice . . . now that I considered every incident, I wondered why none of it had ever proven fatal. The knife wound had been too high. The burr under Black Bob's saddle had only made him toss the child onto the beach. The cake? Hardly enough poison to kill.

Was everything just a warning?

Or . . . perhaps they were trying to make people think that Jared was subject to bad luck. So that when the final, killing blow was struck, everyone would believe it was just his ill fate, this time unfortunately turned deadly.

That meant that the last attempt must look like an accident.

My heart sank. My appetite was gone. I pushed aside the jelly tart, drained the gold-rimmed wine glass, and picked up my shawl. I needed fresh air to calm my worrisome thoughts, or I would never sleep.

As I entered the garden, I wondered, still unable to stop my speculations: How could I help Jared? How could he be saved from that fatal accident? And who was at the bottom of it all?

As before, Katherine Warwick headed my list of suspects. But I could be wrong. Someone else might be the instrument of death.

I shivered, drawing my paisley shawl tighter, although the night was mild. It was my own fear that chilled my blood. *What could I do?* I had no plan as yet, but I must keep my eyes and ears alert. At least, I was conscious of Jared's danger; unfortunately, there was no one else I could trust to help me.

After pacing back and forth, I decided firmly on one thing: Whatever happened, I must not leave here until this awful matter was resolved. The villain might just get tired and quit. (But I didn't really believe that for longer than a minute.)

I raised my skirt and took the path across the dew-wet lawn until I reached the wall. Far below the sea rushed back and forth on its endless, sweeping tides, moaning, grinding relentlessly until it wore away the rocks to crumbling sand.

So might this insidious war of frightening near-misses wear away even the rocklike strength of Jared. But to what purpose? A divorce? A life permanently established in London? A return to the arms of a woman he had scorned? All seemed too puny for such extremes, such diabolical actions.

Unless . . . the perpetrator was mentally unbalanced. My heart beat faster. I knew full well from nursing experiences how an apparently normal person could hide a twisted, malevolent mind that sometimes strayed from its regular paths to move in dark labyrinths unknown — thank God! — to most of us.

Still the question hammered at my brain: Who? Who? Only the seabirds answered, crying: "He! He!" Or did they answer: "She! She!"

Sighing, I leaned my arms along the wall, feeling the warmth of the past sunny hours captured in the stone, and gradually my shivering stopped. As I idly watched the waves, my eyes strayed to the point. And there I beheld Jared. He was sitting on some flat-topped boulders, arms around his bent knees. A white, full-sleeved shirt belled out in the breeze. His dark hair was blowing, too. And though I only could see his profile, he seemed to be wrapped in concentration.

My first instinct was to speed down the cliffside to

join him. But then I thought: Ah, no. Katherine Warwick might see me and be furious. "There's that infatuated nurse chasing after Jared. Just like all the others." *That* I would not be. I was no chaser. Certainly I would have enjoyed some quiet moments in Jared's company. We could have talked. Perhaps discussed the peril I was sure surrounded him. Yes, a talk would be in order, but not at night on a darkening, deserted beach. I drew my shawl around my arms and marched resolutely back into the house.

I lit a lamp when I regained my room, and it was then that I saw it. A folded, sealed note on the bedroom carpet. My name in bold, black letters, the white square contrasting loudly with the bright green carpet. Curiously, I turned it over in my hand, then broke the seal, stepping closer to the lamplight's glow to read it:

> My dear —
> I must talk to you about a very important matter.
> Meet me on the beach tonight at ten o'clock.
>
> Jared Warwick

I felt elation flood me. Now I could follow my first instinct and rush down to the beach to be with him. Nobody could censure me for obeying a summons from my employer. After all, the hour was a good one for a conference. At ten o'clock the music and party-making was at its peak, while Harriet would be sound asleep. Undoubtedly Jared wanted to confer with me about his daughter.

I had my shawl on once again and my hand was upon the china knob when another idea assailed me.

Suppose Katherine Warwick had gone to him with her complaints about my conduct and demanded that he terminate my stay? Perhaps that was the real "important matter." But why should he choose the beach to tell me? Ah—perhaps he wanted to soften the blow in private!

I drew a rather shaken breath. Whatever the reason, I had no excuse for not going to meet him. I picked up the note and thrust it in my pocket. When could it have been delivered? Not by Jared. He was on the beach. Was I certain it hadn't been shoved beneath my door *before* I strolled into the garden? No, I wasn't sure. My mind had been in a seething turmoil, filled with other matters than the carpet at my feet.

Unseen by anyone—at least, so I thought—I hurried back once more into the garden. A glance across the seawall showed me that Jared hadn't moved. He was too far away to call; besides the waves had grown much noisier, just as they did each night.

Shadows stretched, black and secretive, encroaching on the vanishing tail of twilight. But a moon shone fitfully between scudding clouds, and I could easily pick out the wooden steps set into the cliff. Bushes edged the zigzag path, as well as many rocks and boulders, but I descended rapidly, surefooted, eager to hear what Jared had to say, praying it would not be news of my dismissal. If it was—well, maybe I could change his mind.

I felt strangely lighthearted as I sped across the sand toward him, my fringed shawl fluttering, the sea breeze loosening curls from the ribbon I had tied around my hair to confine it at my nape. A hopeless tangle fell about my shoulders by the time I had reached Jared and stood looking up at him from the beach below his perch.

"Mr. Warwick, did you want me?" I shouted.

His eyes flew wide when he turned his head in my direction. "Margaret," he cried. He stared, then smiled, his hard, rugged face changing to something kind and happy, almost tender — as it often seemed to do when he looked at me lately.

He didn't ask what I was doing there or why I had come. He simply reached down his big, square hand and guided me to a perch beside him. I spread my shawl to sit on. He moved it closer.

Suddenly, my heart was beating very fast. It was almost dark, the moon was fitful, to say the least. And Jared, warm, strong, and masculine, was very near, his eyes never straying from my face.

"I was thinking of you," he said softly.

I bit my lip. "I hope you weren't thinking about dismissing me," I burst out, my voice apprehensive.

"What! Of course not. I lo-like having you here. You are doing a fine job. I enjoy your company. So does Harriet. Why should I think of firing you, my dear? What put that idea into your lovely head?" His hand moved and covered mine upon the rock.

I felt an odd, light-headed confusion. Should I tell him about Katherine's visit? This moment seemed so peaceful, so perfect, I hesitated to destroy it. Just the two of us with the lonely sea, the deserted beach. I didn't have sense enough to draw my hand from his. Only later could I marvel, appalled, at this loose-mannered creature who sat with her employer, hand-in-hand, drawing in the fresh and tangy air. I lifted my face to the moonlight, aware of Jared's black eyes that gazed silently at my blowing hair, moved across my face, my throat. Even when I knew he stared at my outlined bosom, my bared arms, I didn't turn away. Or even speak. I waited.

If he had touched me further or placed his lips on mine, I'll never know how I would have reacted.

For he did neither.

His lazily exploring gaze suddenly sharpened on my face. "Margaret, are you all right? Did you come out here to tell me something?"

My eyes met his and widened. "Don't *you* know why I came out here?"

His deeply carved lips quirked. "I'd like to think you craved my company. That was my first, delighted assumption. But then I realized that the discreet and sensible Scottish lassie would never seek a rendezvous with her employer on a dark, deserted beach, unless she had an important reason."

I stared at him blankly. "You sent me a message to come here."

"Not I."

My hand went to my pocket. I held out the note. "This was placed beneath my door tonight. I came at once. Do you mean to say you didn't send it?"

"I never saw it before." He read it, frowning. "It's printed. Not handwritten."

"That's true, but I never thought to question it." I looked at him, bewildered. "What does it mean? Why was it sent? And who—"

He sprang up, lifting me to my feet. "Come! We must return at once. This may be a trick. A trap—"

"Harriet!" I gasped, scarcely aware that his arms were about me tightly as he swung me to the sand.

155

"Hurry!" I stumbled ahead of him, raising my annoying, impeding skirts, my shawl slipping and fluttering.

"Go ahead," I panted when we reached the cliff.

"No, no," he said impatiently. "I'll follow you. It would be too easy for you to miss the steps in this darkness. I'll be right behind."

We scrambled upward until we were halfway there. Then, suddenly, Jared uttered a sharp cry that froze me in my tracks. *"Look out, Margaret!"*

A large rock bounced downward, missing us by inches. Then another. And another. Jared pressed me flat against the cliff, shielding my body with his own. He jerked my shawl from my shoulders and flung it to protect our faces as a regular rain of rocks and earth drummed past, clattering, bounding. Some were huge stones, judging by the crashing sound; the rest must have been a torrent of pebbles.

Fortunately, nothing struck our bodies, and finally the deluge ended. Jared drew away the scarf and we both coughed and coughed.

"Are you all right?" he asked hoarsely, brushing at my hair, my gown, examining my arms for marks. "You're shaking, Margaret. It's all right — it's over now."

He swept the dust from himself and applied a handkerchief to his face. He peered downward into the darkness, then looked up above, narrowly scanning the seawall.

"What caused that?" I croaked, following his gaze. I felt my fear subsiding slowly, leaving me weak and trembling. "We could have been severely injured!"

"Or killed. I guess that we've survived a landslide."

Grimly, his voice and face like granite, Jared steered me upward to the top. We could then see where rocks and earth had been loosened to plunge downward just when we were in the path. An accident? Or deliberate? A sick feeling of horror almost gagged me. Had the villain struck again? This time aiming at us both?

"That message — it was to get me to the beach," I gasped. "Do you usually walk there at this time of night?"

"I have been lately. There are problems to be solved. I have to think."

His hands reached out and gripped my shoulders fiercely. "Margaret, you must leave here! It isn't safe for you anymore. Tonight proved that."

Scarcely aware of what I did, I placed my hands upon his chest, looking up into his angry, shadowed face. "It's not safe for you either. But *you* won't leave. Do you think I'd go with you and Harriet still at someone's mercy?"

"Oh, Margaret —" he whispered brokenly.

As he drew me closer, my weakened senses swam. My lips felt soft, warm, yielding. *I wanted him to kiss me* — to my everlasting shame! I waited, breath suspended.

Then . . . what did I do? That awful Scottish prude inside me said, "Perhaps we should see if Harriet really is all right."

He sucked in a shaken breath. The spell dissolved. "Yes, of course. You're right. As usual."

His arms trailed slowly from around me and we began to climb the hill. Was I a fool? Or was I wise? The moment of surrendering something vital had been so close. When it came again — and it certainly was a possibility — how could we keep our emotions from exploding?

It was going to take all the self-control at my command, for now I knew that Jared was not referring to the attempts upon his life when he had said:

"There is a danger right at my side that I am helpless to combat."

Chapter Sixteen

We found that Harriet was all right and sound asleep. After that, Jared and I bade each other a rather sober goodnight. Neither one of us made further mention of the experience we had just been through. It was almost as though talking about it would unleash the fears we both kept shuttered in our breasts.

Had it been an accident? In view of all the other things, including the mysterious note, I had my doubts. And yet . . . earthslides were not unknown, and certainly Cornwall had a rocky coast and tides of eerie, abnormal strength. I had read of an island off its shores—St. Michael's Mount—where one could walk across the half-mile causeway; yet at other times the roaring sea required a boat, depending on the time and tide.

And we knew now our own tides shook the house.

The trouble with having unexplained, strange accidents was that soon everything took on the appearance of diabolical intent. The slightest upset, the slightest deviation from the norm could cause a leaping pulse, a rush of apprehensive fear.

It was no way to live, and I determined to at least put on a face of calm equanimity toward everyone. No alarm must show, especially when I visited my patient the next morning.

I wondered if Annie would be still visible, and it was Mollie who brought me news of this, along with my rolls and tea. I noticed that she seemed to have acquired a new status of importance — at least in her own mind — since Annie was in disgrace.

While I ate my breakfast, Mollie buzzed about the room, making up the bed and stirring up the fire, while her tongue kept pace with her scampering feet. "Master had a rare set-to with James, I heard. And Annie, too, the silly chit. I coulda told her a thing or two about that hot-eyed laddie-o, but she wouldn't listen. Oh, no. He and Annie was carryin' on in one of the empty rooms, and somebody found out. Guess it was Miss Grey. Anyway, James was told to leave, but Annie can stay if she behaves."

I felt relieved that no one knew I was the one who had informed on James and Annie. I felt rather sorry for the girl. Men like James, young, coarsely handsome, and eager for the chase were probably scarce in her little village.

When I saw her in Harriet's room a little later, I observed her reddened eyes and drooping lips.

"Has that bad James left the island, Annie?" Harriet asked severely, sitting up in her tub while I exercised her limbs in the warm water. I was almost certain there was resistance now in the strengthened muscles, but it was too soon to speak of this.

Annie poured another jug of heated water in the tub

160

and gave a doleful sniff. "I'm sure I hope that James is gone. I was that fearful I'd lose my job, Miss Harriet. He just wouldn't let me be!"

Don't pretend you weren't more than willing to accept his rough lovemaking, I thought sardonically. I had heard her weak protests in the cellars, followed by her complete acquiescence to James's demands for bed and bottle.

I wondered just how much Harriet comprehended of the situation as she admonished Annie: "You must never have anything to do with men like that, my girl. You hear?"

After a fervent promise that she would adhere to perfect conduct in the future, Annie left the room and I lifted my patient onto the bed.

Wrapped in a big towel, Harriet struggled onto her elbows, looking up at me with twinkling eyes. "Don't get out my regular day-dress, Margaret. This morning we're going someplace *special*. Papa's taking us both to Lingrove!"

"What? Lingrove?"

"That's the town by the railroad station. It has lots of shops, an inn, a tavern, a church, everything! Papa's going to the hiring fair and he said we can go shopping while he's there. Won't that be a lark?"

I agreed a little dazedly. Lingrove . . . the home of a certain Rosie Mason. Mrs. Warwick had said she had a shop there now. Perhaps I would devise a chance to see her. Excitement bubbled in my brain. I wouldn't question her. No, *never*! Jared's private life was none of my concern. I was just curious to see the type of woman he might have fancied in his lighter moments.

It was rather puzzling to me. Jared just didn't strike

me as one who carried on affairs right under his own roof. Besides, he was married to a beauty who seemed to crave him madly. Then there was Lady Sylvia, who admired him openly and would perhaps have accepted him quite readily as her "protector."

On the other hand, if Jared had grown cool to Katherine she might have sought retaliation by telling me those tales about his lustful appetites. At the time, I had denounced her remarks as the silly utterances of a petty, jealous woman, but now I wavered when I recalled her saying that I could find Rosie Mason, the ex-nurse, in Lingrove and ask her for myself. Heavens, how I could ask her such a thing? And why would she confide in a complete stranger?

At that point in my thoughts, I was jerked back to the present by Harriet. "Margaret, you're not listening! I asked what you thought I should wear? The rose moiré dress? The blouse and plaid skirt? Queen Victoria loves plaids and they're ever so fashionable now. Or should I wear my blue dress and jacket? It has white frogs down the front and little tassels."

"I vote for frogs and tassels."

When Harriet was dressed, she added a wide-brimmed hat trimmed with purple pansies and then surveyed her reflection in the cheval glass with great approval. "Can't I leave the lap rug home today so everyone can see my pretty outfit?"

"We'll just tuck it behind your back in the chair, lassie, in case you should get chilly. Now I must whisk next door and don my cape and bonnet."

But when I removed my apron and covered the upper portion of my muslin stripes with a short, brown mantle, I couldn't suppress a groan. I looked so dull and drab for such a bright spring day. My heart sank even further when I examined my best bonnet, which never had recovered from its exposure to the rain. As I tied the wrinkled bow beneath my chin, I had a sudden vision of a hat that I had seen once on a fashionable lady in New Bond Street. It had been pale leaf-green, swathed in tulle, and trimmed with gooseberries and pearls. Imagine how . . . everyone's . . . eyes would light up with admiration if I appeared in such a beautiful creation.

Ah, well. Smothering a sigh, I thrust a highly censored letter to Cousin Octavia inside my reticule, slipped on a pair of cotton gloves, and collected Harriet and her wheelchair.

Even before we turned the corner, we could hear Katherine Warwick fuming in the hallway. "I can't just run off and leave Vivienne alone. I don't see why you insist on going, Sylvia—"

"La, dearest, this is my last chance to visit the quaint town of Lingrove. We leave day after tomorrow, you know."

"Why must you go back so soon?" Katherine wailed, catching Sylvia by the arms. "It seems you just arrived."

The countess gently disengaged herself. "I have to meet someone. Vivienne is having an important soirée, mainly in my honor."

Katherine still looked sulky. Neither of them appeared to notice Harriet or the insignificant nurse waiting by the wall.

"Anyway," Sylvia continued. "I am in dire need of some handkerchiefs. Brendan's Isle is rather damp, you know."

"Yes, especially at night," Katherine agreed with a resigned sigh that didn't lighten her querulous expression.

My eyes flew to scan her face. Had she been abroad last evening? Had she thrust the note beneath my door? Then waited—perhaps with someone else—to push the rocks and stones at us? Perhaps Bascom of the weasely face had been paid to help. He looked the sort for whom money would salve every twinge of conscience.

Or maybe Timothy? For love of Katherine? I scrutinized the present company. What was I looking for? Earth lodged under someone's nails? Or a guilty glance, scanning my person for possible injury from the rocks? Alas for my attempts at sleuthing, I found nothing suspicious about anyone.

My gaze returned with reluctant admiration to rest on Lady Sylvia's white lace shawl that she wore today to relieve her somber taffeta. A little hat made entirely of snowy doves was an added touch that made me yearn with envy. How could Jared not notice the difference between the fashionable countess and myself?

When I heard him speak behind me in the hall, however, he sounded slightly irked at the growing assemblage by the door. Timothy was hurrying toward us, also.

"What a party this is turning into," Jared drawled. "I never dreamed my casual remark at supper yesterday would cause everyone to eagerly accompany me to Lingrove. But, of course, I am delighted," he added. "Ah, Tim is going also?"

He stared with little joy at his wife's cousin, who had arrived on the scene in checked trousers and a bright blue coat. Timothy had a large bunch of lilacs and narcissus in his buttonhole, in the current style of certain London "swells," and against his chest he clasped a curly-brimmed grey beaver hat.

"I say, have I kept you waiting? Sorry about that, ducks, but I had to pluck some fresh posies to complete my outfit." He sniffed happily at his bouquet.

"Oh, Timmy, are you deserting me, too?" Katherine wailed.

"What? Aren't you going, love?"

"I have to stay with Vivienne. She doesn't feel quite the thing today and asked me to sit and read to her. After all, she is my guest."

While Timothy muttered consolingly, (although still not offering to stay behind), Katherine's petulant blue gaze came to rest on Harriet. Then on me. "Well, well, I see even the nurse is going."

"I must go along to take care of my charge, madam," I answered tightly. Our eyes clashed, measured each other, then broke away.

"Why aren't your legs covered, Harriet?" her mother suddenly demanded cruelly. "People don't like seeing crippled limbs."

A flame of resentment seared through me. How small of Katherine to pick on the one least able to defend herself! But I had underestimated my young charge.

Harriet's face flamed and her lip quivered briefly, then she raised her chin. "I—I simply didn't want to draw attention to my legs. And the rest of me is all dressed up, you see." She smoothed her coat, then calmly looked away.

Everyone but her mother quickly made assenting

comments. Sylvia swooped down to kiss Harriet's pink cheek. "You are quite right, little one. And you look enchanting in your sweet blue coat and pansy hat. Doesn't she, Papa?" She threw a teasing glance at Jared, and, leaning toward him, clasped his arm with both her hands.

He winked at Harriet. "Indeed she does." Then he transferred his regard to Sylvia. "My daughter is not the only charming lady present," he said gallantly. He threw me just a fleeting glance with the barest lifting of his lips, but I was glad that no one noticed.

At that moment, Bascom appeared at the door and announced that he was ready to drive us to the harbor. Harriet's chair was folded, she was lifted outside, and for just a moment I looked back. Katherine stood before the door. Above her was a row of the strange carved creatures. Dragons with claws raised, wings outstretched for flight, grinning faces, angry faces. They were the gargoyles that had frightened me on my arrival. Katherine looked perfectly at home with them.

I turned into the coach, so glad that we were leaving her behind. What an unpleasant woman Katherine Warwick was—at least toward some people. She fawned rather sickeningly upon her guests from London. Jared must have been completely seduced by her beauty when he married her. Was it still enough to hold him? I could discern no real warmth or sweetness or concern for her family in her nature. But then, I didn't view her as a man would.

A little humor crept into my thoughts. At least the inmates were an interesting group. Fascinating, even, although not always in a pleasant way. I leaned back in my corner and quietly watched. The countess alternately flirted with Tim and then with Jared, occasionally teasing Harriet, while Jared smiled inscrutably at them all. Tim had his arm around his young cousin, whose cheeks were flushed with color, her dark eyes bright with laughter. I sincerely hoped the trip would not be too tiring for her.

Harriet met my glance and leaned toward me, touching me upon the arm. "You haven't had a good look at the village yet, Nurse Margaret, but you can see it now."

As the horses' hooves clattered into the town along the cobblestone streets, I peered out of the window at the rows of whitewashed houses tightly jammed together in the lanes beneath the hill. Some had little tidy yards of vegetables and flowers all growing companionably together. On the seawall, nets fluttered as they dried; a few old men in stocking caps were busy at their mending. Boats sailed in and out of the harbor, with mounds of shining fish upon their planks. I declared it was a very pleasant, pretty village.

The ferry was waiting at the wharf when we arrived, and as soon as we went aboard the barge moved out, its big paddlewheel churning up a wake of foam. There were a few woman passengers traveling with small children. The little ones stared at the strange chair in which Harriet reposed. They knew her, of course, and only giggled when Harriet stuck out her tongue at them.

"How pretty and attractive that makes you look, my girl," I whispered in her ear. "So grown-up, too."

"Well, they shouldn't stare at me," Harriet replied, but it was a shamefaced mutter.

"Perhaps the crown princess of Brendan's Isle should

set an example of good manners for them, then."

Harriet was much struck by this description of herself. "Did you hear that, Papa? You're the king of the island and I'm the crown princess."

Timothy chortled. "I say, that's quite a rags-to-riches story for you, old boy. From gutter to grandeur, eh what?"

Jared didn't answer, but he looked at Timothy a little scornfully, and I wondered what it was all about. Sylvia's next words added to the mystery.

Her narrowed green eyes swept Jared, who was lounging carelessly against the rail, the ends of his black silk cravat blowing in the wind. His clothes were very fashionable today. A ruffled shirt, a coat of pearl-grey cloth with just a hint of satin waistcoat underneath. His trousers were black and tapered at the ankles.

Sylvia moved up close to him, walking her fingers along his sleeve. "You're a fascinating brute, you know that, darling? All that rough, slum strength encased in silk and super-fine. Like a wild beast in a deceptive sheath."

Jared's eyebrows elevated sardonically. "My humble origins don't repel you, then?"

"Quite the contrary," she purred. "They only make you more interesting. You're so different from the men one meets constantly in London soirées. Besides, your origins were only partly humble, darling. Though your mother was a village lass, your grandfather owned the island."

Well, well, here was a revelation! I averted my eyes to stare out at the sea so that the sense of shock I felt would not be noticed. Did this explain Jared's appearance at my door? Did he have a connection in the slums? Was that why he had been meeting someone in Holborn? And how he knew such jargon as thieves' cant?

I thought about Lady Sylvia's words just now. It was true Jared wasn't like the typical picture of an aristocrat. There was that hard toughness in his face and his occasionally unorthodox behavior. With a pang, I realized how little I really knew this man called Jared Warwick. I didn't know his past history at all.

And, of course, that included his love life. Could there have been a grain of truth in Katherine's allegations? Perhaps he *had* turned to some of the willing nurses who came and went. I didn't want to believe it, somehow. I *couldn't* believe it. I had only heard one side—Katherine's.

Impulsively, I decided I would seek out Rosie Mason if it was at all possible and, somehow, learn the truth. Why it was suddenly so important to me, I didn't stop to fathom.

Chapter Seventeen

While I stood alone beside the railing, my mind bent upon the best way to approach Miss Rosie Mason, Jared startled me by speaking in my ear.

"Here, Margaret, take this money." His hand was filled with banknotes, which he held out to me. "Part of it is for Harriet to spend on anything she wants. The rest of it is your wages."

With a surprise murmur of acceptance, I placed the money in my reticule, only to find Jared now extending a handful of golden sovereigns as well. "This should be enough to buy your new shoes. Or—" his glance went to my head, "a new bonnet, perhaps?"

My dreadful hat! I knew I flushed with shame and my voice came out more stiffly than I intended as I straightened with a kind of ridiculous pride. "Thank you, but I can use my own money to buy clothes."

He gave an exasperated sigh. "Margaret, I must insist. You lost some garments in the performance of your duty while in my employ. It is only right that I replace them. Besides . . . I never can make it up to you — all that you have done for us — for me — first in London and now for Harriet."

"I wish you wouldn't feel that way. You owe me nothing."

Covertly, I studied him while he stood, head bent, frowning at the rejected money in his hand. I felt a sense of curiosity after hearing Timothy and Sylvia's disclosures about Jared's humble birth. Would I now discover a taint of commonness in his features? A coarseness I had not noticed heretofore?

Inwardly, I shook my head. No, he looked just as attractive as ever. In my opinion, he was handsome. Many Scots had strong, deeply chiseled features like Jared's. No soft weakness diluted his extremely masculine angles. My employer's black eyes looked out clearly at the world, with no evasion. True, he seldom laughed, but his mouth had quirked with humor on occasion, and, besides, I knew the recent months of his life had not been filled with jollity. I could see that he was often worried, thoughtful, his face strained with some inner conflict. Perhaps connected with his book — perhaps connected with a personal problem.

He raised his eyes, deep-set, magnetic. Our glances locked, each trying to read the other's mind, I suppose.

"Please let me do this, Margaret. It's such a small repayment."

"But I was *glad* to help you. Don't you know that your recovery was my best reward?"

"Yes, I know that much about you. And by this time, you must know what a stubborn brute I am." With a little grin, he thrust the coins into my reticule. "There!" A *fait accompli*."

171

He strode across the deck and I knew it would be ungracious of me to argue further, so I called out a meek, "Thank you," and turned my attention to Harriet.

The ferry had pulled into the wharf and everyone was hurrying to get off. After we disembarked, it was but a short walk down the road to the heart of town, and I found myself as excited as my young charge at the prospect of seeing the bustling town and all the shops. And in my purse was more money to spend than I had ever had before!

A crowd had converged on Lingrove, undoubtedly drawn by the hiring fair, which was proclaimed by a huge banner strung across the street between two tall trees. We all paused for a moment, staring down a side lane where long lines of laborers offered their services for hire. Each one carried some indication of his trade. Shepherds bore a crook, carters a whip, dairymaids a pail, and so forth.

The hiring fair had also filled the town with shoppers. Horses were tethered by their owners at every hitching post, and gigs, carts, and carriages thronged the streets. Thirsty farmers hurried in and out of the tavern, while their wives and daughters patronized the busy shops.

"I'll leave you here," Jared said, "and see if I can find some servants for Brendan's Isle, although I've not had too much luck in the past. However, there seem to be quite a lot of services being offered today."

His gaze encompassed Timothy and Sylvia. "Will you two be joining us for lunch?"

"Why, of course, old chap," Tim exclaimed, widening his eyes.

"Jared, why must you leave us?" Sylvia grabbed his

arm and shook it playfully. "I would love to have your opinion on my purchase of a hat. That shop over there has quite a nice selection, judging by the window." She leaned against him with half-shut eyes and teasing lips, looking exceedingly fetching in her white lace shawl and the dove-trimmed hat. "I insist that you come with us, darling."

Jared shook his head, removing her hand from his arm with a little pat. "Timothy will be a far better judge than I, my dear. Women's folderols are a mystery to me."

He bent down and pinched his daughter's cheek. "You must buy some playthings, little one. A fine new doll, perhaps?"

"Papa," she cried indignantly, "I'm too old to play with dolls."

"You are?" He looked astonished. "Well, Margaret has your money. I'm sure you can find something to your liking. I'll see you all at noontime in the Silver Swan." With a general wave of his hand, he strode away.

Sylvia raised her brows at Timothy. "Did you hear that? Jared referred to the nurse by her first name."

"A slip of the tongue, my lady," I said stiffly. "He's used to hearing Harriet call me Margaret."

The countess didn't glance at me. "That would be a little too familiar for my taste, if I were nurse to a young child." She directed a thin smile at Timothy, who merely looked uncomfortable.

Harriet, however, was swift in showing displeasure with her idol. "Why shouldn't he call her Margaret? She's our friend. Didn't she save my papa's life?"

Sylvia's green eyes rolled heavenward. "Oh, yes, I've

heard about that heroic deed."

"By Jove, I haven't," Timothy cried, looking from one to another. "What's this all about?"

Sylvia heaved an exaggerated sigh. "It seems that Jared went to visit an old friend in London and got caught in a bad fog. Someone tried to knife him on the nurse's doorstep and she attended to his wound. Jared claims she saved his life. That's all."

"All? I would say that's heaps." Timothy looked at me with new respect and cried heartily, "Good show, Nurse MacNeil!"

Sylvia twitched her lace-clad shoulders impatiently. "Oh, do let's get on with our shopping. I have lots of errands to perform today, and, Harriet, I'm sure you want my advice on a new bonnet, don't you, poppet?"

She sailed off, pushing Harriet's chair and chattering in a most beguiling fashion. But Timothy went on his own way to survey the haberdashery farther down the street, saying his eye was caught by the fine display of striped cravats.

Before I followed Harriet and Sylvia, my eyes darted up and down the street, searching for the shop of Rosie Mason. Suddenly, I saw it. "The Toy Box, E. Mason, Prop." My heart beat faster. "Harriet," I called, "I must mail a letter to my cousin. Please wait in the hat shop till I return."

"Yes, yes." Harriet bounced a little. "Oh, hurry, Sylvia, do!" Already Harriet's youthful female instincts seemed to be aroused by the joys of a well-stocked millinery, that happy wonderland designed to capture every lady, young or old.

I would return to the store in a few minutes, but first I had something else to do. I had my letter stamped and mailed, then I went on to the small bow-fronted toy shop a little farther down the block.

Naturally, the place was bursting with young customers, exclaiming and pointing to toys in cases and on shelves. There were colored balls, tops to spin, bags of jacks, bright new knives for mumblety-peg. There were boxes of lead soldiers, sets of dishes. Stuffed bears, ponies, and woolly lambs to pull on wheels. And there were little dolls galore.

It certainly was a spot to capture children, but it was the woman presiding behind the counter who intrigued me. I couldn't see her clearly yet, so I pretended interest in the shelves of mechanical toys behind the counter. Being more expensive as well as fragile, they were not within the reach of careless children.

One in particular caught my eye. A china-headed lady pushed an open carriage in which sat another doll, a child dressed all in blue with tasseled boots and a tiny pillbox on her painted china curls.

Scenting a bigger sale than the dolls of penny-woodens and Frozen Charlottes under discussion at her end of the counter, the woman sought me out with an unctuous smirk.

"Would you care to see a wind-up toy, then, modom?" Her flat, Cornish accents had an overlay of hard-won culture.

I turned my gaze on her, trying not to stare too openly. "You are Miss Mason?"

"I am Miss Rosie Mason, yes. My father is the proprietor." She gestured vaguely to an older, grizzled man across the store.

I didn't take my eyes from her. Brassy curls, bold blue eyes. She was rather short, her bosom tightly outlined in flowered muslin. My heart hammered. Was this . . . Jared's most recent conquest?

I muttered indistinctly, pointing to the doll and carriage, and Miss Mason placed it on the wooden countertop, winding a key in the toy to make it bob along.

"Veddy rare, modom," she purred. "Made by Goodwin and sells quite cheap, it does. Only a quid—er—that is to say, one pound."

Hardly cheap! I pretended interest, however, and bent a considering eye on the quaint toy. "It reminds me of a nurse and her young charge," I murmured. "There is such a one on Brendan's Isle."

"Oh, aye." She brightened. "I know quite a lot about that place. Worked there for two months, I did. I used to be a nurse."

"Indeed? I imagine they hated to lose a fine young woman such as yourself. I understand help is hard to come by over there."

"You are right again, modom. But I was forced to leave."

She shoved the toy closer to me. "Do you fancy this, then? Perhaps you know the young cripple on Brendan's Isle, Harriet Warwick?" Her glance grew sharp. The woman was no fool. She took in my starched, clean cottons, my genteel voice, my manner. "Are you the current nurse, by any chance?"

"I am." Pushing the doll and cart with an idle finger, I continued casually. "It's a very nice place to work. Except for . . . someone . . . I must contend with. I'm sure you take my meaning?"

Miss Mason turned her shoulder on the other customers and lowered her strident voice. "I do, indeed. You mean *him*. Every place I've worked it's been the

176

same. Chase, chase, chase. Fair wore me out, it did, until I had to leave. Now I'm through with all that. I work here now, with me — my — pa."

"I've really not had too much trouble until I came to Brendan's Isle," I murmured. "Pray tell me just what happened to you?" I tried to suggest an avid leer.

"Oh, I couldn't repeat tales. I'll just say this: I never could be alone with *him*. Tried to take advantage of a poor, lone girl every chance he got. Folks say I'm awfully pretty and admire my figure, but sometimes it's a plain curse. Big, strong men like Jared Warwick forcing kisses, pushing their hot hands against you —" Her common, little face looked far from worried by the memory. In fact, she smiled and licked her lips.

But when she caught me staring at her, she quickly cleared her throat and became all business. "Now, then, modom, about this doll and carriage. Shall I put it in a box for you? Just the thing for your young charge, I'd say."

"I think not. I'm afraid it might upset Miss Harriet to have a doll that had to stay in a carriage and be pushed. It would remind her of herself and, you see, I'm hoping to get Miss Harriet on her feet."

The rather fat, obviously reddened lips turned downward. "Huh! Well, I wish you luck with that young crosspatch. And with *him*!" With that, she flounced away, hips bouncing even beneath her full skirt and several petticoats, one of which trailed an inch of dirty lace upon the floor.

I told myself fiercely that the Jared Warwick I knew never would pursue a hussy with broken nails and suspicious color on her face. But as I hurried back to the hat shop and my charge, I found myself remembering the startling disclosures about Jared's early life made by Sylvia and Timothy. Perhaps he did harbor a secret side that found a thrill in taking common doxies to his bed. I felt unnerved and upset. As if I now worked for a perfect stranger — who might be far from perfect! *And even have designs on me.*

I drew a deep breath and clenched my hands on my reticule. I heard the crackle of bulging banknotes, the clink of golden coins. Jared had put them there. Wasn't he always a generous, kind and thoughtful man to me? Didn't I sense that he truly liked me? How dare I judge him? Why should speculation about his secret love affairs upset me?

Yet it did.

Trying to put the matter from my mind, I stepped briskly into the hat shop and looked around for Harriet. I found her leafing rather dolefully through *Le Mode Parisienne*, with Lady Sylvia nowhere in sight.

Harriet looked up and frowned. "It's about time you got back. Sylvia became bored and went on to other shops. Now, will you *please* help me choose a new *chápeau?*" she demanded grandly.

"Yes, indeed. They seem to have a fine selection here."

There were shelves of hats in every material from Milan straw to rainbow-hued crushed velvet. And if you wished for more adornment, there were cases of feathers, ruching, ribbons, and paste jewels by the dozens. To say nothing of the trays of artificial flowers, looking like a summer garden in full bloom.

Harriet's good nature quickly returned as she and I began to try on hats before the mirror. It was a heady feeling to have money to spend on frivolities, and I ook my time before finally settling on a perfect love made of straw-colored silk edged with gauze ribbon and a veritable posy of blush roses, ferns, and violets inside the coquettish brim.

Harriet said she couldn't decide and so took two: a small white velvet bonnet trimmed with tiny plumes, and a yellow leghorn featuring blue birds nestling among forget-me-nots. This last creation matched her coat and promptly went on Harriet's head for the remainder of the trip. She persuaded me to do the same with my new bonnet — and what a joy that was! The saleslady packed our other hats in round, floral-printed boxes tied with ribbons.

Our next destination was the dry goods store, where we examined bolt after bolt of summer cloth, from silks to voiles. Harriet stated that a dressmaker would soon be coming to the house to sew for the family. "Her name is Miss Pynns," she giggled. "I wonder if she just made that up?"

"Well, it's certainly appropriate," I murmured, holding a length of soft green silk beneath my chin.

"Oh, Margaret, that's your color," Harriet declared. "Buy it to wear at Mama's ball. Miss Pynns can make it up for you."

I gave a rueful laugh. "It's hardly likely that the nurse will receive an invitation to her employer's ball." I stroked the shimmering folds, sorely tempted. Once in my life to own such a thing . . . just once . . .

Harriet ordered a great variety of cloth to be delivered to the island, together with patterns, ribbons, and lace trimming. I bought some deep blue twill and some sheer gold mull for myself; one for a walking suit, the other for the warm summer months in Cornwall. I also bought a length of rosy poplin as a present for my cousin.

Then Harriet urged me again, thrusting the emerald lure into my hands. Weakening, I counted my money . . . and then recklessly ordered enough silk to make a modest gown.

By that time, the clock on the Town Hall had already rung for noon and Harriet began to groan. "Come on, Margaret, it's time for lunch. I'm hungry as a horse, aren't you?"

I propelled her out to the street, her wheelchair strung with purchases. "I'm certainly hungry, but not as a horse. No hay for me, thank you very much."

Harriet giggled. "Me neither. Today I want roast chicken, stuffed fish, vegetables vinaigrette, buttered muffins, iced pudding, and Neapolitan cake."

"Stop, stop," I groaned. "I can't stand any more. Even hay is beginning to sound good. Ah, here's the inn, and we can go right up this ramp into the foyer. I wonder if our group is here yet?"

For a few minutes, we both stared around the crowded lobby, with its brown wainscotting, dusty palms, and sagging leather chairs. It was bursting with a great many people, evidently all anxious for their food. There were red-faced farm types squeezed into their town clothes; gentlemen in stovepipe hats and frock coats; ladies in wide, bright skirts and lacy shawls. And all were clamoring for a table in the dining room beyond.

I couldn't see Jared Warwick anywhere. But as my eyes scanned the doorway, someone else appeared. A tall, burly young fellow with high color in his lips and cheeks and tousled black curls beneath a rough cloth cap.

James!

I moved my hand a little awkwardly, then dropped it. Did he know that I was responsible for his dismissal? His bold black eyes met mine, and then he smiled with the old, suggestive leer. But now his hands were clenched upon his hips, his legs spread arrogantly apart.

I backed up to the counter. Suddenly, even in this roomful of people, I felt a wave of fear. There was something different and dangerous now about James. No longer did he look sly but still servile. Now he looked exactly like an animal that had erupted from its cage.

Chapter Eighteen

Where was Jared? I turned desperately to the bald-headed innkeeper behind the counter. "Do you have a table for—"

"Wait your turn, madam, *if* you please!" he bawled, mopping at his reddened face. "Now, then, mister—"

Harriet rapped her knuckles on the wood and received an angry glance. "Go away, little girl. Can't you see I'm busy?" He turned once more to the surging, importuning horde.

Fearfully, I glanced back at the front door. It now was jammed with a new crowd of people, and James had gone. My eyes searched everywhere for him in vain, and at last I allowed myself to draw a thankful breath.

However, just the thought of James anywhere nearby made me feel uneasy. If he found out that my informing Jared had lost him the job at Brendan's Isle, I felt certain he would retaliate. What was to prevent his slipping up to the house any time he chose? He could enter my room, overpower me with ease—and then disappear in a flash. He knew the island well and undoubtedly had many friends who would hide him. It was not a pleasant thought, and I decided that, until he left the area for good to find another job (and Annie probably would know), I would keep my door locked at all times.

I still was worried that James might pop back into the inn and cause an unpleasant scene. "I wish your father would arrive," I groaned to Harriet.

"I'm sure he's here," she said. "Probably in the dining room. If that odious creature behind the desk will just pay some heed to us—"

She suddenly raised her voice, drowning out everyone nearby with her shrillness. "Listen to me, my man! I demand attention! Has my father, *Jared Warwick*, reserved a table?"

The name produced a magic change in the harassed, rotund innkeeper. He gasped. "Are you in *Mr. Warwick's* party? Ah, yes, yes, indeed. He is in the dining room awaiting your arrival." He mopped his dripping face. "I was just about to look for you, but, er, hum—Boy! Take these ladies to Mr. Warwick's table at once."

His beady eyes swept us anxiously. "I hope that you will forgive the short delay, dear ladies?"

Harriet favored him with a glacial nod, and a path was cleared for us through a large, sunny room gleaming with white damask, twinkling silverware, and bouquets of bright flowers. Voices hummed, dishes clinked, as quick-stepping waiters balanced laden trays around the crowded room.

Jared rose and greeted us from a large, round

table in the corner, a choice spot for a favored patron—or at least one who had slipped a few bills into certain pockets.

"Why, who are these two beauties in their brand-new bonnets?" he exclaimed. "What an honor to have them at my table."

Harriet preened, stroking the long brown hair behind her shoulder and straightening her brim. "If I do say so myself, I think we look pretty nice."

"An understatement, if there ever was one." Jared held my chair, his eyes on me so intently that I felt a little flustered and quickly opened the large white menu.

"I wonder where Mr. Banks and Lady Sylvia are?" I murmured, hoping we would not have to wait too long as my eye went over the list of mouth-watering selections. Plain fare, for the most part: Yorkshire pudding, boiled mutton with fresh vegetables, stuffed roast fowl, and suchlike; but I was very hungry and could see from nearby tables that the food was being eagerly devoured and smelled divine.

"Our friends have evidently been delayed by all these tempting shops," Jared replied. "Let us order, ladies; otherwise there is no telling how long we might have to wait for our companions."

After we had decided what to eat—and it included most of Harriet's desired items—Jared told us about the hiring fair.

"I had a most profitable morning, I'm glad to say. I found a couple to work for me on the island. An older man named Robert Barnes, who can replace James in the stable, and his wife, Mattie, who will help with the cooking and other housework."

I cleared my throat. "I—I thought I saw James near the inn today. Did you ever tell him that I was responsible for his dismissal?"

"Of course not."

With Harriet present, that was all that could be said, but I drew a breath of relief. Probably Jared had burst in and surprised James and Annie in the bedroom, as if by accident.

"What will happen to Annie?" I asked.

"Since you requested it, Margaret, I agreed to let her stay, as long as she behaves." His eyes rested fondly on his daughter. "She also was quite a help with Harriet, wasn't she?"

Hearing her name, Harriet turned eagerly from her survey of the room. "Papa, do you remember the last time we came here? We went to Castle Crumbly after lunch."

"Good heavens, what a memory! You were only seven years old at the time." Jared smiled. "We went there for your birthday, just you and I. And now your childhood's nearly gone. Too old for dolls, she says." He sighed.

"What is Castle Crumbly?" I looked from one face to the other. "It hardly sounds attractive or quite safe."

Both pairs of dark eyes danced and father and daughter spoke at once.

"It's a Roman ruin," Jared said.

"It's a castle," Harriet proclaimed just as firmly.

"Oh, Papa, let's go there today, please, *please*! Just as soon as we have finished lunch. Margaret has never seen it, and it's not that far."

Jared raised an interrogative eyebrow at me and I nodded promptly. "I would love to go, since you claim it is so interesting. Roman ruin or castle—both descriptions sound intriguing."

We finished eating, and still Timothy and the countess had not arrived. I wondered if we would have to wait for them, certain that neither would care to accompany us this afternoon. As for myself, I would much prefer their absence.

As we rose from the table, however, I felt compelled to ask, "What about Lady Sylvia and Mr. Banks?"

Jared shrugged indifferently. "I imagine they lost track of the time. I'll leave a message for them at the desk in case they care to join us. Which I doubt."

In a short time, we were on our way, Jared driving a hired gig to convey us to our destination. After leaving the town, the road wound upward through meadows of grazing sheep and groves of fluttering green trees surrounding little farms.

At last, on the top of a hill, the lichen-covered walls of a square stone building came into view. It had ruined towers, broken arches, and gaping holes for windows. Several families in open phaetons, carriages, and even carts were also taking advantage of the fine weather to explore the ancient site today. Jared tied the gig to a post near some other conveyances in a cleared area and then started pushing Harriet's chair up a rather steep incline.

When we reached the top, I was a little out of breath and glad to sink down on a mossy wall and stare around in awe at the Roman castle built when Britain was just a land of savages in skins.

Jared rested a booted foot upon the wall, pointing to the outline of an underground room directly below us. The weathered blocks contained great, worn holes. "That is where the vents of steam came out to heat each room. A central fire warmed the water through pipes. Ingenious, and much more efficient than our present drafty fireplaces, I would say."

"Indeed! It's very clever," I agreed. "They built their castles like fortresses, didn't they, high upon a hill to repel invaders, with a moat for added protection."

"Only now the moat is filled with earth almost to the top, instead of water," Harriet commented. "And so many pretty wildflowers are growing there. May I sit on the edge and pick some, Papa?"

"Certainly." Her father lifted Harriet from the chair to a spot closer to the moat. Another young girl and boy wandered over to talk to her, and, after a few minutes, Jared and I strolled on a little way by ourselves.

The wind blew sweetly over the green spears of grass thrusting through the ancient stones; leaves rustled in a grove of elms and beeches; and a few brightly hued birds warbled as they flew off in the azure sky. The voices of other sightseers came to us, muted by the distance.

I felt as if I were floating in a lovely dream, until Jared unwittingly shattered my composure with a quite innocent remark. "What did you do in Lingrove today, my dear? See anything of interest?"

"I went into The Toy Box—among other places." I had spoken almost without thinking. Now, I stole a worried glance at Jared.

His expression was merely bland and inquiring. "Did you buy a toy?"

I felt uncomfortable, but continued doggedly. "No, but I met a former nurse of Harriet's, a Miss Rosie Mason."

"Ah." His face changed subtly. I couldn't read what his expression meant. "What did Miss Mason have to say?"

I looked away. I toed the grass. "Only that she has quit nursing in private homes because the masters bothered her."

"Did she say I bothered her?" he asked harshly.

I didn't speak. I bit my lip.

"Well?" His voice grated with a hard bitterness.

"Yes," I whispered. "But I don't believe her."

He gave a bark of quite unamused laughter. "You shouldn't, my dear. She lied."

I knew it! My head shot up as relief flooded through me and I expelled my breath. "What happened?"

"Do you really want to hear the story?"

I nodded.

Our eyes clung for a tense moment. Then he tore his glance from mine, as though it were an effort. He stared across the moat and I stared at him — at the black hair blowing in the breeze (did he never wear a hat?), the compressed lips, the muscle twitching in the flat plane of his cheek.

Finally Jared began to speak, quite unemotionally, whereas I listened with bated breath.

"It's a very mundane story. A young woman looking for romance tries several ploys. In my house, they met with no response. At first, Miss Mason

188

seemed mild-mannered and polite, and, even when she became more and more familiar, I kept her on because it was so hard to find a nurse for Harriet. I told myself my own attitude would keep her at a distance. But I was wrong.

"One night, contrary to my usual habit, I left my bedroom suite unlocked and went down to the beach to swim. When I came back, Miss Mason was sitting up in my bed—stark naked. I told her to get out. She pleaded. I grabbed her and hauled her to the door, flinging her robe around her. She then decided on more forceful tactics designed to punish me, and so she began to scream. My wife came to investigate, took in the scene at a glance—Miss Mason naked, I in not much more. Katherine believed the woman's hysterical raving and dismissed her on the spot."

I *knew* Katherine had been wrong, I told myself triumphantly. "Had you no way of proving your innocence?" I demanded indignantly.

"Only my word. Once I had told my side to Katherine, I would speak of it no more. But I will not have Miss Mason reviling me to perfect strangers." He clenched his teeth.

"She actually said very little—only veiled, vague hints. And that was because I was another nurse. Don't you think it might be best simply to ignore the matter?"

"Perhaps you're right," he sighed, after a moment. He drew out his pipe. "Do you mind? I seem to need the soothing effects of some tobacco."

"Of course."

I cast about in my mind for a change of topic.

Anything. "I was interested in hearing Timothy and Sylvia's remarks about your early background. Did your parents die, so that your grandfather had to raise you?"

"Yes." Thankfully, I saw that Jared was diverted. The fragrant pipe smoke drifted upward on the air. "It's a common enough tale, Margaret. A pretty girl from the village was working in the manor and a handsome young man was home on army leave. They fell in love, and when he had to return to London he took her with him. However, it was during the Napoleonic Wars, and he was suddenly recalled and killed in action before they could get married."

Jared turned his head and regarded me gravely. "My mother soon discovered she was pregnant, with no husband. I was born a bastard, Margaret. Are you . . . shocked?"

Slowly, I shook my head. "No, but I feel so sorry for your poor mother. I have seen so many young girls like that in the hospital. Bewildered country girls, their lives in ruins. Usually, they give up their child for adoption or place it in an orphanage and run away."

"My mother did neither, I'm proud to say. However, she couldn't return to Lingrove in disgrace or go begging to my grandfather. Her parents were both dead. So she stayed in the London slums and became a factory worker and found an old woman in Holborn to care for me.

"As soon as I was old enough, I went to work earning a few coppers at anything I could: rat-catching, chimney sweeping, factory running. I wouldn't steal; my mother had taught me to be honest, you see." He added grimly: "And that was quite an accomplishment in the world we lived in."

I listened enthralled. After a minute Jared continued, rather sadly, "When my mother became ill and knew that she was dying, she told me she had finally written to my grandfather and he wished to see me. She had letters from my father, and, since I was the image of him as well, no other proof was needed of my parentage. She . . . she died in a public ward when I was fourteen, and soon after that I went to Brendan's Isle"

He sighed deeply, and my heart went out to him. "I missed my mother for many years. My grandfather was a widower and a stern old fellow, but gradually we grew quite fond of each other. He sent me to good schools, and I became his heir."

Jared walked away a few feet, gazing at the moat, while I sat silent, trying to adjust to this new picture of my employer. He must have endured a hard, rough life in the slums. I knew well those leaning, odorous buildings that teemed with vermin and helpless humanity. I had seen the gaunt dogs, the starving children. In the wards, I had cared for women who were emaciated, hollow-eyed, old before their time, riddled with disease or destroyed by gin, which often was their only solace in a ghastly world. No wonder Jared had once called the wards "those pits of hell." He had known them at first hand when his poor mother had lingered there and died.

I felt so sorry for Jared and longed to comfort him, to erase those grievous pictures from his mind. As I rose from the wall, about to go to him, something flashed among the trees. I saw light strike a long, metallic bore. *A gun*, I thought, in stupefied surprise.

"Jared," I screamed and spun around.

Beside the wall, he had bent down to knock the dottle from his pipe, and, as he did, there was a shattering explosion. Across the moat, chips flew from the ancient masonry.

Somebody had fired a shot.

Chapter Nineteen

Jared had just missed being killed!

I saw him straighten slowly, his face chalk-white with shock. "That was a gunshot!" He started running toward his daughter and I flew after him, my legs unsteady with the fear that suddenly unnerved me. *Was this another attack aimed at Jared?*

Other people had heard the noise and recognized it. They milled together, staring this way and that, all talking excitedly, although no one seemed to have actual knowledge of who had fired the shot. They all agreed, however, that it had come from the belt of trees.

"Damme, these poachers grow more reckless every day," one old gentleman expostulated, blowing out his moustaches. "They ought to string the blackguards up when they're caught shooting in a public place."

His lady put out a hand to me. "The little gel is quite unharmed. You and your husband don't need to worry."

Obviously, Jared was struggling to contain his anger

in order to avoid frightening the child. "Harriet, are you all right?"

"Of course." She raised puzzled eyes and stared around, hands clutching her lapful of daisy chains. "What is everybody talking about, Papa? What happened?"

"Someone took a shot at a pigeon or a rabbit, I guess," Jared responded tightly. "Almost caused an accident. Wait here with Margaret while I take a look around."

"Be careful," I cried, putting out my hand to him.

He gripped it briefly, his taut glance going from me to Harriet.

I watched anxiously as he ran off toward the woods, followed by some of the other men. The rest of us stood around and waited. Some people still seemed shocked, while others were already laughing a little too loudly, ridiculing their unnecessary fright.

Of course, it was apparent that no one had been hit. But was it luck? An accident? Or — what?

It wasn't long before the men returned, looking disgruntled. Jared strode toward us, strands of black hair tumbling across his forehead. His cravat had become untied and he shoved the ends impatiently inside his waistcoat.

"Did you find anything? Did you see who it was?" I demanded urgently.

"We saw no one and found nothing except some trampled grass and broken plants near the grove of trees." Jared ground his teeth together. "Whoever it was, he vanished without a trace."

"He got away extremely fast, I'd say."

"That's right. But everyone here was so stunned after

194

hearing that shot so close by, they couldn't move fast enough to flush him out. And I was just as slow."

Jared cast a grim glance at his daughter, noting the worried paleness of her young face. "I think we better go home now, Harriet. We don't want you getting too tired. Isn't that right, Nurse Margaret?"

I uttered a firm agreement.

Jared lifted Harriet in his arms and carried her down the hill, a rather fierce protectiveness in his face and arms.

But Harriet's eyes sought mine across her father's shoulder, and I could see fear in their dark depths.

Trundling the wheelchair behind them, I hastened to speak reassuringly. "Nothing happened, lassie. No one was hurt. It was just a poacher in the woods taking a rather bad aim at some poor bird, most likely."

Harriet nodded bleakly, tightening her arms around her father's neck.

If it had indeed been another attempt on her father's life, I thought with a pang, was the mysterious enemy now intent on committing *murder*? Heretofore, the attempts had been more in the manner of threats, a wearing away of the nerves. But—this . . . The watcher in the woods might easily have been intent on a human target in the form of Jared Warwick.

It didn't bear thinking about, not if I was to keep Harriet from becoming as frantically upset as I was inwardly. So I steeled my face and voice to give no inkling of my turmoil. And nothing more was said about the shooting, although each of us, I'm sure, struggled with our own disturbing silent questions.

When we reached the town, Jared stopped the gig at the inn to inquire about the other members of our party. In a few minutes, he returned and told us: "Tim and Sylvia arrived after we had left the inn. They wrote a message to me that they wished to spend the rest of the day in town on additional shopping expeditions. They will come home on the last ferry. All we have to do is send the carriage to the island dock when they are due to arrive."

Personally, I hadn't missed them in the least and was glad I'd had an afternoon alone with Jared—in spite of the fright we had sustained. The rest of the time had been delightful.

The day was fading as we boarded the ferry, the setting sun merging into shadows tinged with coolness. The paddlewheel splashed across a molten sea crested with streaks of crimson. But I don't think any of us felt in the mood to appreciate the beauty of the scene. Jared stood at the prow of the boat, the wind ruffling his black hair. The lines beside his mouth were deep, and he looked quite unapproachable. After a keen glance at him, I went to sit by Harriet, who was huddled by the railing in her chair, her thin face pinched and worried.

"Do you think that shot was meant for Papa?" she asked abruptly, turning a very adult, searching glance on me.

I squared my shoulders, mentally as well as physically. "Why, I doubt that, lassie. You know the hills are filled with hunters seeking small game. Someone just grew careless, that's all. We can't become obsessed with seeing danger where none exists. That would not be healthy, and soon we would find ourselves unable to think clearly about anything." I pressed Harriet's fingers, which were plucking restlessly at her lap rug. "We must stay cool and canny. That's our watchword, remember?"

Harriet smiled wanly. "Yes, I remember."

I could see she was trying hard to obey my injunction. Briskly, I spoke of other matters, recalling the good lunch we had had at the inn and the pleasures of our shopping expedition. The next step was a discussion of possible fashions for the material we had bought, and pretty soon I had the satisfaction of seeing Harriet's face relaxed and even smiling.

As for me, however, I was beginning to feel drained and weary. It had been a day of nerve-wracking events, beginning with my confrontation with Miss Rosie Mason, then hearing Jared's further disclosures and his heartbreaking tale about his early life and the death of his poor mother. The climax — the shooting — had capped it all.

Now, all I could do was think longingly of my quiet room, a light supper on a tray, and a night of peaceful rest.

But the day was not over yet.

A blast of noise greeted us the minute we stepped inside the front door of the manor. Laughter, loud voices, and lively music came in a bombarding wave from the front parlor.

Jared groaned aloud. "I guess my deserted wife has consoled herself by organizing a party. Heaven deliver me! What next?"

At that moment, Madame Lelong appeared in the hallway and sailed toward us, champagne bubbling in a glass she held aloft. "Ah, dear Jared, we are having such excitement, such a jollity. A few friends of Katherine's invaded us from the mainland and, *voilà*, your wife invited them to spend the night." For the first time, the Frenchwoman seemed as bubbly as the golden wine she sipped, her painted maquillage cracking into lines of laughter.

Jared surveyed her with a weary sigh. "Where is Katherine? In the parlor?"

"Ah, *non. Pauvre petite*, she took to her bed with the aching head and asked that I play hostess until the dinner hour. I trust you do not mind, *mon cher*? I am going to invite dear Katherine to be my guest for a few days in London to repay her so-generous hospitality. She complains of the *ennui*, you comprehend? I would ask you also, but—"

"No, no," Jared interrupted. "Thank you, madam, I can't go at this time."

"*Quel dommage,*" the Frenchwoman murmured automatically. She craned her pea-green turban with its waving feather and peered past all of us at the empty doorway. "*Tiens*, do not Sylvia and Timothy accompany you?"

"We went our separate ways," Jared answered. "Bascom will return to wait for them at the harbor."

He drew a labored breath. "We are all very fatigued, but I suppose I must greet our guests." He glanced at Harriet who was edging her wheelchair toward the parlor, her brown eyes snapping with anticipation. "I think a nap is in order for this young lady, Nurse MacNeil."

I hastened to agree and grasped my charge's chair without delay, wheeling Harriet away down the hall, ignoring the usual cries of protest and fierce demands to see the company.

In spite of everything, I soon had her settled in her bed and saw with relief that her lids had already begun to droop with weariness and her protests had sunk to a mere token whimper.

My own fatigue was almost as great. Perhaps I, too, had time for a short nap. As soon as I entered my room, I removed my gown and took down my hair, uttering a groan of relief when the weight of steel pins lay before me on the marble-topped dressing table.

Wearing only my low-necked undergarments, I began to brush my hair. It proved so relaxing that when a knock sounded at my door I only mumbled, "Come in," without getting to my feet, certain it would be one of the maids with a query about my supper. I knew this was not a night I would be dining with the family.

Drowsily, I glanced into the mirror, and then I gave a cry of consternation. It was Jared!

He closed the door and walked toward me, jolting every shred of sleepiness from my mind. For a moment, I couldn't move as our eyes met in the mirror. Mine were wide with dismayed embarrassment, a crimson tide sweeping to my hairline as I saw him drop his gaze to take an intimate, masculine survey of my unbound curls, the bareness of my arms and shoulders, the rapid rise and fall of my irregular breathing.

I sprang to face him, arms crossed on my exposed bosom. "*Mr. Warwick!* What are you doing here? Can't you see that I'm not dressed?" My voice rose shrilly.

"I see very well," he grunted. "However, you have as much on as a ballgown." Still eyeing me, he began to undo the buttons of his jacket.

What ailed the man? Hardly able to speak, I grabbed up my robe, knotting it frantically around my waist. "Mr. Warwick, wh-what do you want?"

I backed away in growing apprehension until I suddenly realized that his thoughts had shifted from the state of my deshabille and now were centered on a package that he withdrew from beneath his coat. It was quite bulky, wrapped in oilskin paper, and securely tied with twine.

He held it out to me. "Margaret, I would like to ask a favor of you. Will you keep this package for me? It's the manuscript of my book."

Wonderingly, I stepped forward and took it from his hands, my pulse resuming its normal rate. "Why . . . certainly." The thick pad felt very heavy and was certainly wrapped to conceal its contents from any prying eyes. I wished that I could take a peep at it . . . this mysterious book that Jared evidently valued.

"No one must know that you have it, Margaret," Jared admonished me. "So hide it carefully. It will just be for tonight when there are so many strangers in the house. Even a locked door won't keep out a determined snoop."

He glanced around the room. "Where will you put it?"

I considered carefully before I spoke. "I think my portmanteau would be as good as any place. It's in the back of the closet and I can put some clothing on the top so it will look quite natural."

Jared nodded, and, when the manuscript was safely stowed away, he regarded me quizzically. "No questions as to why I ask this of you? No curiosity concerning the nature of my book? Or why I am afraid for anyone to see it but myself?"

I tightened my robe and looked away. "Oh, I am curious, all right. But I won't pry. If you wanted me to know I'm sure you would tell me. And if you didn't, no amount of questioning would do me the slightest good."

"I have always thought of you as a most unusual woman. Now I'm certain of it." Jared's mouth twitched and he moved closer to me, drawing out a small white box from the pocket of his coat. "Please do me one more favor, Margaret. Turn around and face the mirror."

Now what? I looked from him to the small white box he held. He stared back, one hand defiantly on his hip. Puzzled, I gave a shrug and did as he requested.

"This is just a slight token of my gratitude and not a bribe for taking care of my book, you understand."

He brushed back my hair, and I saw a flash of green and gold as he draped a chain and lavaliere around my neck. His fingers fumbled with the clasp and then an emerald stone enclosed in a circle of filigree swung from a golden chain. It came to rest in the hollow of my breast where my robe had parted.

For a moment, I was too stunned to speak and could only stare into the mirrored image.

Jared rested his hands on my shoulders and turned me around to face him, his eyes traveling warmly across my face and throat to the valley where the green jewel lay. "It becomes you, Margaret. Simple, cool, and beautiful—just like you." His voice was strangely husky.

I was hardly aware of what he said. There was a roaring in my ears. I felt appalled, shocked, by the indiscretion of Jared's gift.

I swallowed and whispered hoarsely, "I—I can't accept this. Surely, you must know why—"

His face changed and his hands fell from my shoulders. "No, I don't know why you can't accept a small

201

token of my gratitude, and I refuse to take it back. Can't you see that I am just as determined to repay this debt I owe — as you are to declare its nonexistence?"

"It isn't proper —" I began falteringly.

He swung away to the door. "Put it down to my crude upbringing, then. I don't always act the gentleman. Besides," he flung over his shoulder, "it's just a trinket. Don't make so much fuss about it."

I took a step toward him. "Jared —" The name burst uncontrollably from my lips, but the door closed behind him with a decisive click and the remainder of my protest died unspoken.

Oh dear heaven, probably I had hurt his feelings. No doubt he had expected a delighted response of gratitude from me. With a moan, I undid the clasp and stared down at the winking jewel. It was a small but perfect emerald set in the finest filigree and certainly too valuable to be considered a mere "trinket." It was gorgeous! I had never dreamed of owning anything like this. For a few yearning moments, I turned it this way and that, watching the play of light, wishing there were some way in which I *could* accept it . . .

But I knew there wasn't. Imagine what Jared's wife would say — or Sylvia — or Vivienne Lelong — if any of them should see it on me. They would then believe without a doubt all their prurient speculations about Jared and myself. No decent woman accepted jewelry from a man unless they were married or engaged. That was the social law in Queen Victoria's rigid code, to which every proper person adhered. Regardless of my employer's opposition — or even his disappointment — I must return the lavaliere as soon as possible.

I lifted the green gem and watched it flash and shimmer almost blindingly. What would it be like to own such a lovely thing? To have the right to wear it? The next step in my dreaming jumped to wondering what it would be like to be married to a man like Jared Warwick, a man so generous, so magnetic, so attractive . . .

For just a moment, the jewel slipped unheeded to the dresser and my errant thoughts contemplated Jared as a lover. I remembered how his black gaze had fastened on my half-bared bosom, highlighted by the emerald fire. What was he thinking? I placed my hands upon the marble top and dropped my head and closed my eyes.

What would have happened if I had accepted Jared's gift in the manner of a Lady Sylvia, for instance? Suppose I had cooed, "Ohhhh, thank you, dearest Jared. How unutterably sweet of you. I simply adore it." If I had raised my lips invitingly, would he have kissed them? And then my throat and shoulders? And then . . .

A shudder swept me and my head jerked up, shocked at the direction of my thoughts. I was mad to indulge in such fantasies.

What was happening to me?

Unseeingly, I gripped the bureau's edge. Should I leave this place before it was too late? This unsettling island with its mysterious accidents? And a man who was becoming increasingly disturbing to my senses?

Then I remembered Harriet and the improvement I had noticed in her recently. And Jared had entrusted me with his manuscript. I couldn't fail them . . . I couldn't leave just yet.

But I determined to be on my guard with Jared and

return the jewel as soon as possible. With this decision made, I placed it in a drawer wrapped in some handkerchiefs. Now there was no time for a nap, so I dressed again, planning to have a quiet evening with my charge and an early bed for both of us.

At least, that was my intention. I was completely unaware of what this night still held in store — for everybody in the house.

Chapter Twenty

Harriet and I dined in her room on a light but nourishing repast of vermicelli soup, codfish with oyster sauce, sliced mutton surrounded by larded sweetbreads, and bowls of charlotte russe covered with whipped cream. After this, we both declared we felt greatly revived.

The meal had been served before the fireplace, and when it was cleared away Harriet used the table to display several current fashion periodicals. "Now, Margaret, we must decide on styles for the materials we bought today."

Harriet's finger tapped a page of children's dresses made almost exactly like their elders, with much flouncing, puffing, and trimming. "A little too fancy for my taste," she decided after due deliberation. "What do you say?"

I murmured noncommittally, finding it hard to concentrate on berthes, worked points, or Swiss insertion. An emerald pendant held my inner vision, swinging back and forth like my own vacillating will. Oh, how I wished that I could keep the lovely gift and avoid angering Jared. On the other hand, a good woman would never accept a jewel from her employer. Accepting the gem might indicate consent to other liberties, I thought uneasily, remembering Jared's ungentlemanly inspection of my person. The thought of submitting to Jared's passion was like a dark tide, frightening . . . yet . . . somehow fascinating.

With a start, I realized that Harriet was speaking to me. "Margaret! You're not listening."

"Oh, what is it, dear? I fear my mind was wandering. What did you say?"

"I asked how you wished your green silk to be trimmed? Do you prefer ribbon, flowers, or beadwork? Do you want the skirt ruffled or ruched or—"

By concentrating on frills, fancies, and furbelows, I was temporarily able to forget the pendant as well as the other article Jared had brought to me: the mysterious book.

But later, when I went to bed, it was not so easy to control my thoughts. After I fell asleep, I started dreaming. At first, it seemed so real I could not be sure if I were really asleep or not . . .

I heard a knocking on my door, and when I opened it I discovered Jared on the threshold.

He was fully dressed, but his white silk shirt was open part way down his chest and his hair was flung roughly across his forehead as though he had been running his fingers through it many times. His black eyes had a hot, bright shine to them, and he looked aroused and forceful, as though his veneer of culture was about to crack.

I tried to speak calmly above my clamoring senses. "Have you come to get your manuscript, Mr. Warwick?"

"Not yet," he grated.

"Then—the pendant? Have you realized how improper it would be for me to accept—"

"To hell with the pendant."

His violent language terrified me and I started to back away, but his hand shot out and gripped my wrist. He kicked the door shut with his foot.

"You know what I've come for. You're not that naive. I've desired you ever since that night I kissed you in your home. Why do you think I hired you on the spot?"

I tried to speak or move but found I couldn't. Before I could draw another breath, Jared jerked me to him and put his full-lipped mouth upon my own. It was a long, voluptuous kiss, as though driven by an unchecked force. Fear, astonishment—all deserted me in the wake of the strangest emotions I had ever dreamed of. A searing fire? A sweeping tide? What could I call it? I only know that when he halted his drugging kisses, I felt that I would faint.

But Jared's arms still held me tightly as we gazed into each other's eyes. "I love you, Margaret. I want you to come away with me."

"N—now?" I whispered, dazedly.

"Yes. Tonight. We'll go to London—"

The room seemed to be spinning. I couldn't think . . .

Jared's lips sank to my throat, my bosom, wherever he could find the skin exposed. "Come away with me tonight, my darling. Forget your practical good sense."

Those last two words cut through the throbbing haze that had enveloped me, and, with an effort, I pulled myself away.

"Jared, we can't!" I moaned. "There's Harriet. And Katherine. Oh, listen, do you hear that knocking at the door? Perhaps your wife has come—"

The pounding went on and on and someone shouted . . .

I seemed to be swimming up through layers of cotton wool. And, all the while, the sounds continued. Until, suddenly, I jerked upright. I had been dreaming! Jared wasn't in my room. He hadn't kissed me or asked me to run away with him; and with that knowledge came a stab of pain.

But—what was all that noise out in the hall? Struggling into my robe and slippers, I flew to unlock the door. A fearful, acrid odor rushed into the room. Smoke!

Annie had Harriet in her wheelchair, a shawl around her shoulders. "Hurry," they cried in unison. "There's a fire!"

"Get outside, miss," Annie said and coughed.

Managing to tie my sash, I tore down the hall behind them. "Where is the fire?" I gasped. "Are they trying to put it out?"

"It's in the wing where Mr. Warwick sleeps," Annie shouted over her shoulder. "I think he—"

Harriet let out a piercing shriek. "Papa, Papa! *They're trying to kill my papa again!*" She reared up, hands pushing frantically at the sides of her wheelchair. Her labored breath sawed in and out, and

208

beads of perspiration stood out on her skin as she heaved and struggled, almost overturning the rocking wheelchair.

Then—with a wild cry—Harriet stood up and ran!

Annie screamed, "Miss Harriet!" And clapped her hands across her eyes. "Owww, I'm seein' things! Dearest God, what's happening?"

I shouted and tore after Harriet, reaching her just as she sagged and fell against the wall, her strength exhausted. I clasped the slim form tightly, and I sobbed, "Oh, my dear, you walked! You *walked*!"

Harriet didn't seem aware of what she had accomplished. She tried to push away from my enfolding arms. "They're going to kill him! Margaret, let me *go*!"

My eyes followed the direction of her waving arms. Swirls of smoke eddied from the ell where Jared had his rooms, and, suddenly, the house was filled with the noise of clattering feet and shrill, excited voices. Katherine and her guests swarmed down the stairs. Servants appeared carrying pails of sand and water, and I was forced flat against the wall, holding Harriet in my arms.

"Go to my papa, Margaret, please, please! See if he's all right."

"Yes, yes, but you must promise to stay here. Annie, keep Miss Harriet in her chair and make her go outside."

"No, no," Harriet shrilled. "The smoke's not bad right here."

I couldn't stay to argue. I was just as fearful for Jared's safety as Harriet. I turned and tried to push my way through the half-dressed guests and the servants who were running up and down the hall. The smoke thickened whitely as they doused the fire with pails of water. The vapors filled my nose and throat as I shouted, "Jared! Jared!"

Katherine, in a clinging purple nightrail, gave me a hard, frowning glance for presuming to use Jared's first name. Sylvia stood close by in a fur-edged robe, and Timothy had donned trousers but wore no shirt.

He panted as he came up to us, hauling a dripping pail. "Kate, shouldn't we ring the bell outdoors to alert the villagers? We may need more help—"

Just then, Jared appeared in the doorway to his room, completely if carelessly dressed in boots, breeches, and an open shirt. "The fire's out," he croaked and began to cough, wiping his soot-streaked face against his sleeve.

The next moment Harriet flew down the hall straight toward her father. Everyone fell back, shocked into silence, gaping at her.

At first, her father couldn't move or speak, but as Harriet flung herself into his arms he swept her up, pressing her head against his shoulder. Brokenly, he repeated her name over and over, while tears streamed down his cheeks.

"Harriet, Harriet, am I dreaming?"

"Papa," she sobbed into his neck, "I was so afraid that you were dead!"

The crowd all surged around them, then, and a joyful babble arose, eclipsing the excitement of the fire.

"Harriet walked!"

"My God, did you see her?"

"It's a miracle, that's what it is."

Vivienne Lelong exclaimed in French. Timothy kissed Harriet and wiped his eyes. Sylvia took the opportunity to pull down Jared's head and kiss him fully on the mouth. Which he didn't even seem to notice.

Katherine alone spoke calmly. "I always said that Harriet could walk if she wanted to. Thank goodness, now we can dispense with nurses and she can return to school." She disregarded Harriet's protesting cry and turned toward her husband. "This fire — how did it start?"

Jared shook his head a little groggily, still staring at his daughter. With an effort, he lifted his head to speak to Katherine.

"I don't really know. Luckily, I hadn't gone to bed — I fell asleep reading in a chair. The smell of smoke awoke me and I found a fire in the next room burning by the hall door. Perhaps some sparks fell from my pipe on a nearby table."

"Oh, Papa," Harriet wailed, her arms tightening around his neck. "Your book — did it burn up?"

"No, only some penciled notes and a few rough drafts. My book was unharmed." Briefly, his glance touched mine, then he looked away.

Instantly, it came to me. It hadn't been his pipe. He must have been expecting that something would be tried tonight. That was why he hadn't gone to bed and why he had given his manuscript into my keeping. The trouble was, he had drifted off to sleep before the fire was started.

All the so-called accidents, could they have been

attempts to suppress his book? And perhaps its author? The idea was so stupefying, I could only lean against the wall, making no sense of my churning thoughts. Around me, servants bustled up and down, carrying the charred remains of papers, wet ashes that gave off an unpleasant stench, and a scorched rug and chair. The acrid smoke was clearing through the open doors and windows.

As Jared started past me with Harriet smiling on his shoulder, my own eyes suddenly grew misty. "This horrible night produced a miracle," I breathed.

Timothy turned to me and laid a hand upon my arm. "And if anybody deserves a vote of thanks for helping to bring that miracle about, it's you, by Jove."

I was touched by the seriousness of his remark. But just the same, I examined him covertly. Tonight Timothy's red-rimmed eyes and soot-streaked face gave him a much older, harder look. *Could Timothy be the culprit?* Was he still in love with Katherine and trying to set her free from Jared? I didn't like that idea in the least—Timothy was Harriet's beloved playfellow.

"I didn't do so much," I told him now. "Harriet's own will had to break through her barrier of fear. The exercises helped her to be ready when the time came, that was all."

I left him then and hurried down the hall to Harriet's room where Jared was just depositing his daughter on the bed.

Seeing me, she reached up to grab his hand. "Papa, you won't send Margaret away yet, will you?

212

I don't think I could have walked tonight if she hadn't made me exercise so faithfully these past weeks. I'll still need her for a real long time, won't I?"

"I have no intention of dismissing Nurse Mac-Neil," Jared said, glancing at me with a rather deep expression.

"Papa, wouldn't this be a good time to give it to her?" Harriet hissed. "You know what I mean."

"I already have, sweetheart."

She bolted upright. "Margaret, where is it? Are you wearing the pendant underneath your robe?"

My hand went to my bare throat. Of course I wasn't! My horrified glance swiveled from Harriet to Jared. Had he discussed such a compromising gift with his *daughter*?

Harriet continued to stare at me expectantly.

"N-no," I almost choked and had to clear my throat. "It's too—too valuable. I c-can't accept it." Dear heaven, how could you explain the indiscretion of this gift to a child?

Harriet thumped the counterpane. "Margaret, I insist that you accept the pendant. It's just a little thing that belonged to Papa's grandmother. We both decided it would look nice on you and that you should have it."

I managed to make an inarticulate sound of protest, avoiding Jared's eyes, and shook my head.

"Yes! You saved my father's life and you helped me walk again. Isn't that worth something?" Harriet thrust out her chin. "Papa, why don't you persuade her?"

He spread his hands and looked as though he

were biting back a laugh. "You seem to be doing a better job than I did." With his soot-streaked face, tousled hair, and unbuttoned shirt, there was something rather vulnerable and endearing about this man who had endured so much lately and cared so deeply for his daughter. I felt my stubborn heart go out to him.

"Well, I — I thank you both very much. It's a very generous, lovely gift, but I'll have to — er — think about it."

I bent down and settled the covers around the child. "Now it's time for everyone to get some rest, especially you, my dear. The most important thing right now is that you can walk again. We are all so very thankful tonight." I kissed Harriet's cheek and felt the slender arms go around my neck in an unprecedented hug.

I had to brush tears from my eyes when I followed Jared into the empty hall where the smell of smoke and ashes still hung heavy on the air.

"I'll take my manuscript now," Jared said in a low tone. "I'm sure there will be no more attempts tonight." He entered my room and lit the lamp in a rose-painted globe beside my bed.

I hastened to the closet and returned carrying the manuscript. I turned it over several times, then, drawing a deep breath, I looked him straight in the eye. "Have all these so-called accidents been caused by this book of yours?"

He hesitated. "Perhaps. All right, Margaret, I'll be frank with you. God knows, you've earned the right to know. I just thought it might be safer — Well, anyway, yes, someone wants to stop the publication of my book."

"Who, Jared?" I gasped. "I—I—mean, Mr. Warwick."

"Call me Jared. I love to hear you say it."

I felt the color sweep my face. "About the book," I said hastily. "That fire tonight—"

"The fire was set deliberately. A rag dipped in oil had been lit and forced through the keyhole, which is very large and old-fashioned, in my writing room. Some papers were slid underneath the door to help start the blaze. Fortunately, I woke in time to put out the fire before much harm had been done. It really was more in the nature of a warning. You see, I had received a note—"

I broke in with a cry. "A note? From whom? What did it say?"

"Just that my book should be suppressed unless I wanted to have more trouble." Jared gave me a harassed look and raked the tousled hair back from his forehead. "That's absolutely all I am going to tell you."

I shook my head at him. "I think you should confide in me. I don't like fighting shadows."

"I'm sorry, Margaret. I really don't have any idea yet who sent the note or who instigated all these 'accidents.' I never should have involved you in all this. But you don't know how—how glad I am that you did come here. If that sounds mixed up, I can't help it." His naturally husky voice had grown quite unsteady.

But when he put out his hand to me and touched my arm, it all came rushing back: the dream, the passion of his kiss, the way I had responded to it . . .

I thrust the book into his hands. "Here, take it," I jerked out breathlessly. "Goodnight. I'm sure you must be as exhausted as I am."

He hesitated briefly, his lips parted as though he wished to say something further. But then he pressed them together tightly, muttered his thanks, and the door closed after him.

Weakly, I staggered to the bed and leaned my head against the post. The green room with its flickering golden light still seemed to vibrate with the presence of the heavy-shouldered man, hard-faced, and shaggy-haired, whose strong masculine appeal threatened more and more to overwhelm me.

Chapter Twenty-one

My problems had no ready solution, and, after Jared left, I felt too tired to think. I soon fell into an exhausted slumber that brought me to the breakfast room rather late the next morning.

I had heard the other guests leave earlier and now only the three Warwicks, plus Lady Sylvia and Timothy, were finishing their morning repast at the table.

Evidently an upsetting conversation was in progress as I entered. Katherine faced Jared across the table, her angry color almost disfiguring her beauty. She wore a traveling costume of pale mauve twill, with a short moleskin cape slung behind her chair.

"Jared, you know that Madame Lelong invited me to go to London today." She glared at him. "And you agreed to let me go. You said so last night in front of everybody at the supper table."

"But after everything that's happened—the fire—Harriet's recovery . . ." Jared's voice held a strange note of pleading quite at variance with his usual commanding tones. "I thought you might like to spend the day with your daughter."

"You thought wrong, as usual. Why should there be all this fuss about Harriet's so-called recovery? You'd think it was a miracle! I believe now, as I always have, that Harriet could walk any time it suited her. No. You said that I could go and I'm holding you to your promise. Tim, Sylvia — you both heard what Jared said last night."

"Lord, ducky, don't embroil me in your domestic squabbles." Timothy rolled his eyes heavenward and rose hastily, patting his lips with a linen napkin. "I'm going upstairs to finish packing. It's a shame we all slept so late and missed the morning train. Now we'll have to pig it in a stagecoach." He gave a gusty sigh and tugged his flowered waistcoat into place.

He was the only one who acknowledged my presence, giving me a little wink as I slipped into a vacant seat after helping myself from the dishes on the sideboard.

Sylvia rose and placed a hand on Jared. "Why don't you come to London with us, darling? It would be such fun."

"Thanks," Jared replied curtly, his eyes upon his plate. "But I have urgent work to do finishing my book. I may come up later to see my publisher, however."

"Oh, divine!" Sylvia brightened. "We can all arrange to meet at the Great Exhibition."

"Mama, Mama, let me go with you!" Harriet cried, bouncing up and down in her chair. "Please, please! I can walk now, and I could attend the exhibition with you."

218

"Are you mad?" Katherine threw her a look of incredulous horror. "Why, you are still not well enough."

"Mama, I promise I wouldn't be any trouble," Harriet wailed. "I do so want to see all the pretty things—the wax flowers, the wooden toys, the silver statues. Margaret's been telling me all about the Crystal Palace—"

"Then let her go on telling," Katherine snapped. "I fear that is as close as you will get."

She turned her gaze on Jared with an implacable expression. "I will be gone about a week, so don't look for me any sooner. It isn't every day I receive an invitation to be the guest of a wealthy society woman like Vivienne Lelong. Don't begrudge me my little pleasures, Jared. You have no right to! After all, if you insist on keeping me a virtual prisoner on this horrible, remote island, what can you expect?"

"What indeed?" he grated, glaring at her. "Go, my dearest wife and enjoy your 'little pleasures.' They seem to be of paramount importance to you."

Harriet let out another howl.

"Stop whimpering," Jared told her. "You have so much to be happy for today." His voice grew milder. "Count your blessings, child. I'm sure I do." His somber gaze followed Katherine out the door.

I bent above my scrambled eggs and kippers, trying to be inconspicuous and to eat as quietly as I could while the room emptied. Soon only Jared, Harriet, and I remained seated at the table.

Jared, in a full-cut shirt and dark grey waistcoat sprawled back in his chair, one hand toying with his cup while he frowned at the snowy damask cloth.

What was he thinking? That he had a feckless, shallow wife? Or did he have a thwarted feeling of desire for her affection and wish that he could have made her stay with him today?

Before I could stop myself, jealousy shot its tongued flame into me. To tell the truth, I was more pleased by Jared's disagreements with his wife than by the thought that he really loved and desired her in his heart. I felt dismayed and heartily ashamed of myself for feeling this way. And I didn't know what to do about it. Except sternly to suppress such maunderings whenever they occurred.

Suddenly, I heard my name and realized that Jared was addressing me. "What do you think of my idea, Margaret?" he asked. Miraculously, the worried lines had smoothed out of his face and he actually looked happy and expectant.

"What idea is that?" I asked, bewildered.

Harriet then piped up. "Papa says he will take time off today to celebrate my walking again, and we can have a picnic. Just the three of us. He'll get out the dogcart and drive us to the meadow." Harriet's face had cleared, with a child's usual resilience when presented with another idea.

I looked from one to the other with a smile. "That sounds fine to me, but we should not neglect your regular exercises and massage, Harriet, even though you're walking. Perhaps we can be ready in an hour, if we get right to work. Will that suit you, Mr. Warwick?"

"It will suit *Jared*," he emphasized. "Say it, Margaret. There is no one here to raise an eyebrow now.

And I'm sure that Harriet will not be shocked."

"Very well . . . Jared," I murmured self-consciously, while Harriet hid her giggles behind a napkin.

Jared's gaze had settled on my neck. "Where is the controversial pendant?" he drawled. "Buried in a bureau drawer like a guilty secret?"

"I have it on, but un—underneath." I stuttered a little beneath his probing glance and only drew the pendant from my high-necked bodice for a second, before I slid it back again.

"Afraid of comments from the staff?" he grunted, shoving back his chair. "Very well, *Miss MacNeil*, always sensible and proper to the core. At least, you aren't flinging it back at me."

I flushed painfully. "Please—don't think I am unappreciative," I begged, wishing he would understand. But Jared only threw me a rather taunting smile before he left.

I wouldn't admit exactly why I did it, but when it was time to get ready for the picnic I removed my cap and apron, took down my hair, and tied it back with a ribbon at my nape. As I smoothed the close-waisted dress of blue-sprigged calico, I told my mirror, a little defiantly, that now maybe I wouldn't look quite so prim and proper. I flung a white crocheted shawl around my shoulders, and topped everything with the new silk bonnet and its delectable flower trimming.

The small dogcart and pony were waiting in the garden. Jared lifted Harriet to the front seat and I climbed onto the leather-padded seat behind. A hamper rested on the floor, as well as several rugs and cushions. Jared snapped the reins and we moved off briskly past the greenhouse, past the stableyard, onto the tree-lined road beside the cliff.

I inhaled deeply of the wonderful fragrance of sea and meadow, gazing around blissfully at fluffy clouds, deep blue sky, and winging birds. "How unusual this weather has been lately for an English spring," I remarked.

"I predict that it won't last much longer." Jared cocked a weatherwise eye at the horizon. "We might have rain by nightfall."

"Did everybody leave for London?" I ventured to inquire, wondering if, by some miracle, Katherine had been persuaded to stay home.

Jared answered grimly, "We three are all that remain, except for the servants."

At his words, a faint twinge of alarm sounded in my brain. Here was a handsome, virile man, rejected by his wife, thrown together with a young, single woman for whom he had declared he felt much admiration and much gratitude. He had even seemed to be drawn to me physically when he had stared his fill at my partially exposed figure the other evening. And on other occasions there had been warmth and awareness when he spoke with me — too much, perhaps.

Inwardly, I groaned. I knew I must halt these wild conjectures before they took possession of me. Probably it was just my imagination, anyway. Why must I persist in looking for signs of Jared's interest beyond the bounds of friendship and gratitude? Or of mere normal kindness?

It was almost as though I *wanted* to see such signs!

Which, of course, was *utter nonsense.*

I sat up straighter, settled my hat and shawl, and determined fiercely that nothing must mar this lovely day of sun and birdsong—and the miracle of Harriet's recovery.

True, the child's legs were still weak, but every step increased her strength, and I had no doubt that by the end of the week Harriet would be in full command of her limbs and able to run, as well as walk, if she didn't overdo it.

During the ride, Harriet commented ecstatically on all the flowering plants, "laughing seagulls" (her own description), and then the perfection of the tree-enclosed, sun-filled meadow. Everything she saw seemed to have gained a new brilliance and wonder in her eyes. It was as though she had never expected to enjoy any of it again.

When rugs had been spread on the choicest spot of ground and pillows propped against the sunny boulders, Harriet was not content to rest but soon wavered off, a little wobbly but determined, to pick wildflowers and explore.

I settled myself a few feet from Jared, who leaned back on the rock. Both of us watched Harriet a little anxiously at first, but, as her steps grew more confident, Jared exhaled his breath and turned to me. "She's going to be all right."

We smiled at each other from full and thankful hearts. Then Jared sobered. "While we have the chance, I think I better give you some long overdue explanations. I have thought about what you said last night, and I realize that it isn't fair to keep you blindly in the dark. Even though I reasoned that I was protecting you."

I looked back at him eagerly and moved a little closer, "Well, perhaps I could help you better if I knew more about the problem."

Jared nodded. "My book is nearly finished now and soon I'll deliver it to the publisher. And since everyone is gone except the servants and ourselves, I think it might be safe to tell you a few things."

I gazed at him expectantly, my lips parted.

"To begin with, I nearly always write about slum conditions—"

"That sounds reasonable," I interrupted. "Things you know about."

"Yes, the mills and factories employing tiny children from five a.m. to ten p.m., the ragged orphans sleeping at the base of lampposts to keep warm because they have no one to take them in, the thirteen-year-old girls given to rich men, the overcrowded tenements, the sewers running with disease, the putrid meat called 'Tommy Rot' sold from butcher shops. It's all a hellish nightmare!"

I nodded soberly. "I know. There are dreadful, depressing subjects, but if you can help—"

"Sometimes changes can be brought about if people in authority are made aware of them. Also, public conscience can be a powerful weapon if aroused. So—I write about these subjects in my books."

"Why have I never seen any of them?" I inquired. "Oh, I remember, you use a pen name, don't you?"

"I write under the name of Henry Verite."

"Verite—Latin for truth." I frowned thoughtfully. "How many people know this is really Jared

Warwick?"

"Several." He shrugged. "Katherine and my publisher. Sometimes I used my pen name when I went into the slums to research my material. I imagine my questioning this last time caused suspicion, and, possibly, an old acquaintance leaked the secret of my identity to the wrong people. For a good price."

"What is your present book about? Something so important they would kill you to suppress it? Or can't you tell me about that?"

He spoke so softly that I had to lean closer, even though there were no other ears but mine to hear his words. "I have uncovered a scandal in a housing plan for the slums of Holborn. Most of the present dwellings are horrendous, as you may know. No heating, no water, no privacy, overrun with vermin, a breeding ground for crime. As many as fifteen people or more sometimes share one room, and fifty have to share a common water pump in the courtyards, which are usually awash with sewage. A certain industrialist has been given a contract to tear down these tracts and build new rows of model homes."

"Oh, I've heard of that," I exclaimed. "I thought it sounded like a wonderful idea."

"It would be, in the proper hands. But this particular man has built slum dwellings in Scotland under another name. His firetraps burned hundreds of people one night, but the person responsible for this outrage vanished into thin air."

"And you know who he is?"

"I know the names he goes by: Grainger Dodge in

England. Gordon Knox in Scotland. My book will bring his past crimes to light and, hopefully, trigger an investigation. I know I have him worried. I have been threatened numerous times by anonymous letters and told to halt my investigations. One letter, however, came from an informer who said he would talk to me at a tavern in Holborn. He never appeared, and that was the night that I was stabbed."

"A trap, of course. Jared—" How easily the name fell from my lips. "—have you gone to the police?"

"Yes, but how do you arrest a shadow? A fleeing footstep? A shot fired in the crowd? I have hired surveillance on the island, but this identity must remain a secret, even from you."

I opened my mouth to argue this point. Then I thought: Jared had confided quite a lot to me. I must not push him too far.

I settled for another point. "Perhaps the industrialist hired an agent to persecute you. Someone who could get close." I bit my lip and hesitated. How could I say that I suspected his wife, or Timothy, or even one of his other guests?

My thoughts began to race. There might even be two different people after him. Suppose only the stabbing had been done by the infamous housing contractor or his hireling? The other attacks might have been perpetrated by any of the three guests: Madame Lelong, Timothy, or Lady Sylvia. As well as Katherine, who certainly had a strong motive for getting rid of Jared. And Timothy might be helping her. Lady Sylvia? Revenge, perhaps, because her favors had been refused? I dismissed Vivienne Lelong from the list of suspects. She, alone, seemed above suspicion, only because I could discern no motive.

However, all of them had had the opportunity. All had been at the manor on every occasion that the "accidents" had occurred. When the rock was thrown at Jared's horse, they had all been out on the grounds, going their separate ways, searching for him. When the shot was fired in the ruins, Timothy or Sylvia easily could have been there, too. Katherine had been in bed with a headache . . . *but had she*? Couldn't she secretly have slipped over to the mainland, or even hired someone else to fire the shot?

Jared's somber gaze roved across my face as though he looked into a mirror and could read my mind. "Yes, it could be anyone. I wonder . . . have I been wrong to risk so much to write this book? Even to the point of endangering my own family?" He looked broodingly across the field at Harriet seated in the grass, examining her store of harebells, daisies, purple violets, and the like.

After a moment's reflection, I said carefully, "I don't know how you could not write about this grave injustice once you knew about it. It must have been a hard decision for you to make. But, Jared, *you* are the one who has been in danger. *You* have been the target. And I—I admire you for your courage."

"Do you?" Jared leaned toward me and his hand came up to touch my cheek. A jolt went through me but I didn't move. He trailed his fingers slowly, gently. Then as light as air, he traced my parted lips, through which I was breathing quite unsteadily.

"Margaret," he whispered in a husky, shaking

227

voice, "how could I ever bear to let you go?"

I couldn't look away from the dark-steel glance that impaled me like a helpless moth. An invisible current seemed to stretch between us. I, for one, could not have uttered a single sound of protest if he had caught me to him—right there in the open field—and kissed me thoroughly. No, I would have let him . . . and enjoyed it! That much was clear to me . . . and perhaps to him . . . in the heady, vibrating silence.

But the moment was shattered by Harriet, who suddenly plopped down beside us, showering us with flowers and laughter. "Whoops! My legs are tired now. And I'm awfully hungry. Let's eat."

I turned to her quickly, making sure she hadn't overdone. All the while, I was experiencing mixed emotions: regret that the wonderful, shared emotion between Jared and myself hadn't lasted longer, and relief that it had ended before an irrevocable step was taken.

Hands trembling slightly, I set out the contents of the picnic lunch while Jared talked and laughed a little overloudly with his daughter. Ample justice was done to the cold roast chicken, the sandwiches of tongue and beef, the pickled vegetables, cherry turnovers, cheese cakes, cider, ginger beer, and claret wine. Everyone was very jolly. Then very sleepy. We all closed our eyes, the talk grew desultory, and I know I napped, feeling more peaceful and happy than at any time since I had arrived on Brendan's Isle. The breeze blew sweetly from the sun-warmed grass and meadow flowers. The ocean waves and mewing gulls were a distant harmony. We three were together. And Harriet could walk . . .

When I awoke, Harriet and her father were conversing in low tones, and they both smiled at me. "It's time to leave," Jared said. Shadows were stretching across the field and the air was cool.

As we wended our way homeward in the dogcart, the thought came to me: Today we had been like a happy, complete little family, all in accord.

The next minute, horror filled me. What was I thinking of? Jared was a married man with a child. He never would divorce his wife and impose such scandal on them all.

And I was just the nurse, who soon must leave. At all costs, I must try to keep my head. That reflection was as depressing as it was sensible. Sensible! I was beginning to hate that word with all my heart and soul.

Chapter Twenty-two

Jared's prediction for the weather soon came true. By nightfall, rain rattled the long, draped windows and wind moaned down the chimneys, sometimes sending out an annoying belch of smoke.

During the next few days, Jared secluded himself in his rooms, evidently immersed in his writing. He only appeared at the dinner hour, then retired directly afterward. I couldn't help but wonder if he were trying to avoid me. Perhaps he was as aware of the dangerous emotion building up between us as I was. In a way, I felt relieved by his absence, even though I missed him. It was easier to control the disturbing conflicts in my mind when I didn't see him constantly.

However, I frequently found my thoughts returning to the startling disclosures he had made to me in the meadow. I had never heard of "Henry Verite," but, of course, the circulating library to which Octavia and I belonged catered more to the taste of lady patrons who preferred poetry and novels. The Brontes, Jane Austen, Dickens, Tennyson, and Wordsworth — these were all great favorites of ours.

It certainly was to Jared's credit that he pursued such a singular, hazardous type of writing. An exposé so dangerous that someone might have been hired to stop him. Perhaps now, with Katherine and all the guests out of the house, there might be a lull in the attacks. Of course, there was no guarantee that it was one of them. A stranger could right now be lurking in the village. . . .

Now that I thought about it, the ferret-faced Bascom was more in evidence than ever: often standing staring silently in the rain-drenched garden or slipping along the hallways from the wing where Jared worked. Had he taken over some of James's duties? I didn't have occasion to observe the pair named Barnes, but with their help Miss Grey ran the house as smoothly as ever, even with the mistress far away.

I determined not to be led into a sense of false security by this oasis of peace. I still must be on my guard. But . . . how? I groaned to myself. And against . . . whom?

Only Harriet seemed completely carefree these foggy, chill spring days. Since she had regained the use of her legs, her strength had increased quite rapidly, and she was usually to be found jumping up and down the stairs, sliding in the marble hallway, or dancing to a tinkling music box. It was almost as though she felt afraid that she might suddenly find her limbs immobile again unless she used them constantly.

The activity couldn't hurt her, and I watched her antics with a heart full of thanksgiving, even admitting a little credit to myself. I had made her exercise and had dispelled some of the fears that had kept her in the house listening to whispering voices. That had not been good for her at all. The only problem now was that I still had to make her get sufficient rest, and this often took all my powers of persuasion.

However, when Miss Pynns, the dressmaker, and her assistant arrived, they proved to be a new diversion. Harriet and I soon became engrossed in pouring over the periodicals they had brought, which displayed the latest styles from Paris. It was a delicious feeling to have three lengths of new cloth at my disposal, and I wanted to make the most of it.

The dressmaking details frequently were discussed at the dinner table, much to Jared's amusement. He usually made no comment, but one evening he remarked to me quite seriously, "Your own material must also be made by the professional team, you know. Miss Pynns has been hired to remain for the whole week. So why not use her talents?"

"Thank you, Jared, but I learned to sew from my Cousin Octavia," I replied. "I believe I can manage a few simple styles."

"Always so damnably independent," Jared muttered under his breath, frowning into his glass of ruby claret. "Won't you ever give some man the pleasure of doing things for you?"

Not someone who doesn't belong to me, I thought sadly to myself. But I didn't speak, I only flushed and looked down at my plate.

While I was floundering for a reply, Harriet intervened. "Papa, Margaret has a length of perfectly gorgeous green silk cloth. You must insist that she let Miss Pynns make it up in one of the new French styles."

"I insist, Miss Independence," Jared said, looking at

me over the rim of his glass.

How could I resist that dark and forceful glance? "It isn't fair. Two of you against one." I laughed helplessly. "Very well. Thank you. If Miss Pynns has the time, I will be grateful for her assistance. But I have nearly finished my walking suit, and the gold mull afternoon dress will be quite simple."

After all, I had learned a thing or two from Octavia and need not be ashamed of my efforts. However, it would be nice to have Miss Pynns attend to my best gown. It was by far the loveliest material I had ever owned, and I would hate to see it ruined. Though I doubted if I would have any occasion to wear it before I left.

Unfortunately, whenever I visited the sewing room, I seemed to encounter the disdainful eye of Miss Grey as she passed in the hall. I could almost hear the haughty housekeeper thinking: "What airs our nurse gives herself these days. A seamstress for her clothes, indeed! Who does she think she is? This never would have happened if the mistress were in residence. *She* sees through the hussy."

I always held my head high when I saw Miss Grey, since I had done nothing to be ashamed of. I was only following Jared's wishes in allowing Miss Pynns to sew for me. And he was my employer, not Miss Grey. In his generous, rather autocratic way, he was attempting to do me another favor, that was all.

In the sewing room, Miss Pynns and her assistant reigned supreme. They were both thin, austere London women, absolutely rigid in their opinions. They gave the impression of possessing the ultimate knowledge about the world of fashion, "the Top of the *Ton.*"

Both of them had eyes that appeared to assess a figure and a personality at a glance — and then they would decide the proper style and brook no argument.

Harriet and I both bowed meekly to their edicts, except for me, when it came to the low neckline on my green silk gown. The amount of curving breast displayed was startling, but when I ventured to object, Miss Pynns stiffened ominously.

"Since the queen herself wears the most extreme décolleté, how can a loyal subject suggest that this is wrong? Surely you do not question our glorious sovereign's taste or morals?"

I subsided.

But the assistant seamstress snickered. "Our short, plump ruler knows that low necklines are the most becoming ones for her, that is why she favors them."

Miss Pynns glared at her as if treason has been uttered, and the assistant quickly buried herself behind a billow of white organdy which she was scalloping for Harriet.

"My mother must have seen Queen Victoria when the Great Exhibition opened," Harriet stated importantly, twirling around in her new pink velvet skirt and jacket, much to Miss Pynns's annoyance as she tried to measure the hemline.

"Too bad your mama couldn't have postponed her visit until after we made her clothes. Goodness knows when we can return. Everybody wants new garments for this Exhibition Summer."

"Papa is taking us to London as soon as our clothes are finished," Harriet said, causing me to turn and gape at her.

A trip . . . to London?

Disregarding me, Harriet continued blithely, "When *will* our things be ready, Miss Pynns and Needles?"

"Much sooner if you will just stand still, young lady. And kindly keep a civil tongue in your head," the seamstress snapped. "We, too, are anxious to return and view the celebrated Crystal Palace."

Harriet began to talk of nothing else, and I found that I was infected with the same anticipation, though I hardly dared to hope . . . was I included in the trip?

That night Jared verified that I was to come with them. "I promised you, remember? We spoke of it that first night in London at your home. I have business in the city with my publisher, which should not take long; then we can have several days at the exhibition."

The three of us were at the dinner table finishing our bowls of apple duff, and immediately Harriet began to jabber excitedly while I glowed with anticipation. I must be sure to have my blue traveling costume pressed and ready, as well as the yellow mull. Thank goodness, I have my new straw hat. . . .

"I have just received the *London Times* with its account of opening day," Jared said. "Would you care to see it, Margaret?"

Harriet gave a gleeful yelp. "Oh, Papa, won't you read it aloud to us? Then we can all hear it together. Can't you spare some time from your old book tonight?"

He smiled at her indulgently. "Very well. If everyone has finished, let us adjourn to the library."

In the dark gold room lamps were lit, and Jared struck a lucifer to start a fire crackling in the hearth. I sat next to Harriet on the damask sofa, while Jared stood before the fireplace searching for the article.

Whenever we were together these days, no matter

how briefly, I found myself observing him covertly, adding to my store of memories against the days when memories of him would be all I had. If it was a dangerous indulgence, somehow I didn't care. My eyes feasted on the thick, unruly hair curling on the back edge of his velvet collar, savoring his dark, introspective gaze that could turn so quickly to demanding force. Like the strongly carved lips, which were sometimes warmly sensual and sometimes fiercely masterful. His whole appearance was very masculine, from the square, cleft chin and broadly-muscled chest to the strong limbs parted arrogantly in his usual stance. Wouldn't any normal woman wonder if she could attract him? Katherine must be singularly cold-blooded. . . .

With a start, I realized that Jared had begun to read, and I made myself concentrate on his low, deep, slightly husky voice:

" 'Today London was given a public holiday for the eagerly awaited opening of the Great Exhibition. Multitudes of people from all over the world had converged on the city in recent days to swell hotels and rooming houses to the bursting point. At dawn on May Day, thousands lined the avenues leading to Hyde Park.

" 'After a cloudy morning, the sun burst through to shine a benediction on the royal carriage containing our beloved Queen Victoria adorned in her favorite pink silk, her hair and person sparkling with diamonds, Prince Albert and the two eldest children at her side.

" 'Crowds cheered and roared, cannons boomed, bands played, trumpets pealed. Flags of every nation fluttered from the roof of the Crystal Palace as the queen and her entourage made their way across the park into the building where one hundred thousand exhibits waited to astound the public. The main hall rose three stories high, with galleries for spectators, tall elms growing in the center, fountains spraying crystal shafts of water, all shimmering in the sun slanting through hundreds of glass panes.

" 'Seated on a blue and silver throne, the queen smiled fondly on her "dearest Albert," whose persistence in the face of many obstacles made this exhibition possible.' "

There was a great deal more, describing the dedication ceremonies, the dignitaries present, the astonishing displays, and the innovative facilities for rest and refreshment inside the hall.

When Jared put down the paper, he beamed at his audience. "Well, ladies how soon can you arrange to leave?"

"Tomorrow, tomorrow," Harriet shouted, flinging herself upon him.

"Not so fast, sweetheart. I will need another day or two," he laughed. "Then my manuscript will be complete." "How about you, Margaret, what do you say?"

"Miss Pynns is almost finished. Harriet and I will need another day to pack. We can be ready in two days' time. Will that be satisfactory?" I couldn't keep the joyful anticipation from my voice.

"That sounds fine," Jared replied. "Now, Harriet, run along to bed. Ask Annie to attend you. I wish to speak with Margaret about some details of the trip."

"I can sleep at Cousin Octavia's," I stated when we were alone. "It will give me a chance to visit with her."

Jared still stood by the fireplace, one foot resting on

the fender, his arm along the mantelpiece. He gave me a little, cryptic smile. "If you wish. Madame Lelong invited Harriet and me to stay at her townhouse whenever we came in, but we will go to the Clarendon for the two or three nights we are in London. I have no love of parties or society such as Vivienne delights in."

He came to sit beside me on the yellow damask sofa and looked down at the hands linked between his knees. "You must think we have a strange relationship—my wife and I."

My mouth suddenly felt dry, but I managed to say, "It—it really is none of my affair."

Jared ignored my statement. "Katherine was eighteen when I first met her, and it was like confronting a beautiful young goddess. I was struck down at first glance, dazzled with wonder and desire. Her father had been a nobleman of extremely frivolous habits, which sent her mother to an early grave and dissipated every cent they had. Since Katherine had to marry for money, she conferred herself on me—the jacked-up slum boy who now had plenty of brass. My grandfather had died the year before and I was his only heir.

"Unfortunately, besides her beauty, Katherine also had some far from endearing traits, which didn't surface until we had been married a while. Especially after I had made her pregnant. At any rate, though I was proud to become a father, motherhood was not for Katherine the Great. She soon refused to have relations with me any longer and moved into another bedroom on the upper floor. And we began to live a life apart, two strangers under the same roof."

I didn't speak or move. I, too, stared down at the carpet, wondering what to say. Jared was a splendid man with many admirable traits of character and personality. Katherine, in my opinion, was a peevish, vindictive fool.

Jared's next words strengthened this opinion. He sprang up and went to stand once more before the fire. "It didn't help that I spent all my days writing and wouldn't leave the island except for research in the slums. I can't blame Katherine too much for what happened to us." (Poppycock! I thought scornfully.)

"Katherine wanted a social life of gaiety and excitement. She was her father's daughter, after all. She yearned for London; I despised it. I wanted more children; she told me all children were brats. She would taunt me, flaunting her charms, then shove me away with scorn and loathing until I learned to stop reaching for her love. And eventually, I didn't want it. Katherine still tries to raise my hopes that she will share my bed, but the truth is, she disgusts me now."

Jared swung around and asked me in a grating voice, "Are you shocked by these disclosures, Margaret?"

I looked him squarely in the eye. "No, Jared. Why do you always expect me to be shocked? Do I seem so narrow-minded and rigid in my views? After all, I have seen the seamy side of life, working six years in a public hospital ward. Dissipation, prostitution, crimes of many kinds . . . none of these things are unfamiliar to me. I've seen the results of them at first hand. And heard the bitter tales in detail from the victims' lips. No, Jared, I am not shocked easily — as are many other women in this protective age."

Jared's look softened. "Innocence does not always come from ignorance. You have kept your cool, sweet

239

tolerance even though you walked through slime. You haven't let it soil or harden you. I love to see that in you. And I hope you never lose it."

He swung back to the mantel, gripping it with whitened knuckles, his eyes bent upon the flames. "And God help me not ever to take it from you."

When I left the library, I pondered Jared's strange remark with a feeling of acute uneasiness. Was he involved in something else that he had not disclosed to me?

Or did he only mean the dangerous attraction building up between us?

I think both of us now realized that we were faltering on the edge of an abyss and must draw back or be destroyed.

Chapter Twenty-three

When I arrived back in my bedroom, I was still engrossed in my thoughts of Jared.

Absently, I began my preparations to retire. I cleaned my teeth with some Fleer's powder on a tooth twig, performed my nightly ablutions with the can of hot water left in my room, then, donning a long-sleeved cotton nightshift that buttoned to my throat, I sat down to brush my hair.

The window draperies were slightly parted, and I stared a little blindly at the moonlight flickering through the garden. It had been another storm-filled day, but now the trees swayed in an errant wind that had temporarily dispelled the rain. But it was not far off; I could hear muted thunder mingling with the roar of a wild surf.

My thoughts were every bit as turbulent as the waves. What was I to do about this thing that had sprung up between Jared and myself? It had come so subtly, grown so insidiously, like a creeper in that hot-house of his: suffocating, frightening and — dearest

God—yes . . . it was also a wonder and a joy.

Was it love? Would it endure to haunt me after I no longer feasted on the sight of Jared Warwick? Right now, every nuance and facet of his masculinity drew me like iron shavings to a magnet. My heart beat faster just to think about him. When his hand touched mine, my blood grew hot and coursed wildly through my body. If that beautiful, demanding, male mouth should press itself to mine, I was afraid that I—sensible, cool, level-headed woman that I was (or used to be)—would suddenly lose all reason, all coolness, all control. Jared's will would bend my will to his with hardly any effort.

The brush dropped unheeded in my lap. What was I thinking—Jared would never seduce me! My head bent down, my long, red hair falling forward, covering my clenched hands. He was the stronger now. Tonight his words had made that clear. He had a very deep, strong sense of right and wrong. Of honor and fidelity. He was married. And though he no longer loved his wife, he would respect his vows. But what would become of me? Was I doomed to days, months, even years yearning for a man I couldn't have?

I sprang up and flung aside the emerald drapery, gasping for a little air. I opened the window and breathed deeply, my eyes closed, praying for a return of sanity. The wind blew over me with a fragrance of wet leaves and rain. It was brisk and cool. It steadied me.

And at last the madness passed. I must guard against those tempting dreams of abandoning myself to Jared. Whenever I felt them encroaching on my thoughts, I must get busy and distract my mind.

Thank goodness, we would soon be on our way to

London. And then Katherine probably would be here on our return, and, as soon as Harriet was pronounced able to go back to school, I would resign my post. I breathed a silent prayer that I would be sustained in this time of trial, the like of which I'd never known or ever dreamed I would encounter.

I knew that a walk outdoors would do me good before I went to bed, but when my gaze surveyed the garden I saw something moving in the trees. Was it Bascom? I strained my eyes. A flash of moonlight through the scudding clouds revealed a form, dark-clad, taller than the gardener. I drew back quickly. It must be Jared. And I certainly dared not encounter him alone in a midnight garden—not so soon after the emotions I had felt such a little while ago.

I left the window part way open, turned out my lamp, and crawled into the softness of my featherbed. I told myself I would not think of . . . him. My heart felt as though a hand had caught it in a painful squeeze, but, fortunately, the hour was very late, I was fatigued, and almost immediately I drifted off to sleep.

However, in a short time I was awake again. Some sound had banished sleep and I sat upright, listening, brushing back my hair with one hand while the other caught the blanket to my breast.

It came again. A rattling on the window. Pebbles! Someone was trying to attract my attention. Was another outbreak of trouble about to begin? Had I been wrong to think the attempts on Jared were ended with the departure of his wife and guests?

I slid my feet into my slippers and tiptoed to the dark oblong of the window. The noise that had woke me was gone. A wind blew the long lace curtain into the room.

And then I saw it. A note upon the floor. A folded paper! My heart began to pound as I lit a candle and read the printed message:

Margaret: meet me *now* in the greenhouse. We must talk. J.

Uncertainly, I stared at it. Was this another trick? Was the printing the same as that of the former note luring me to the beach? I didn't know. And the initial J—for Jared? But *was* it from him? I squinted at the clock. It was only twenty minutes since I had seen him walking in the garden. Perhaps he *did* wish to have some words with me in private.

I ran back and flung the window wider. There was no sign of anyone loitering in the garden. But then it was so dark whenever clouds disguised the moon.

I chewed my lip, wondering, and began to pace back and forth. A trap? A trick? Surely no one had any reason to harm me. But then I thought: it could be jealousy on the part of Katherine. Even in her absence, she might have hired someone.

Well, what could they do? Nothing could hurt me in the greenhouse. Perhaps the note really was from Jared and he had something to tell me in secret . . . and it was urgent. I didn't let myself speculate any further. The note said "now," so time was of the essence.

I flung a cape around my shoulders and tied it at the neck. I put on stockings and shoes, my fingers trembling, finding I must swallow frequently against the dryness of my mouth and throat.

But before I left the house, I determined to follow

my own watchwords: cool and canny. Carrying a flickering candle, I sped down the silent, empty hallway and rapped urgently at Jared's door. If he was there, I would know the note was false.

I called his name. When there was no answer, I called louder. I rapped again, even tried the knob. The door was locked and Jared wasn't there. So. I would go to the greenhouse as instructed.

For a moment, I couldn't remember how to find it from inside the house. We had left the dining room that day, gone down a hallway . . . holding my candle aloft, I felt my way along. Yes, yes! I saw a glass door, black, unlit, but surely the entrance to the conservatory. When I pressed the cold metal handle of the latch, the door creaked faintly and opened wide.

A rush of hot, moist air engulfed me as I stepped inside. There was a smell of the heavy fragrance that I had found so sickening, also an aroma of leaf mold, and the dankness of thick-fleshed orchids feeding on the rough bark of the banana trees, drawing air into their greedy gold and purple throats. My candle lit them here and there, but most of the glass house was dark. Only an occasional streak of lightning flashed outside and showed the winding paths, the crawling vegetation, and the blank panes of the walls.

"Jared?" I cursed the quavering weakness of my voice, but I couldn't help it. "Jared, I found your note. Are you here?" Suddenly, I felt terribly afraid. Something was wrong. *But what?*

The next moment I found out.

My candle was knocked from my hand and died instantly. A powerful, hot hand clamped tightly on my mouth while a strong arm was flung across my bosom, pinning my arms helplessly to my sides. I knew the body in back of me was a hard wall of male muscle. I also knew it wasn't Jared by the smell. There was fish and horse and stale wine about this person.

"Not Jared," came the husky whisper. "Nay, 'tis James who sent the note."

James! Fear drenched me and I struggled wildly, making choked, incoherent sounds, trying to kick backward, trying to twist away. A flowerpot crashed against a rock.

There was the sound of heavy breathing, and then my assailant spoke into my ear. "Naw, then, sweetheart, stop your strugglin' and I'll let you be. But promise not to scream. Nod your head."

What did James want with me? Terror swamped me and my legs threatened to give way. Had he come to exact revenge? I sagged, shaking in every limb, and nodded, determined to yell the house down at the first opportunity.

But I was not given the chance. James turned my body so I lay across his arm while his other hand still effectively insured my silence.

He chuckled. "Those big, wild eyes! I'm not sure I can trust you, pretty nurse. First, you must hear what I came to say. I like you, see? Always did. And I want you to come away with me."

Astonishment turned me rigid. He was asking me to *go away with him.* Then he didn't want revenge. He wanted *me.* I was further assured of his intent when he suddenly released my mouth and slid his hand beneath my cape to investigate that area he had always eyed so hungrily.

I let out a yell and struggled with his groping hand.

"Stop that! I'll see you land in jail—you rotten cur!"

"Listen," he wheedled, withdrawing his hand. "I've got money now, Margaret. Lots and lots of pretty money. Come away and help me spend it, eh?"

My thoughts raced. James had lots of money? What did this mean? After a second, James let me stand upright. Just one powerful hand still gripped my arm beneath the cape as he eyed me intently.

I could see the avid excitement in his face when the lightning flickered. "Come with me tonight to London. I'll have lots more brass when I get there, too."

Somebody must have paid James to cause all those accidents! I was certain of it.

I cleared my throat. "This money, where is it coming from? Who is paying you? And for what?"

He drew back a little warily. "Nay, then, no questions, my girl. You'll take me as I am, see? I promise you the best time of your life in London. Lots of pretties, a fine room in a big hotel. With me, o'course." He chuckled. "You'll come, then?"

I noticed that he wore a high-necked dark-red shirt and a coat of loud black checks with a gold watchchain across a satin vest. Quite the dandy. His tale of sudden wealth was obviously true. But where was it coming from?

"Well?" he urged.

I slid a step away and looked down, twisting my fingers, trying to appear helpless and undecided. He would not believe a too-easy capitulation. Besides, I was undecided. I couldn't figure out how I was going to gain the information that I sought from James.

"I'm tempted, James," I whispered. "You catch me at a weak moment. Jared—Mr. Warwick—oh, never have

247

I been so humiliated by a man! So mistreated!"

"Ah-ha, I knew somethin' was afoot the way his black eyes used to stare at you. So hot they looked." James's voice thickened. "What did he do? Kiss you? Make free with your person?"

I flung up my head. " 'Tis none of your affair, my man. Only — only after everything, he's still sending me away. Because Miss Harriet won't need me."

"And he's tired of you, eh?" James leered. "Then the time is right to flit. Right to me."

Before I was aware of his intention, James caught my cape in his fist and whirled me up against his body. He clamped his mouth on mine, hard and wet, grinding back and forth until I tasted blood. I thought I would faint with revulsion before he had to lift his head and draw a breath.

He gave a crow of exultation. "Bet you never had a kiss like that, eh, pretty nurse?"

How I ached to rake my fingernails against his loathsome face! I even felt like using some of the slum tactics I had heard and seen. But, while I trembled, seething with thwarted fury, I reminded myself that before me stood the key to all of Jared's troubles.

"Not so fast!" I gulped, pushing him away. "Some things must be cleared between us. This money — who is paying it to you?"

"Come with me to London and mayhap I'll tell." He raked the black strands from his perspiring forehead. "God's teeth, 'tis hot in here. Anyroad, what do you care where the money's from? Come away and leave all these mucky goings-on . . ."

"Hold on there, James. What do you know about these mucky goings-on?"

"Nothin'," he growled. "Nothin'!"

"You just admitted you were getting a lot of money. And I think someone has been paid to torment Jared. *Was it you?*"

"No, no!" He ran a finger around his neckband.

"You'll have to be more honest with me, James. I won't go away with someone who isn't straight with me."

"Gawr, not here. Not now. Not till we get to London. Someone might come in at any minute. 'Tis a fearful risk my comin' here."

"Why did you choose the greenhouse?"

"Where else could we meet and have no one see us or hear you scream?" He moved a little closer. "I was that afraid you'd yell when I kissed you. But you didn't. So you must like me, eh? Want another sample of the good times to come, my pretty?" He reached out his hand.

"No! Not now." I jumped quickly, but not before my cape slipped off and James's scrabbling fingers had torn my nightrail halfway down. His face contorted with unholy glee and a stab of fear swept through me. This man was unpredictable! James would tell me nothing unless I accompanied him to London and I had no intention of doing that. But if I could rouse Jared . . . unfortunately, James was between me and the hallway. Where, oh, where was the garden door?

I whirled away and darted down a path just as lightning flashed, then there came the crash of thunder. I circled a mound of thick-leaved plants, crowding bushes, rocks, earth. My toe hit a stone bench. Panting, gasping for air in the smothering moistness, I ran—directly into James!

He caught my shoulders. "Ah, I like a gal with spirit."

I held him off, speaking in rapid gulps. "James, I can't run off tonight. I'd never get a character from Jared. But soon Harriet won't need me. We're all going to the exhibition in London and then—"

He nodded exultantly. "I'll be there every day at noon. We'll meet." He took another survey of my heaving, exposed bosom and then—although I tried to jerk my head back—he planted a disgusting kiss upon my outraged lips. And vanished out the door.

I saw now that he had used the *garden door*. The next second, I was after him. He must be stopped and made to talk! But James was tall and fleet of foot and knew the grounds. Even while I screamed for Jared and tore across the lawn, I heard the clopping of a horse's hoofs.

Rain was falling now, but I was scarcely aware of it or the fact that my shift was soaked through and clinging in tatters to my shivering body.

"James, wait!" I shouted. But he was too far away to hear me.

Then Jared called my name.

Spinning around, I saw him run toward me from the opening in the seawall. "God in heaven, what's the matter? Your gown—did you have an accident? Are you hurt? What happened?" He gave me a quick survey, then caught me against his chest.

Ashamed, my fumbling fingers tried to close my gaping nightshift. I couldn't help it, I sobbed wildly as I clung to Jared, his own muscular body as wet and cold as mine.

"J-James was in the greenhouse. Go after him—he knows what's been going on. I'm sure of it! He's been getting a lot of money from someone—" I had to stop and gulp for breath.

Jared gripped my shoulders and looked down at me, his face a frightening mask of anger. "What was he doing in the greenhouse? *What did he do to you?*"

"N-nothing! He sent me a note to meet him in the greenhouse signed J. I thought it was from you. Oh, Jared, you must go after him!"

"He didn't try to harm you? Why is your garment torn?" Jared ground out between clenched teeth. *"What did he do?"*

"A kiss, that's all, I swear. He wanted me to run away to London with him. But, Jared, he knows some answers. Please, please, don't delay any longer —"

"I'll get him," He barked. "Go inside, Margaret. You'll catch a chill."

Then he disappeared into the night.

Sleep was out of the question. I scrubbed my face and every place that James had touched. Then I changed my shift, put on my robe, and sat down by the lighted lamp, staring unseeing at the painted globe.

I prayed that Jared would not act heedlessly — not for James's sake, but for his. However, I hoped he would catch up with James and force some answers from the cur. If James had been the instrument, who had paid him? That was the question hammering at my brain. I could see that he was leery of disclosing any names, perhaps a little fearful.

Was he planning blackmail when he got to London? Or was he just going to collect the remainder of the money due him? But from whom? Katherine was in London. So were all the guests. As well as the industrialist responsible for the housing fraud. I still thought Jared might have two separate enemies.

Round and round the questions and speculations

raced until the ticking clock announced that two hours of the night had sped by while I sat immersed in thought. Soon it would be dawn. But still I waited tensely, hoping for a word with Jared.

When I heard his knock and low-voiced inquiry, "Margaret, are you asleep?" I sped across the carpet and flung wide the door.

"Come in." I gestured to the fire. "Get warm."

He came wearily into the room, clothes and hair plastered with the water that still poured from the heavens. He rubbed his face and hands with the towel I handed him.

"James — did you find him?" I asked, gripping my hands together.

"No," he answered tersely. "I went all through the village, waking the good folk until I found a friend of his who admitted lending him a boat earlier in the evening. James had told him he had urgent business in London, and when we went down to the harbor the boat was gone. His friend knew nothing more. He's a good man and I believe him."

He flung down the towel. "I must change my clothes immediately. I'm dripping on your rug. I was walking on the beach when it started raining, so I headed back to the house. Then I heard your shouts. My God, how terrified I was." he threw me a heavy glance beneath his lowered brows. "Are you sure you're all right, Margaret?"

I nodded, feeling a flush mount to my cheeks. I felt ashamed, soiled by my contact with James, yet I knew it was insignificant beside the more important thing that had been learned tonight. James's confession about acquiring sudden wealth was startling — the first light in the long, dark tunnel. The first clue, so to speak.

I told Jared *nearly* everything that James had said. But not his offer to meet me in London at the exhibition. If I met James alone, I might extract some information. But Jared would never let me go alone, and once James saw Jared, he would bolt. I would have to use all my wiles and shrewdness. Once I discovered the name of the mysterious hidden source behind all the attacks, it would be up to Jared to make the next move toward apprehension. He would have to call in the authorities.

So all was not lost this night—even though James had escaped. It was even possible that, with the publication of Jared's book, further harassment would end.

But then I thought, with a pang of fear: *there still remains revenge.*

Chapter Twenty-four

Another good thing came out of James's visit (terrifying and horrible though it had been). It pushed back the tide of emotionalism that had been rising between Jared and myself. We were back to our previous concern about the attacks, wondering if our trouble could be over, but not daring to feel secure.

Both of us were astounded by James's revelation. Jared berated himself for not suspecting James, especially as several of the attempts involved the horses, and as James was known as a good shot.

"Evidently he had been instructed merely to frighten you," I said one evening as we waited for our dinner. "None of the attempts were fatal."

"They were nearly fatal," Jared frowned. "And look what happened to Harriet. I also never dreamed he'd ask you to go skylarking."

I responded crisply. "Neither did I. It was both astonishing and revolting."

"I wonder who's behind him?" Jared mused.

Neither of us had an answer.

Just then, Harriet appeared in the dining room doorway, so we dropped the subject. We hadn't told her a word about James's reappearance, as we both agreed it wouldn't be advisable to worry her.

Also, we didn't want the London excursion to be shadowed. Fortunately, there were a lot of preparations to occupy our time and minds: planning and discussing what to take, refurbishing certain articles of clothing (mine), then the packing of portmanteaus, carryalls, and hat boxes. Many last-minute details arose unexpectedly, of course, and had to be attended to.

But finally all was ready. I became filled with a happy anticipation, and I could see that Jared responded the same way. At least, so he appeared. And I felt I knew him well enough by now to judge his moods.

On the day of departure, we consumed a solid breakfast, crossed the bay on the ferry, and boarded the early train for London. Jared had secured a private drawing room of astonishing elegance. The furnishings were of yellow satinwood upholstered in blue moiré silk. The metalwork was gilt and the walls and ceiling had been padded to deaden noise and vibration. There was a solid table with four chairs, and several more chairs were bolted to the floor, with cushions on the back and seats and big, puffed arms.

Our cook on the island had packed a sizable hamper and spared no pains to make everything delicious. There was no chance for hunger to overtake us on this trip, with the many sandwiches, pickles, tarts, fruit, and jars of bottled tea.

Naturally, the ride was also more enjoyable than

my former one because of my companions. Jared sustained his jovial mood, attending to our every comfort, while Harriet made us laugh with her excited questions as she bounced from one window to the other.

It seemed to me that our troubles had been left behind on Brendan's Isle, each receding mile making us more secure and happy. I determined to enjoy myself as much as possible and see that Harriet and Jared did the same. I would only think about each day as it came along and put the future firmly from my thoughts.

It was late in the evening when we arrived in London, and though I protested that I could take a hansom cab, Jared insisted on depositing me personally inside Cousin Octavia's small house.

I introduced him proudly, and he, all warmth and charm, invited Octavia to accompany us to the exhibition the next day. But she declined, saying she had seen it twice and that was quite enough to thoroughly fatigue her.

As soon as Jared and Harriet took their departure, I turned eagerly to my cousin. "Well, what do you think of my employer now that you have met him?"

"He's a gentleman," Octavia pronounced promptly. "He seems generous, kind, and intelligent. Not handsome but attractive. Mind of his own, I'd say. Hope he doesn't spoil that youngster, though. I could see that she's a handful and that he dotes on her."

I agreed. "But she's a darling, too."

Octavia shot me a keen glance above her steel-rimmed spectacles and cleared her throat. "I'd wager Mr. Warwick thinks you are rather a darling, too."

"Octavia! Why should you think that?"

"Well, bringing you up to the exhibition in that private car, and the little gel said he'd had your room at the manor specially furnished for you."

"He—he's very kind and generous, that's all," I faltered. "He's also very grateful because I saved his life and helped his daughter."

"Hmmm," was Octavia's final remark on the subject, much to my relief.

It felt wonderful to be back in the little house that had represented home for the past six years. But after the gifts had been distributed and every bit of news exchanged, I began to feel strangely restless.

Somehow, I didn't seem to belong in the city anymore. It was much noisier than I remembered, and the air was heavy and foul-smelling. London seemed so old and dirty. I found myself yearning for salt-tanged air, a rocky cliff, and a garden by the sea. Already I missed both Jared and his daughter. How on earth would I ever endure the lonely future without them? A wave of something close to terror threatened to engulf me and I fought against it. I wanted to enjoy these last remaining days with them. Well, then, there must be no more sad thoughts.

I was ready and waiting early the next morning when Jared and Harriet came for me in a hansom cab. Harriet was bursting with praise for the teeming city. To her, it was all so new and exciting. She was thrilled by the red, two-decker omnibuses drawn by big grey horses. She delighted in the clanging bells and singsong cries of street vendors and wanted to stop the cab for everything she saw: the baskets of fresh violets, the trays of ribbons and pins, the hot potatoes sold from little stoves . . . She "adored" the tall, soot-streaked buildings with their elaborate carvings, the shops of Bond Street, the dashing carriages. She was certain she beheld royalty at every turn.

Seeing holiday London through Harriet's eyes made my own spirits soar, and Jared obviously felt the same way.

We had to leave the cab when we reached Hyde Park and proceed on foot along the Serpentine Lake as the hordes of people, plodding horses, and conveyances of every kind clogged all roads converging on the exhibition.

"We must rent a wheelchair for you as soon as you feel tired," Jared said, sending his daughter a keen glance, even though the happy face beneath the velvet bonnet denied the slightest touch of weariness.

"There it is," she suddenly shrieked, pointing to the Crystal Palace. "Oh, look how big it is — look at all the flags — oh, it glitters just like a castle in Fairyland!"

"I also see eight miles of tables and a building covering nineteen acres," Jared groaned. "And thousands and thousands of people trying to see each exhibit. A little daunting, wouldn't you say?"

"Ah, but so light and graceful in spite of its size," I exclaimed, gazing upward at the immense square walls of glass, three stories high, sparkling with clear, golden light.

We entered through the arched opening where two Beefeaters stood on guard issuing tickets for five shillings each. Inside, in spite of the huge crowds, it was still cool and airy, with currents circulating from a canvas covering the south elevation and a fountain spraying jets of refreshing water high into the air. Music came from organs in the background, almost inaudible against the swelling murmur of awe from the throngs of people navigating through the rooms.

In the center hall, the clump of elms towered to the crystal dome, and, looking at them, Harriet intoned deeply: " 'Try sparrowhawks, ma'am.' " She then asked me to tell Jared the story of the Duke of Wellington's victory over the Crystal Palace Birds.

When I finished, Jared chuckled and pointed to a sign beside the gallery stairs. " 'No alcohol, no tobacco, no dogs permitted at any time' They should have added: 'And no birds.' "

Harriet whooped. "But the birds couldn't read, Papa!"

After we had all laughed, we began to inch our way along the displays, exclaiming in delight and astonishment. There was every kind of beauty, novelty, and wonder from around the world. Silks and embroidery from China; swords encrusted with jewels, brasses, and lacquerwork from India; pottery, lace, gold and silver plate from England; elaborately carved wooden objects from Switzerland. My favorite items were an inkstand made of silver trees and ebony fawns; a lady's desk of carved white wood at which one could write either standing or sitting; and vases of wax flowers almost breathing life.

Jared eagerly studied the newly invented deadly Colt revolver and the McCormick reaper from the United States. He told us that the latter invention would revolutionize farming with its speed and efficiency. "And also put many a laborer out of work," he added wryly.

After about two hours, seeing that her father was heading for a long row of inventions, Harriet suddenly wailed, "Papa, I'm getting tired. And hungry, too."

"What am I thinking of," he exclaimed. "You must rest immediately."

I looked around. "There's a sign pointing to the Food Pavilion. Why don't I take Harriet there and find her some refreshment?"

"Good idea." Jared consulted his gold watch. "I'll meet you there. I want to visit the American exhibit a little longer. By George, this is fascinating stuff, isn't it?"

I agreed with slightly less enthusiasm than a couple of hours earlier. Pushing my way through the crowd, I decided that a chair must be obtained for Harriet as soon as we had finished eating. I felt ready to rest myself. But first we would build up our depleted energies with a little fuel.

The catering for the exhibition was furnished by Messrs. Schweppe & Company, so many soda waters were in evidence. No cooking was permitted on the premises, but there was a plenitude of cold meats, cheese, buns, sandwiches, fruit, and pastries, all served from a long buffet.

I left Harriet leaning in a corner since no tables were available at the moment. Then I pushed my way through the crush of people, noticing the foreign dress of turbaned East Indians, Mandarin-coated Chinese, and the unmistakable elegance of Parisians. Though there was a babble of many different tongues, they now all shared one common desire and that was to be fed.

After a long struggle, I obtained a tray of sandwiches, three apples, a pot of hot tea, and a bottle of ginger beer requested by Harriet.

But, when I returned to the corner where I had left my charge, there was no sign of the pink-clad figure. Anxiously, I peered around, calling Harriet's name. But the noise drowned out my voice. Plates and utensils rattled on trays, booted feet resounded on wooden planks, and everyone seemed to be talking and laughing at a much higher pitch than usual.

Where could the weary child have gone? Perhaps to one of the newly innovated lavatories or retiring rooms? Perhaps she had even fainted and been carried away! I sat my tray down on a table and began to question everyone nearby. But no one had noticed a small dark-haired girl in pink, waiting in the corner. Everyone was too intent on assuaging the pangs of hunger or attending to the demands of their own families.

Fighting a mounting alarm, I pushed people ruthlessly from my path, calling Harriet's name as loudly as I could, disregarding the curious stares and heads that turned in my direction. Some of them showed sympathy and suggested that I should contact one of the guards.

Deciding that was good advice, I made my way out of the Food Pavilion and headed toward a door. At the exit, a large, burly figure moved directly in my path, effectively blocking my progress.

"Excuse me," I muttered and tried to dodge around him. When he didn't budge, my glance rose to the man's face and my annoyance was supplanted by surprise.

"James!"

He stood before me, flamboyantly dressed in black and white checks with a vest of blinding crimson. Big and dark, his eyes raked me boldly while he grinned. "Well, well, if it isn't the pretty nurse. Did you decide to look me up, then?"

"I came with the Warwicks to look after Harriet." I hedged, wondering how best to handle this.

"How long before you get the sack?"

I had forgotten my lie about an imminent dismissal. I wet my lips. "N-not too long. James, I have to talk to you. Can you wait here until I find Harriet? It seems I've lost her—"

"Aw, she's outside with her papa. Everyone's goin' to see the queen ride by. So you and I can talk right now." He leaned back against the wall, eyes narrowed. Yet for all his devil-may-care stance, I sensed that he was keyed up to a hair-trigger alertness. His gaze kept leaving me to scan the people hurrying past. *Who was he searching for?*

The crowds so eager to view their sovereign and her consort pressed James and me against the corner. We were as isolated as if we had been quite alone. No one gave us a single glance.

"Have you decided to throw in your lot with me,

then?" James murmured, staring over my head. His hand moved up and down my arm just to remind me of what delights might be in store. "When do you leave the Warwicks?"

I tried fiercely not to shrink away. There was the taint of spirits on his breath. And something else seemed to exude from James. I could almost smell the fear.

"I'll be leaving — soon." That much was true. "James, you said you'd tell me how you got that money if we met in London. I can't help being curious. You must be a pretty clever fellow. Don't you want to tell me all about it?"

He shifted uneasily. "Not until I get it all." He eyed me up and down. "My offer still stands, my girl. You should leave Brendan's Isle at once and come to me. Eh, that's a right dangerous place!"

"Why?"

"You know. Things happened there."

"And in Lingrove. Like the shooting. *Did you do that?*"

"No," he jerked out hoarsely, eyes darting.

"James!" I hissed. "The truth!"

He was breathing rapidly. "Well, see, I was that riled at Master. He kicked me off the island —"

"Who paid you?"

He shook his head and shrugged. "Just before I left, I got a note beneath my door. No name."

"Was that the first one?"

No answer.

"Well, what did *that* note say?" I tried to hang on to my patience, but this was like prying mussels from their shell.

"It said: 'Follow Jared Warwick tomorrow in Lingrove. Fire at him but do not kill. Five sovereigns will be waiting at the same place.' "

"Which was?"

"The inn at Lingrove. An envelope with my name on't left at the desk."

"So you've been paid before?"

"Not much," he muttered, caught off-guard. "This was lots more. But not enough since I've lost my job."

I gripped the iron bar of his arm. "Don't tell me you don't know who hired you?"

His lips pulled back from his teeth. "Not till lately." His eyes were fastened on the thinning crowd. Suddenly, his gaze sharpened. "Ah-ha!"

Cockily, he looked at me, once more sure of himself. "All right, my girl. If you wanta know who's payin' me, come to Astley's Circus tonight. And be prepared to come away with me." In a flash, he was out the door, mingling with the surging throng.

I darted after him but could see no sign of his checked coat. There were so many others! Everybody had swarmed close to the road, cheering and yelling. I could hear the approaching drums, the marching feet, the horses' thunder. I could not resist the thrill that swept me as the cry went up: "The queen! The queen!"

Carried forward by the throng, I saw a gilded carriage roll into view. A small pink figure waved and nodded, then was borne swiftly along, the guard of cavalry cantering protectively behind her.

The very next instant, a scream rang out and several voices rose in shrill alarm. "Look, look!" "A man's been knocked down by the horses!" "Someone pushed the lad!" "Guard, help him!"

Immediately, I thought of James and the dangerous people he was involved with. Dear God, was it possible someone had killed him? Feeling faint and dizzy, I tried to see past the press of bodies, the shocked faces, the excited voices. The guards cleared a path for a man with a doctor's satchel and the people closed in behind him.

I tried to push through the impenetrable wall of dismayed people. "I'm a nurse," I shouted. "Maybe I can help!" I was met with curious, disbelieving stares. A woman nurse? What was that?

Then a collective sigh went up from the knot of observers. "Gawr, he's awright," someone shrilled.

A beefy man, mopping his red face, pushed through the dispersing mob, speaking to no one in particular. "Got up, he did, and ran away without a word o' thanks, ungrateful beggar."

I grabbed his arm and the man gave me a startled look. "Please, sir, did the victim have on a red vest and checked coat?"

"Aye, that he did, mum. Know him, did ye?"

Nodding, I turned away. Was it an accident or had James's contact tried to kill him just now, knowing James was never going to stop demanding money?

Deep in thought, I turned my steps back to the building and found myself confronting a familiar group. Jared was pushing Harriet in a wheelchair. Katherine, Sylvia, and Timothy suddenly appeared from different directions. Had they seen the accident? *Had one of them caused it by a well-aimed push?*

Before I could open my mouth, Harriet bounced up and down and waved me closer. "Margaret, Margaret, I saw the queen! Oh, she looked ever so nice, sweet and smiling, all in pink with diamonds in her hair. Prince Albert was on the other side of her. Oh, it was capital! Did you see them, too?"

"Yes, I saw the queen. Harriet, where did you go when we were in the Food Pavilion? I looked all over for you."

"I'm sorry, Margaret. I saw a school friend and went to speak to her. Then Papa came along with a wheelchair and said we didn't want to miss the queen. We looked for you, too."

"Nurse MacNeil," Katherine Warwick snapped, twirling a purple sunshade, "if you were brought to London to look after Harriet, I would say you are not doing a very conscientious job."

"Harriet was all right. I had her, didn't I?" Jared intervened smoothly.

Timothy greeted me, but Sylvia bent down to chatter with Harriet, admiring her pink outfit, asking what she had seen so far.

Then Vivienne Lelong appeared. Evidently the party had arrived together but dispersed according to different interests. In the midst of all the chatter, my ears pricked up when I heard Madame Lelong invite Jared and his daughter to attend Astley's Circus in the evening.

"The child would love it, *n'est-ce pas*? And if she needs the nurse's care, she can come also. A *petit répas* at my town house first, then my two carriages can convey our party to this exciting show. What do you say, *mon* Jared?" She flicked his chin with a long white glove.

Sylvia's green eyes sparkled. "Oh, lovely! Jared, you must not deny Harriet such a treat."

Jared looked at me questioningly and I nodded eagerly. This would be another opportunity to confront James. If I managed it right, perhaps I could follow him and see the person he was meeting.

I wondered if I should confide in Jared? The thing that stopped me was the thought that I could do a better job of sleuthing and get close to James without arousing his suspicions. If there was danger in such a venture, I pushed it from my mind. Larger issues were at stake. Evidence must be obtained against the person who was paying James, or the attacks of vengeance against Jared might end with his death.

Chapter Twenty-five

I dressed that night for Astley's Circus in the manner of a decorous, unobtrusive servant; a simple black alpaca with white lace at the demure neckline, a plain, garnet-colored cape, and an untrimmed bonnet.

I had brought the emerald pendant to London and always wore it, but I kept it completely hidden underneath my high-necked bodices. I knew Octavia would be shocked if she knew I had accepted such a gift, even if it was from a grateful employer.

When I was ready and waiting in the parlor, Octavia surveyed me keenly. "Such a dark cape! And that winter bonnet — why don't you wear the new silk one you bought in Lingrove? That becomes you so — "

"I don't wish to appear in the least conspicuous," I said, stepping across the room to part the parlor drapes and peer into the street. "Besides, no one will pay the slightest heed tonight to Harriet's nurse."

"*He* might," Octavia muttered darkly.

I didn't question her or turn around. I knew the other ladies in our party would outshine me like a peacock outshines a wren. And if I wanted to slip away and track down James, I must merely be a gliding shadow in the crowd.

My palms felt damp in their crocheted black mitts and my bonnet strings felt too tight. Desperately, I prayed that I'd stay "cool and canny." I was still not certain if I should tell my plan to Jared. . . .

There was no sign of him yet in the darkening street, but, thank goodness, the night was clear. The lone gas lamp at the far corner gave a very dim illumination, and in a bad fog it was completely useless. I watched idly as carriages rattled by, then a cab or two. A few pedestrians hurried past, headed for home and hearth now that the shops and businesses were closed. I barely registered these facts as my mind wrestled with the coming problem.

Then at last I reached a decision. I would not tell Jared until after I had made the attempt tonight by myself. If I failed to encounter James — or if I was in luck and found him receiving bills from someone — then I would lay it all before Jared and let him take the necessary action. I was sure I stood a better chance of trailing James than Jared did, but if he knew of my plan, he would scotch it, sure as fate.

With this final decision, I grew calmer. When Jared emerged from a carriage, I went to let him in the door. After he had greeted Octavia, we were on our way.

In the rented carriage, Harriet gave me a disappointed survey. "You're not very dressed up, Margaret. This will be a gala evening, you know," she stated authoritatively. She was wearing a full pelisse of light blue velvet trimmed with swansdown, while Jared, casual as ever, yet in good taste, wore white and black, his coat cut to the satin waist in front and worn long in the back. He carried a beaver hat.

"You both look very grand." I smiled. "And, as your nurse, Harriet, I intend to be a suitable background, that is all."

Jared's glance was warm. "That face, those wide grey eyes, the lashes long and curling, that glorious hair—even pulled back now in a knot—you never could fade into any background and remain unnoticed, isn't that true, daughter?"

"Very true. Margaret is a beauty, no doubt about it. She just needs more fashionable attire." Harriet sounded exceedingly adult. "Papa, while we're in London, there are all those lovely shops on Bond Street—"

Still glowing inwardly from Jared's compliments, I interrupted with a laugh. "Harriet, I think your papa is more interested in viewing the exhibition than the shops. I know I am."

Fortunately, our conversation then turned to the exhibits we had seen, and I hoped fervently that I *could* remain unnoticed tonight. So much depended on it. I was in a fever of impatience to reach Astley's Circus and hoped there would not be too much time spent dawdling over supper—that *petit répas* to which Vivienne Lelong had invited us.

The Frenchwoman lived in a Georgian-style house in fashionable Belgrave Square. It was painted white and blue and set behind a black grilled fence. Inside, I noticed she had the new gas lighting in the hall, with jets flaring behind etched glass sconces on the wall.

A liveried manservant hung our wraps in a closet and led us to the parlor from whence came the sound of upraised voices and the tinkle and clink of glasses.

As we entered, I received an impression of great opulence: two rose-veined marble pillars reached to a ceiling of inlaid gold and shimmering chandeliers that would not have been amiss in a French court. Chair backs were carved in elaborate designs of flowers, grapes, and foliage, while sofas in jewel tones of wine and sapphire velvet were tufted and deeply buttoned. Rare blossoms appeared everywhere in gold and silver vases, their fragrance vying with the women's perfume heavy on the air.

Katherine was in her favorite shades of purple, with a great many amethysts in her hair and dripping down into her décolleté. Tonight Sylvia wore green the color of her eyes, the black discarded for once. Several other strangers sat or stood about the room clad in equal elegance.

I heard Jared draw a short, hard breath, and I remembered that this was not an affair he ordinarily would seek. It was the entertainment of his daughter that had overcome his prejudice tonight.

I took a corner chair, demure and silent, but my eyes swept every known face in the room. Would one of them tonight become unmasked? Katherine . . . Timothy . . . or Sylvia? Or would it be a stranger? Some hireling of the unscrupulous housing villain?

When supper was announced, I was allotted a chair by Harriet. The *petit répas* was a "groaning board," in my opinion. Various wines appeared for each course beside the gold-rimmed plates. A towering epergne in the center held pride of place with tiers of sugared nuts, glacé fruits, grapes, and exquisite roses dripping from the top. Trays and silver bowls were circulated by a maid. Bathed in sauce or herbs, they probably were

French dishes, but to me they merely represented a rich array of salmon, quail, calf's head, and pigeon pie.

The ten or twelve diners ate and ate, chattering and laughing all the while. I had never seen Katherine Warwich so exuberant, with an almost hysterical gaiety. The beauty was an accomplished flirt, no doubt about it. While steadily ignoring Jared, she laughed and touched provocatively first Timothy on one side, then an older, grey-haired Frenchman with some title, whose narrow gaze seldom strayed above her bosom.

Sylvia devoted herself to Jared and hung possessively on his arm even when we were all ready to depart. Although Jared disengaged himself to look out for Harriet, as soon as possible, Sylvia's hand flew back like a claw. Outside of actual rudeness, he could not dislodge her.

"Let the nurse attend to Harriet," she purred in Jared's face. "That's what she is here for."

"Certainly, I'll attend to Harriet," I said. "Don't worry about her." Then *I* began to worry. How was I going to be able to slip away and search for James if I had to stay by Harriet's side? Some way, somehow, it must be done.

When we reached Astley's Circus, I had already heard Timothy explain to Harriet that the equestrian acts we were about to see were internationally famous. Philip Astley, an astute horse trainer, had been the first man to teach horses to dance to music. His early crude open-air performances soon caught on in England, and it was he who had popularized the circus. Now he was dead, but the show went on just the same.

Westminster Bridge Road was thronged with people when we reached the building. Posters stated that "Mazeppa" would be played tonight. "A Thrilling Equestrian Drama Starring the Sensational American Star Adah Isaacs Menken."

Harriet's jaw dropped when she saw the flamboyant drawings of the actress in scanty clothing tied to a horse's back, and the other scenes of blazing guns, belching cannons, and troops of soldiers, horses, and other extra actors preparing to annihilate each other.

"You won't be nervous, will you, Harriet?" Jared asked as we all went through the door.

"Who, me? Nervous?" she cried. "Papa, I want to come here *every night*."

Jared and I exchanged a glance of mutual amusement.

As we entered the interior, I gasped at the gorgeous color scheme of white, lemon, green, and gold, with crimson hangings from the private boxes circling three sides of a ring covered with white sawdust. In back of the ring rose a huge stage, its mysteries hidden by a deeply fringed velvet curtain.

For the moment I forgot everything but this exciting entertainment that I had never seen before. I felt Jared's arm go around my waist, and, looking up, I saw him smiling down at me — so tenderly that a tremor raced throughout my body. Unchecked by any common sense, I pressed against him in return. The rest of our party was ahead, including Sylvia. Even Harriet was led by Timothy, and, in the crush of strangers, we were singularly alone.

Jared's arm pulled me as close as possible. I put my free hand out and clutched his vest. Our eyes clung in one of those deep, vibrant moments of awareness. I knew we both felt desire. And more. My pulses raced insanely.

"My very dear—my dearest girl—enjoy yourself to-night. As I shall, knowing you are happy." Jared's voice was low, throbbing, even huskier than usual.

My heart was too full for speech. My lips moved silently: "Jared!" And I knew then—I loved this man. As I had never loved before. This was the kind of feeling that would send me into danger for his sake. That would make me leave him so that he would not suffer a grievous scandal. This was the feeling that would endure past age and beauty and desire.

Weak and dizzy, elated and despairing, sad yet happy. That was what I felt just then.

When I was seated in the rear row of Vivienne Lelong's velvet box, it came to me with something of a pang that I was not here to muse on Jared—but to help him. And to do that, I must find James.

I rose and peered in every direction, finally borrowing Timothy's binoculars so I could examine the cheaper rows of seats below us and the balcony on the third level. I saw checkered coats aplenty, rough black heads, and crimson vests. But I was too far away to pick out James. I must get closer.

The orchestra began to tune its instruments, the row of lights illuminating the stage flared up, and everyone grew hushed.

It began with an explosion followed by noise, color, and spectacle that consumed everyone's attention as the saga of the Polish Page unfolded. There were horses, chariots, flags, applause, cries, cheers. The audience was enraptured, and so was I, wishing I could stay and watch it all. But Jared's future safety was of the uppermost importance, and I decided I would not be missed f I slipped outside the box. People frequently moved about, searching for refreshment, I supposed, or greeting friends. An intermission was almost due, but by hat time the halls and stairs would be too crowded.

I crept out past the crimson velvet curtains into the hallway and descended to the cheaper seats, gazing intently in every direction.

At last I spotted James. But he did not see me. A large gentleman shuffled just ahead of me, and I kept in his shadow.

James stood up, staring right at the box where I'd been sitting. He waved his hand, and then I knew—his contact was seated in our box! I turned and stared back, but, just then, everyone rose as the curtain fell to a roar of whistles, stamping feet, and clapping hands. People began pouring from their seats to stretch their legs while the orchestra kept up a loud, exciting interlude.

I pressed back against the wall where I could watch James, yet not be seen. He waved again, his grin cocky and assured. He held out his palm and pointed to it. The orchestra grew louder, cymbals crashed, drums rattled, and someone fired a shot. Crash! The music ended.

And so did James's life.

His mouth became an O of round dismay. He fell, sprawled in the aisle. Then the crowd enclosed him, pointing, screaming, jabbering. Police blew shrilly on their whistles. Feet thundered up the aisle.

Shaking so that I could barely stand, I pushed against the wall.

"Did you see who shot him, miss?" a guard inquired.

"No," I answered hoarsely. Strangely, I felt a stab of

pity. For all his faults, James had not been a killer. He had really liked me. And he had been so full of life just five minutes earlier.

I looked back at our box. It was empty. But someone had slipped out to fire a fatal shot, to close James's mouth forever and stop his greedy demands for money.

Someone in the plot against Jared was here tonight. But I still didn't know who on earth it was. And I felt sick with self-recrimination and regret. Jared might have handled it much better.

Chapter Twenty-six

In all that crowded confusion, the police didn't seem able to find a single witness to the shooting. And though I believed that James had been about to contact someone in our box, I had no proof. Not one shred of evidence. I hadn't seen who fired the shot. It seemed that no one had.

James's body was removed and the people on the main floor drifted back to their seats. "There has been an accident," the manager announced briefly from the stage. "When quiet is restored, the final act will then proceed."

I met Jared outside Madame Lelong's box. "It was James," he said without preamble.

I nodded. "I know."

"Did you see anything? Were you questioned?"

"I knew nothing concrete. I only thought James looked up at our box before he died." I let the implication remain unspoken. "I haven't mentioned this to anyone but you."

Jared made no comment. His face looked hard and

introspective, his jaw rigid. "I almost wish you weren't returning with us to Brendan's Isle."

"Do you want me to stay here?" I faltered.

"It's the danger I'm concerned about. I'm not sure it's over. If anything happened to you, I'd never forgive myself."

"With James gone and your book almost ready for the publisher, don't you think the danger will be over now?"

Frowning, Jared was silent, leaning back against the white and gold wall, his hand thrust in his pocket, his eyes upon the carpet. Finally, he nodded. "Perhaps you're right. We'll stay here two more days, then go back as planned."

He raised his eyes. "My dear, of course I want you with me—if I can keep you safe. You know that, don't you?"

Though I felt like a drab little wren in my plain attire, Jared's words raised me to the status of a queen.

We went back inside, then, and the play resumed.

The next morning, Octavia asked me about my future plans. I found I was able to hide my feelings and answer calmly, "I will leave the island very soon. Harriet can walk now and has almost regained her full capacities. She is like a different child these days, fearless and cheerful."

"Then you have done a lot for her."

"I banished some cobwebs from her mind and cleared up a mystery that troubled her. When I first came, she seemed to think that walking again would expose her to the lurking dangers. Her wheelchair represented security, requiring someone to be always in

278

attendance."

"Her parents must be very grateful to you, though they sound like a strange pair. Why is the mother gallivanting around London without her husband or her child? Doesn't he mind?"

I hadn't told Octavia about the personal side of Jared's marriage, so I had to answer carefully. "I think he minds. But since he likes her to live on Brendan's Isle—which she hates—Mr. Warwick believes she should be allowed an occasional trip to London with her friends."

"Generous of him," Octavia commented dryly. "Reminds me of the old Regency days, when marriage partners were free to go their separate ways and carry on romantic intrigues. Since Victoria came to the throne, most people follow her moral edicts. I don't know if I like this atmosphere you're moving in, cousin. This man—"

"He's a wonderful man," I interrupted. "His wife simply doesn't appreciate him at all."

Octavia's eyebrows rose and she gave me a long, considering look.

"Well—" I floundered, "how many wealthy men concern themselves in fighting for the poor?"

"He does this? How?"

"Through his books, which expose housing crimes and terrible working conditions of the people who can't speak out for themselves. He writes under the name of Henry Verite."

"Never heard of him. Interesting. Have to read one of his books."

I suddenly wondered if I should have disclosed Jared's pen name. But several people knew it, didn't

279

they? His publisher, his wife, as well as myself. And Katherine probably had told Sylvia and Timothy at some time or other.

Was it really possible one of these people could be responsible for the attempts to halt his book? Now that James was gone, would someone try again? Another accident—perhaps a fatal one?

I had to struggle to suppress the cold fear that engulfed me. There was nothing I could do right now. Surely we were safe for the time being. We had two more days in London and we must enjoy them.

And so we did. We went to the exhibition every day. We rode an excursion boat along the Thames. We took Octavia to a most elegant dinner at Jared's fine hotel.

And then, when we returned to Brendan's Isle, there was another happy distraction. Preparations for the ball were under way. A small army of blue-smocked men and women had been imported from London to prepare the food and refurbish a large room that I had never seen before.

The day after our arrival, Harriet and I stood in the doorway gazing at the scrubbing of white woodwork, the polishing of crystal chandeliers, and the dusting of floor-length mirrors set between the windows. The workers had brought a great many little gilt tables and chairs, boxes of flowers, and crates of fresh green ferns woven in long ropes to be tacked around the walls.

"Umm, smell this." Harriet sniffed at a large box of waxy white flowers packed in moss. "What are these, Margaret, do you know?"

I shook my head. "Must be from a conservatory such as your father has. Goodness, their strong fragrance is overpowering. Let's go outside for a walk and breathe

280

some fresh air. It's a lovely day."

"You go on. I want to watch a little longer."

A curly-headed young boy was grinning at Harriet in her pink-checked pinafore. Watching him demurely beneath her long lashes, Harriet slid onto a chair and crossed her ribbon-tied kid slippers. When I glanced back from the doorway, they were already talking animatedly.

What an effortless way to give a party, I thought wryly, as I drifted across the garden. Katherine would arrive tonight with most of the guests in tow. The ball would be held next day, and all she would be required to do was don her costume and look as beautiful as possible.

Yet the Beauty did not seem to be a happy woman. She denied her husband and child any semblance of affection and really seemed to love no one but herself. How could she live with such a powerfully magnetic man and not feel drawn to him? Just thinking about him sent a wave of fiery weakness sweeping over me, and I leaned limply on the seawall gazing at the waves foaming on the rocks, the gulls mewing in the sunlit air. I drew a long, sighing breath. Soon I would have to leave all this . . .

Perhaps it would have been better if I had never come here in the first place . . . but then I saw Jared trudging along the beach, the breeze lifting his thick black hair, a full white shirt opened on his chest, and my heart contracted. No, never could I regret having known and loved him. I would have my memories to cherish all my life.

"Jared," I called impulsively and waved when he squinted up the cliff, shading his eyes.

His face broke into a smile. "Come down here, Margaret."

I was already moving through the opening in the wall, and I descended the rough, stony path so quickly that I was quite breathless when Jared reached up to lift me over the last few feet of earth and rocks.

His warm hands remained clasped on my waist. "How pink your cheeks are! Do you want to rest on the sand or walk a little?"

"Oh, let's walk. I have so few duties now, I need the exercise."

He took my hand in his and we picked our way across the sand, side by side, wrapped in a contented silence.

At last I spoke. "Harriet is occupied watching the preparations for the ball. It should be a marvelous affair. Do you have a costume for it?"

"Just a black domino and mask. We will provide several of them for guests who don't want to bother with elaborate disguises. A long domino covers both men and women equally well." He threw me a sideways glance and tightened his fingers on my hand. "I am looking forward to dancing with you, Margaret."

"Oh, Jared, how could I attend? It would be most improper."

"No, Margaret, I insist. I want you there. Harriet will be allowed to attend for about an hour and you must see that she doesn't overdo. Isn't that right?"

"Very well. But I—I shouldn't dance."

He lifted his head arrogantly, tossing back his hair. "You will if I say so."

"Your wife would not like it. And what will the other guests think? A nurse dancing with her employer—"

He stopped and grabbed my shoulders roughly. "To hell with the other guests!" His voice was a desperate, low-pitched growl. "Margaret — Margaret, don't you realize how little time is left to us?"

There it was. Out in the open at last. All his longing and feeling for me showing plainly in the trembling of his lips, his burning grip, the dark flame flaring in his eyes.

My heart soared with a thrill it had no right to feel. I couldn't speak. I could only stare at him, enraptured, as Jared drew me slowly, inexorably, into his arms.

I could feel his heart thundering against my own and the heat of his hard body through the thin muslin of his shirt. His mouth descended slowly, his lips were breathless, shaking. Then, after the first touch, he consumed me like a flame. He kissed me with a fierce, wild hunger, and I met it with my own, holding nothing back, giving him everything his probing lips demanded. The world grew dark, silent, and remote. Nothing mattered but this moment — and I wanted it to stretch into eternity.

When he lifted his head to gasp my name, I tangled my fingers in his hair and dragged him back. Lips and bodies locked, we dropped onto the sand. Jared had one arm beneath my shoulders; with the other hand he parted by bodice, covering my throat and breast with kisses.

As his caresses became more intimate, more seeking, my own responses grew more unbridled. I gave a cry of earth-old longing, my hands tugging at his waist.

And it was then that Jared jerked upright and put me from him. "Oh, God! Forgive me, Margaret." he gasped thickly, lowering his head upon his knees, his whole body shuddering. "Another minute and I—I couldn't have held back—"

I struggled up and grasped his arm. "I wanted you to make love to me—you know that! Jared," I moaned brokenly, "I love you—desperately!"

"As I love you." He shoved back the tousled, wet hair from his forehead and drew a labored, rasping breath from the depths of his being. "My darling, don't you realize the consequences if we'd continued?"

"I don't care," I repeated with a sob and buried my face against his shoulder. "It's all we'll ever have—"

"Oh, darling—dearest—" He put his arms around me and held me close until we both grew calmer.

"Listen to me, Margaret, I must tell you something. You made a violent impact on me that first night when you took me into your home. I admired your compassion, your bravery, your skill. Then I became aware of your creamy skin, the lovely hair tumbling below your shoulders, and I became inflamed with an unholy passion for you."

"When you were delirious, you kissed me passionately," I whispered, swallowing.

"I thought I dreamed that." He smiled a little shakily. "Just like all the other dreams I've had. You have no idea of the many nights in which I imagined your seduction." His fingers tightened, and it was a minute before he continued huskily. "Then something happened, Margaret. After you came here, I fell in love with you. And seduction became impossible."

"Why, Jared?" I clutched his shoulders. "I feel as though I've been encased in glass all my life, looking out coolly and untouched. Now at last I've broken out and I'm a different person. I'll do anything you want—

284

go away with you—live with you—"

"Do you think I'd let you sacrifice yourself like that?" With a violent gesture, Jared sprang to his feet, clenching his hands. *"I won't let you!* Even though it's tearing out my heart! You have no idea what it would be like to become my mistress. The hole-in-wall existence, the secret, fear-filled meetings, the scorn of neighbors and relatives. You would have to live alone in some secluded house, waiting for my visits, friendless, ashamed, coming to hate yourself and me—"

"No, no, it wouldn't have to be like that." My fingers fumbled with the buttons of my dress as I struggled to my feet and gazed at him imploringly.

"I saw what it did to my mother, having an illegitimate child, discarded by her village, forced to live in a tenement where morals went unquestioned."

My voice was thick with unshed tears. "What—what about divorce?"

"I have asked Katherine for a divorce, and she always refuses. Partly fearful of a scandal, partly because she loves to torment me. Also, she likes to have a husband in the background, with money to supply a big house where she can entertain her friends."

He added heavily, "And then there's Harriet. Her future place in society might be ruined if Katherine made trouble. Even Harriet's chance for a decent marriage."

I looked down dully at the sand. "You're right. There's nothing we can do. I—I'll go as soon as possible."

He blocked my path. "Don't ever doubt my love for you, my darling. I will never love another woman as long as I live. You must believe that."

I looked at his haggard face through a film of tears and whispered, "C-can't we meet sometimes when you come to London? If we are very careful and circumspect around each other?"

I swayed toward him as a flower sways toward its sun. Jared caught me in his arms, covering my face with kisses, gasping against my eager, open lips, "Yes, yes! I swear this is the last time I will ever kiss you with such passion. I will protect you, my love—my life—"

"Papa! Margaret!" Harriet's high voice piped.

We jerked apart and saw Harriet staring at us from across the beach. How guilty we must look, I thought in horror, seeing Jared's face as inflamed as my own, his body still shaking from the rigid control of unresolved emotions.

"Some guests have arrived," Harriet said calmly, walking toward us.

How would she respond to what she had just seen, I wondered? A violent, unbridled embrace between her father and her nurse?

Harriet simply behaved as though she hadn't seen a thing.

Chapter Twenty-seven

I found it hard to sleep that night. I longed to go to Jared with every nerve within my body. But I knew that he was right in everything he'd said. I would be an outcast if I became his mistress. It was impossible to keep such things secret. Octavia would suffer. And Harriet. Maybe even Katherine . . . in any event, she would make Jared suffer in retaliation.

As I turned my hot face on the pillow, at one minute I was prepared to cry aloud that it didn't matter! At least, I would know Jared's love for a brief time . . . Then would come another thought: Was physical expression of our love all I wanted from him? And I knew it wasn't. I wanted other things almost as much. Freedom to talk and laugh together. To care for him, comfort him. Bear his children. And to grow old together, supporting each other through life's storms and heartaches. Everything enriched, of course, by the physical love we'd share.

But it could never be. I would have to give him up. My tears fell until I had no more.

Finally, a weary calmness overtook me, and I had one thought before I slept: There was something I could do for him before I left. Perhaps I could unravel this dangerous mystery that ensnared him.

The next morning, I considered the problem carefully from every angle. Katherine had arrived with her London cronies, as well as other guests, but I was concerned only with those who had been on the island six months ago when the trouble had started.

I marshaled my ideas as keenly as any criminologist — or so I hoped. The person responsible for these acts would be doing it for money. Madame Lelong seemed extremely wealthy, if her house and jewels were any indication. But, on the other hand, did the Frenchwoman have a mass of unpaid debts that might be threatening her with prison? Timothy and Sylvia both needed money. Or Timothy might be helping Katherine, who had more to gain by Jared's death than anyone of my four suspects. But would she try to kill her husband after thirteen years of marriage? It was a terrible thought, but I had read of cases where the festering resentment took a long, long time to reach the danger point.

If the housing criminal was paying someone, he evidently had not wanted a murder investigation of an important writer who was unveiling a scandal. So far, there had been only fear tactics. But now it might be carried a step farther in desperation. Or revenge.

Pacing back and forth, I knew I must do something. I could not drift helplessly in the background until the criminal struck again. Time was running out, and I must act before I left.

First, I would prepare some bait. Sitting down at the

small desk in my bedroom, I drafted four short notes, each saying the same thing:

> If you want to know what James told me in London before he died, come to the conservatory tonight just before unmasking.

I left the notes unsigned and wondered: Would anyone respond? I groaned, burying my face in my hands. Was I a fool? What did I know about trapping criminals?

After a while, however, I raised my head. Well, all I could do was try my best. Foolish or not, this plan was all I had. I rose determinedly and placed the four notes in my pocket. If someone responded and met me in the conservatory, I would reveal what James had said and watch for a reaction. I would tell them that Jared had given me the manuscript for safekeeping, and that I was prepared to hand it over for a good price, since I did not believe the dangerous material should be published. There might be retaliations against the family.

Various dialogs churned within my brain, until I had to admit it was useless to try to outguess my opponent. I could only hope and pray for guidance when the time came. For now, I had to wait until everyone was outdoors. In the early afternoon, I stared out of my bedroom window watching the guests strolling past in the garden, laughing, chatting, flirting. Some played games of croquet on the lawn, others shrieked playfully as they batted little shuttlecocks across a net. Indoors there were the sounds of doors slamming, feet scurrying, voices calling orders. Tradesmen arrived from village and mainland with a great neighing of horses and rattling of cartwheels.

At last I saw my four suspects occupied outdoors, and excitement and apprehension rose in me like a choking miasma. It was true that I was unskilled at deception, threats, and intrigue, but there was an overwhelming goal at stake: Jared's life.

At all costs, he must not know my plan. He never would allow me to be put in such a dangerous position. If anyone showed a note to him, all would be lost. He would suspect that I had sent it because I had told him about my talk with James. However, at supper the previous night he had mentioned that he would be locked in his writing room all day and didn't wish to be disturbed.

I knew I should have help, however, when I confronted the person in the greenhouse. If he or she tried to escape, how could I prevent it? There might not be a chance to alert Jared when the final moments came. As soon as I handed over a fake bundle, my own life would not be worth a brass farthing. Especially since the evil-doer would have been unmasked by me.

Who could be my ally? Then it came to me. Jared had said someone on the island was working for the police. Was it the local constabulary? No, Lingrove was too small to furnish anyone full-time. It had to be a person posing as a worker on the island who had probably been hired in London. The men formerly called "Bow Street Runners" had occasionally turned to secret investigation. I had read an angry article about them in the *Observer*, denouncing them because they were a tough, slum-oriented group who didn't always work within the law. Suppose Jared knew one from his boyhood in that area?

Someone . . . such as . . . Bascom!

The name sounded like a clanging tocsin in my mind, sharp and clear: *Bascom*. Instead of being a criminal, suppose he was a Bow Street Runner? He had it all: the tough London accent, a sly, shrewd face, his stillness and swift vanishing, the intent way he observed everything. His indifferent gardening. And hadn't he arrived six months ago? I was certain I was right!

Rushing from the room I determined to find him as soon as I had distributed my notes. I nearly collided with Harriet in the hall. The girl's pinafore was askew, her hair wound up in curl papers, her arms around a basket filled with trailing ferns.

"Barney's letting me help decorate," she caroled. "You know, he's that cute boy, son of one of the caterers. Oh, Margaret, I'm having such fun."

"Where did you get those plants? Did Bascom give them to you?"

"Yes, he's in the greenhouse. He pulled them up for me, roots and all." She giggled. "He's a terrible gardener, but I guess Papa thinks he's all right. They often talk together."

I felt almost choked with excitement. "Well, I must see if there's anything I can do to help your mother or her friends. Perhaps a headache powder, a draught to calm someone's nerves."

"Oh, no one needs a thing, I'm sure. They are all tearing around outdoors like children playing silly games." She sailed down the hall, calling out to Barney, whose curly brown head instantly appeared around a corner.

I knew the upper floors had been allotted to the

guests and I flew up the stairs, glancing swiftly up and down the hall. No one was in sight. Heart pounding, I shoved one note underneath Katherine's bedroom door. Before I could search out the other rooms, Annie appeared lugging a steaming copper jug.

"What a lot you have to do today," I exclaimed. "Can I open this door for you?"

"Thank you, miss," Annie gasped. "Soon everyone will be hollering for water. Master Timothy said to bring his early, so that's what I'm doing."

Tim's room. It was strewn with odds and ends of gay cravats, striped waistcoats, bottles of pomade and bay rum, a jester's costume hanging on a hook. I stepped inside the door and unobtrusively slipped my note onto a nearby taboret.

Two notes delivered. Two more to go.

"Annie, which rooms belong to Lady Sylvia and Madame Lelong? They requested some headache powders from me."

The young maid indicated the doors without any question. Annie was in a high state of excitement. If she ever thought of James, she didn't show it.

The remaining notes delivered, I drew a shaking breath and skimmed down the stairs into the garden. Earlier, I had washed my hair and tied it loosely at the back of my neck. Later I would bathe and dress in my green silk. Yearningly, I contemplated the dance I would have with Jared. One last time in his arms, his compelling black eyes caressing me. That moment might be the only happiness I would experience for a long time to come. The memory of our embrace and words upon the beach passed searingly across my mind. But then I thrust it from me. I would savor the

292

memory of Jared's kisses many times in the lonely future. But now now.

Quickly, I moved through the groups of ladies and gentlemen chatting and strolling along the garden paths. Some were passing in and out of the greenhouse through the outside door.

I heard Bascom's voice and knew I need search for him no farther. "Crikey, folks," he shrilled. "We must keep that door closed now. Lose all the 'ot air, we will."

I slipped inside as the other people left, some with handfuls of orchids stripped from trees and pots. A shame—but what did such things matter now?

Bascom shut the door, heaving a sigh, and turned a harassed glance on me. "You want somethin', Miss Nurse?"

How to begin? Suppose I was wrong about him? I gazed at him helplessly until he moved closer, his small, bright eyes studying me.

"What's the matter, nurse?" he asked softly. "Are you all right? Jared told me to keep an eye peeled on you."

He called him Jared, not Mr. Warwick.

"Did you know Jared Warwick when he lived in Holborn?" I blurted out.

He hesitated only briefly. "Aye, I did."

I glanced to right and left, then whispered, "Are you a former Bow Street Runner?"

His eyes narrowed more than ever and he countered with a question of his own. "What's in the wind, miss? You 'eard somethin'?"

"*Are you a policeman?*" I demanded. "I have to know!"

"Not . . . exactly. I'm 'ere to watch for . . . things."

I had my answer and I was forced to trust him. There was no one else. Recklessly, I poured out my plan and all my suspicions. "One of these people may come here just before midnight to meet me and find out what I know. Will you help me? And Jared? Will you hide nearby and listen?"

"Where?" He gave a grunt. "Up in a tree like a bloomin' monkey? Come off it, miss. This ain't a game for the likes of you. Forget it."

I clenched my hands. "I tell you, something must be done tonight. I'm certain the criminal is in the house. This is our only chance to expose him—or her." I grabbed his thin arm and shook it fiercely. "*Please!* You must help me! What can you lose?"

He pulled away and chewed a rather dirty fingernail. "I dunno—"

"Listen to me! The guilty person is sure to appear after he reads my note. He will want to know what James has said. I will offer the manuscript for a price and try to extract a confession first. The person will be certain of victory by that time and may get careless."

"And kill you after they get the fake book you bring 'em."

"But they can't if you are hidden in here."

He took a few strides back and forth, staring at the path littered with lavender and white petals and tattered ferns. After a long deliberation, he said, "Too much is left to ruddy luck. It won't work."

"*It will.* It has to! There's just one more thing—you must not breathe a word of this to Jared."

"Why's that?"

"He would try to stop me."

"Soft about you, ain't he? Can't say I blame 'im. The wife's a beaut, but a cold dish o' puddin'. 'Course, one of the suspects may tell 'im."

"I don't think so. Everyone is getting ready for the ball and Jared is locked inside his room. And the guilty person will be extremely secretive, you may be sure. He—or she—won't be showing that note around."

People were advancing on the greenhouse again and I whispered hurriedly, "Please, Bascom, say you'll help me!"

"I dunno, miss," he groaned. "Really, it ain't got a Chinaman's chance of workin'."

Chapter Twenty-eight

In an agony of mixed emotions, I began to dress
for the masquerade. My mind was more concerned
with the greenhouse tonight than with the ballroom.
Bascom had made me no promises, seeming to regard the whole ideas as ridiculous and impractical.
I was almost inclined to agree with him. And yet
. . . it *might* work. So far, Jared evidently didn't
know about my plan. Bascom had acquiesced regarding that, at least.

When I was dressed, I surveyed myself in the
mirror and hoped, wistfully, that Jared would admire the gown. Everything seemed to be rushing
toward finality: the last time I would attend such a
ball, the last time I would dance with Jared. Soon it
would be the last time I would ever see him.

The green silk shimmered through a blur of
tears, and hastily I brushed my eyes, struggling for
composure. This was no time for foolish vapors. Tonight I must have all my wits about me. "Cool and
Canny."

With a deep breath, I drew myself up tall, then noticed with alarm how much white skin appeared above the low, square neckline. My fan — that would help conceal the décolletage if someone ogled. I had a simple one of ivory lace that had been my mother's.

I touched the auburn curls looped up with a velvet ribbon, found my fan, and decided I was as ready as possible. I stepped into the hall and turned toward Harriet's door to see if she was ready. I heard the distant sound of excited voices, the tuning of instruments in the ballroom, footsteps coming down the marble staircase, the opening and closing of doors.

Then someone called my name and Jared came along the hall, a full black domino swirling around his ankles. He drew me back into my room without a word and shut the door.

For a long moment, his eyes traveled slowly, sensuously over my hair and face, and my form so artfully displayed in the daring French design, the pendant rising and falling on my breast as my breathing quickened.

"My beautiful girl," he murmured. "Your skin looks like thick cream against that emerald silk and your hair is like a burnished flame."

I felt an ache, a silent cry, a longing beyond words rise up in me. Helplessly, I reached for him. As he caught me to him, my arms went around his waist beneath the black silk domino, which enfolded us like a tent.

His mouth on mine was hard and urgent, and, somehow, violently despairing. "So much for promises," he groaned against my lips. "I feel as though I'll go out of my mind without you. God help us both!"

He clutched me even closer and pushed my lips apart. Our bodies curved and fit as though two halves of a whole were mated. His breath was my breath, his beating heart was also mine. His kiss went on and on, his hand beneath my gown found my straining breast and claimed it.

When we finally drew apart, I felt that I could hardly stand. Trembling, I arranged the gown upon my shoulders and smoothed my hair. When I was sufficiently in command of myself, I looked at Jared. Neither of us spoke.

He, too, seemed to need support. He leaned back against the door, regarding me so sadly, such anguish in his face, I had to look away again and retrieve my fallen fan.

Jared cleared his throat. "I came to tell you something. I don't want to worry you, but I received another threatening note tonight . . . Now we know the person is very close and we must be on our guard."

"Especially you!" My hand flew to my heart. "Oh, Jared—"

"I will not take any chances. And you won't be in any danger at the ball. Probably, it was just one last idle threat and won't be followed up. What can they do with the house alive with people?"

He pushed away from the door. "Come, my darling girl, let us dance and be merry while we can." His glance was anything but merry, but I managed an answering smile as best I could.

We left my room just as Miss Grey passed in the hallway. She nodded coldly, noting our flushed faces and the fact that Jared had been inside my room with the door closed.

Jared didn't look at her and I dismissed the housekeeper's suspicions from my mind. I had much more important matters to concern me — such as the hoped-for rendezvous at midnight. Perhaps more than a satin mask would be stripped from someone's face tonight.

"I have to see if Harriet is ready," I told Jared, and he nodded and walked away.

When I entered Harriet's room, Annie was just putting the finishing touches to the long, glossy ringlets, which were topped by a wreath of rosebuds and blue satin ribbons. She stepped aside and Harriet twirled around for my inspection, showing layers of petticoats and ruffled pantalettes.

"I wish I could have had a costume," Harriet said fretfully. "Instead of this baby dress of white organdy."

"Oh, my dear, it's charming," I said truthfully, admiring the embroidered forget-me-nots that matched the wide blue sash. "Miss Pynns put a lot of skill into your dress."

"I suppose so, but I get so tired of only white for parties. You look gorgeous, Margaret! Everyone will want to dance with you."

As we stepped into the hall, she cried excitedly, 'Listen to the music. Isn't it all just wonderful? My first grown-up ball!" Her feet began to prance.

"Remember, my girl, you can only dance with Papa or Cousin Tim," I said, hurrying to keep up with her. "And after one hour, you must retire."

"What am I, Cinderella?" Harriet grumbled, but by then we had reached the ballroom and both of us were silenced by the enchanting spectacle confronting us.

In the big, glittering room, the mirrored walls reflected a whirling throng of flamboyant costumes and masked faces. There were horned devils in red velvet dancing with Medici ladies adorned with floating, golden gauze and jeweled brocade. There were brown-robed friars, scarlet cardinals, multihued jesters, and ermined kings and queens.

Everything flashed and twinkled and swirled in a kaleidoscope of color and exciting music. The orchestra was playing a lively polka and I glimpsed the unmistakable black curls and beautiful, red-bowed mouth of Katherine Warwick. She wore her favorite purple in a daring copy of a harem girl, a wreath of matching orchids in her hair. She glided in the arms of a black domino, and I wondered if the man was Jared—feeling a prick of jealousy. But there were several other dominoes about the room, the long, full robes completely concealing the wearers.

Some people stood around sipping champagne brought to them by servants carrying laden trays of crystal goblets. Older guests gossiped on sofas placed against the wall. All of them were masked, except for Harriet and me. The air reeked of heavy, expensive perfumes, powder, pomade, garlands of thick, waxy blossoms, and candlewax from hundreds of tapers burning in the gilded chandeliers.

Timothy appeared in the jester's outfit I had noticed hanging in his room. It had variegated satin squares, a cap of bells, and a little scepter fluttering with ribbons. He went down on one knee before a tittering Harriet.

"Dearest lady, will you deign to tread a measure with the King of Fools?"

"Yes, if you don't tread your measure on my feet. Your costume suits you, Cousin."

He hit her with his scepter and they ran off with peals of laughter to join the lively dancers in a spirited galop.

I refused an importuning Pierot and edged back to a sofa. I had no wish to dance with anyone but Jared. I also must try to keep an eye on everyone who was on my list of suspects.

Timothy and Katherine were on the ballroom floor. As for the others . . . a voice spoke in my ear and I located Madame Lelong sliding to a seat beside me.

"You do not dance, *ma petite*?" The Frenchwoman was a strange-looking figure in a too-revealing yellow satin. She didn't wear a costume, just a half-mask rimmed with brilliants. Her throat and fingers sparkled with an astounding array of diamonds.

"I am here to watch over Harriet, madam," I answered. "I am not here as a guest."

"That is right." A gypsy woman stood before us, green eyes glittering. "But I never saw a nurse adorned in silk and emeralds."

It was Sylvia, her blond hair covered by a scarf, her person garbed in black, with long colored ribbons dangling from her waist. Her slitted eyes behind the mask rested on the pendant that tonight I

301

wore out in the open for all to see. What did it matter? I would soon be gone.

Sylvia bent down and touched the jewel, lips drawn back from her teeth. "*He* gave it to you, didn't he? For services rendered beyond the line of duty?"

Madame Lelong cackled gleefully, choking out some words in French.

I twisted away from the touch of those cold fingers and unfurled my fan to cover myself. Too angry to reply to Sylvia's insinuation, I stood up, watching Harriet twirling nearby in her father's arms.

"Papa taught me to waltz just now," she fluted, then missed a step and giggled, but then the music ended.

Jared deposited his breathless daughter in a chair and turned to me imperiously. "Come, dance with me now." He took my elbow in his hand, but, before we could move onto the floor, Sylvia slid between us.

"Ah, dance with gypsy queen, my lover. All night long I wait for you."

"I have a partner, gypsy girl."

"Bah, this one cannot dance as I do, warm and close, exciting you. Come! The gypsy queen commands you."

Harriet laughed in glee and several people turned to stare at us.

Madame Lelong was among them. "Ah, *mon ami*, this time you must choose between two beautiful, desirable women. *C'est la vie!*"

Flooded with embarrassment, I tried to disengage

Jared's fingers, vicelike on my arm. "I really do not care to dance just now," I said in a low voice.

Jared turned, put both hands on Sylvia's shoulders, and moved her firmly backward. "Sorry, gypsy girl. Another time, perhaps."

"I will wait for you," she hissed. "Do not trifle with the gypsy queen."

She whirled away and Jared led me onto the dance floor as the strains of a waltz filled the air. He drew me close against him in a manner not approved, but I didn't care. Closing my eyes, I savored the comfort of this brief moment, letting myself drift with the music, wishing it would go on forever.

But of course it didn't. The music ended. I opened my eyes, and, though Jared's arms tightened for a brief moment as he gazed down at me, we reluctantly moved apart.

He escorted me back to Harriet. "Would you both like some refreshment? An ice or some champagne?"

"Champagne!" Harriet shouted.

"Not for you, missy." He quirked a questioning eyebrow in my direction and I settled for an ice. Tonight I wanted all my wits about me.

A little later, Harriet went off to dance again with Timothy and Jared sat beside me on the sofa, consuming several glasses of champagne.

"You better put Harriet to bed pretty soon," he said, "and arrange for Annie to stay with her tonight. I suppose I must placate Sylvia with a dance or she will create another scene."

Impulsively, I burst out, "Jared, is she in love

303

with you?"

"In love with my money perhaps. She has none of her own, and I don't think she would object to being set up in a flat by some wealthy gentleman."

"And you never cared to accommodate her?"

"Never. Sylvia is too bold for my taste, and, underneath all that ardor, I believe she's hard and cold." His voice sank to a velvet growl. "The type of woman I prefer is right beside me, and if I can't have her, I swear there will be no one." He took my hand, pressed a long, deep kiss upon the palm, then rose and vanished in the crowd.

I curled my fingers tightly around the place that he had touched, blinking back the threat of tears. Impatiently, I shook my head. This was no time for weakness or indulging in a bout of hopeless yearning.

Only one more hour until unmasking—and before that time, I hoped to do some unmasking of my own.

Chapter Twenty-nine

"Why can't I stay up a little longer?" Harriet wailed as I propelled her firmly from the ballroom. "It's not even eleven o'clock and I want something to eat."

When we came abreast of the adjoining room, Harriet planted her feet stubbornly, not moving, her eyes devouring the buffet tables heaped with platters of meats arranged in fancy patterns, towering moulded aspics, salmon mousse shaped like a giant fish, chicken salad in lettuce cups, tiers of tarts, and little iced cakes decorated with candied flowers.

"The food won't be served until after everyone unmasks," I began, giving her a sympathetic glance.

"I don't care—I'm *starving!*" Harriet moaned, clinging to the door jamb.

"Oh, all right, go along to your room and ring for Annie. I'll bring you something to eat." I tossed lobster paté, sliced guinea fowl, cheese straws, and petits fours indiscriminately on a plate. I added a glass of tea and hurried back to Harriet.

She was in bed and gave a bounce of joy. "Oh,

yummy! Care to join me, Margaret?"

"No, thanks. I just hope that doesn't give you bad dreams, my girl." A knot had formed in my stomach like a fist of iron. I paced restlessly back and forth until Harriet finally finished and pushed the plate aside.

She yawned widely. "Thank you, darling Margaret. That . . . was . . . scrumptious. . . ."

She was half-asleep when I tiptoed from the room, after giving Annie instructions to spend the night curled up in a nearby chair, "in case Miss Harriet should need you."

Back in the ballroom, I saw that the dancing, music, and gaiety continued unabated. I stayed in the background, circling the room, trying to keep an eye on everyone I suspected. Timothy was dancing. Madame Lelong moved around to different chairs, chatting with her cronies. Katherine and Sylvia alternately appeared and disappeared.

Where was Jared? It seemed that a great many people wore black silk dominoes. I strained my eyes until they ached. The floor was packed; the very walls seemed to tremble with the noise, and I had to press my fingers against my throbbing temples. The time was drawing near. But even though I was expecting it, the sudden chiming of the clock made me start with terror. Eleven-thirty! Soon everybody would unmask.

The time had come to make my way to the conservatory. And now that it was here, a terrible reluctance filled me, a fear and dread of what might be revealed. With leaden feet, I moved through the throngs drifting up and down the hall and stairs. I hardly saw them — they were merely shadows.

My heart pounded; my mouth felt so dry I could

hardly swallow; and, conversely, my hands became so wet I had to wipe them constantly on my gown.

But, somehow, I reached the greenhouse.

The door stood open. And, to my utter consternation, I saw that it was filled with people. Like a fool, this was a contingency that I had never taken into consideration. However, it acted like a chilling dose of water, and, suddenly, my mind felt clear and swiftly racing.

I stepped inside and raised my voice. "Listen, everyone. Please, listen! Mrs. Warwick has instructed me to inform you that it is nearly time to unmask. After that, prizes will be given for the best costumes." That was true enough, and a pleased murmur greeted my announcement. "You are requested to assemble in the ballroom at this time so that the judges may inspect you."

Little Bo Peep, Mother Goose, kings and clowns, courtiers and their ladies all trailed away, chattering like eager children about the coming contest.

Limp with relief, I watched them leave. When the place was empty, I closed the door and looked around. Orchids still quivered, bruised, falling down the tree trunks, a pot lay broken on the path from someone's clumsy foot. But now the place was quiet.

"Is anybody here?" My voice came out a whispered croak.

No one answered.

Trembling, I sank down on a bench to wait. A dim glow came from the brazier of coals that was kept to warm the air, but no other light shone in the room. Tonight there was only an intermittent moon and no stars. With the hall door closed, it was a place of shadows . . . mysterious . . . a waiting trap.

Would it be sprung tonight? I swallowed the dry dust in my throat and took a few deep breaths to steady my jumping nerves. This was much harder than I had expected.

And then . . . very softly . . . the hall door opened.

I sprang to my feet, one hand pressed against my throat. A sudden chilling of my bare shoulders made me shudder. I strained my eyes. And felt a pulse jerk in my throat.

A figure stood before me in the entrance. A figure in a long brown monk's robe, the cowl drawn forward to hide a masked and silent face.

Excitement and a surge of exaltation flooded me, sweeping away fear. I had done it! Brought the culprit out of hiding for a confrontation!

The brown robe drew a little nearer, and a long drawn hiss came from the mask. "You!"

My shoulders straightened. My chin lifted. "Yes! I sent the note." I felt gratified by the steadiness of my voice. "Will you remove your mask? You have the advantage of me."

"Never mind that. Why did you send that message?" The voice was a disguised breath. "What did it mean?"

Who was this person? Surely someone that I knew — for he/she knew me! A woman, I surmised, as the shape was not too tall. And the hissed words did not sound masculine.

"I spoke to James before he died. He told me everything. He said that he was hired to fire that shot at Jared when he went to Lingrove."

I attempted to draw nearer, but the cowled figure retreated and the sibilant whisper came again. "Did he say who hired him?"

"That's all you'll get from me until we come to terms."

"Terms?"

"I can get the book for you. That's what all these threats and 'accidents' have been about, haven't they?"

"What book?"

"We both know what book. I mean Jared Warwick's exposé of a fraudulent housing scheme and the man responsible. I was given the manuscript for safekeeping during the ball. I am prepared to sell it to you for a price and claim that it was stolen from my room."

"You must be mad! Why should I want this book?"

"Because you are the person who has been hired to stop its publication. You won't be paid, I'm sure, until that has been accomplished. Either by harming Jared—or killing him." I cleared my throat. "Of course, now there's another choice. I can give you the manuscript, including all the notes."

"This is a fantasy—you are guessing—"

"I think not. You are the only one who responded to my note. Why else would you be here?"

"Curiosity. This book . . . you have it in your room?"

"So you *are* interested."

Suddenly, the clouds unveiled the moon, and, for a brief flash, I saw the eyes of the cowled figure gleam through the mask.

That color! I almost reeled from shock. Somehow . . . I had never really suspected . . .

It was a moment before I spoke. "I have the book and I will sell it. I have been discharged now that Harriet can walk and I must leave tomorrow. I will never have another chance to get my hands on so much money. Besides, I really don't think the book should be published. Revenge might be taken against the family."

I paused, then said deliberately, "Are you interested or not . . . *Lady Sylvia?*"

The silence stretched, pulsating. Knowledge on the one side; awareness of that knowledge on the other.

Then Lady Sylvia spoke in her normal tones and casually removed her mask. "So you know who I am. What of it?"

"I know you are the person in the pay of this man behind the housing fraud. You are the one responsible for all these hateful incidents —"

"What nonsense," the countess snarled. "I simply agree that the book should be suppressed. I will take it off your hands."

"For a price, my lady. Don't let us bandy words. I know you have been trying to stop Jared and I know why. James told me all about it. How you left the money at the inn —"

"He lied! A child took the money."

Her face flushed at the slip. I let it pass and simply continued smoothly. "No one needs to know about our transaction. You want money; so do I. I have the book and will sell it tonight. Shall we say a hundred pounds? I'm not greedy. Part of the money now — or some jewels will do — and a note signed by you promising the remainder in a day or two when you are — ah — in funds."

"If . . . if I take the book, how can I trust you not to tell someone?"

"We both hold equal weapons. Disclosure would harm either of us. Besides, I have written down a full account and left it in a safe place to be opened by my cousin if anything happens to me."

"Get the book."

"Before I do, will you satisfy my curiosity about a few small matters? How did you become acquainted with the head of this villainous housing scheme? And what trail led you to Jared Warwick?"

"I can answer that," a harsh voice exploded from the doorway. "The housing villain was her uncle. And I provided a very handy trail to Jared."

Katherine Warwick stood framed in the hall doorway, glaring furiously.

Sylvia and I both froze while Katherine swept forward in her robes of purple gauze, her eyes blazing in a wild, white face, her hands curled like jeweled claws. She sucked in a rasping breath. "So, Sylvia, it was you all along. Using me, flattering, fawning. I thought you liked me — were my dearest friend." She gave an angry sob. "In an idle moment, I told you that my husband wrote under the name of Henry Verite and was investigating the new slum housing. Immediately, you went to the enemy, hatching out a plot for money." Her voice rose shrilly. "You are vile!"

Sylvia wet her lips, her voice placating. "Why should it concern you? You don't love your husband."

"It's the fact that you deceived me — all of us," Katherine hissed. "You said once that your uncle dealt in dark and secret matters to make money. And so do you! False friend!" Eyes almost starting from her head, Katherine swung her hand against the countess's face with all her might.

Sylvia staggered backward, clutching at her cheek. "You hypocrite! You're only furious because I fooled you. At least I had some feeling for Jared and never harmed him to the point of death. It was mainly to

311

scare him—"

"You stabbed my husband," Katherine interrupted fiercely. "Tried to poison him, fixed the horse's saddle so my child was lamed, set the fire. You are a fiend! A monster!"

"My uncle arranged the stabbing," Sylvia babbled. "I had not part in that. I slipped a drop of poison on the cakes, set the fire, yes, and pushed the rocks down from the cliff." She looked at me with jealous hatred in her eyes.

"What about the death of James? He was blackmailing you after he had made a shrewd guess as to your activities. And so you shot him." I began to move toward her.

The countess jerked around, for the first time looking frightened. I dived and pinned her arms against her body. "Quick! Go get Jared! She has just confessed to many crimes, and we both heard her."

"You traitor!" Sylvia writhed and flung herself about. The next instant, she was free.

And a pistol was in her hand.

Several things happened at once. Katherine snatched up a flower pot and threw it at Sylvia with all her strength. It smashed against the glass and blood spurted over Sylvia's face. I ran to the hall door, screaming for Jared.

And Bascom emerged from the far corner of the greenhouse. "Nobody moves a step," he bawled. "I represents the law!"

Sylvia, clutching blindly at her cheek, wrenched open the outside door, fired wildly into the greenhouse, and fled into the night with Bascom after her.

And then disaster struck in earnest. The glass, shattered from its wrought iron bands, suddenly crashed inward. Orchids rained down, pots smashed, trees toppled — all jabbed by the deadly points of crystal shards. The noise was obliterated by my screams as I saw Katherine slip and fall, a dagger of sharp glass protruding from her breast. In seconds, she was covered like a pall with purple orchids and slivers of glinting, jagged horror.

As soon as the glass stopped falling, I struggled to Katherine's side, knowing all too well what I would find. Excited voices rose in the hallway, and Jared dashed into the conservatory.

"My God! What's happened?" he shouted. "Margaret — are you hurt?"

I shook my head and managed to say hoarsely. "It's your — your wife —"

People crowded at the door, white-faced and staring. Wind blew cruelly through the gaping roof, and Jared, like a figure carved of stone, made his way across the carnage to his wife.

With her purple garments spread around her and a darker stain upon her breast, Katherine Warwick looked strangely like a dying orchid. Like the flowers she had loved so much in life.

I felt the cold, blue-veined wrist, knowing there would be no pulse. Speechlessly, I raised my eyes to Jared and slowly shook my head.

A terrible sob tore from his lips as he gathered his dead wife in his arms and pressed his face against her hair. "Kate, Kate! Oh, no, my poor, dear girl. Not this way —"

Everyone grew silent. At last, Jared — with a look I never hope to see again — lifted Katherine in his arms.

"My wife is dead. Everyone — get out of my way."

Huddled on the ground amid the crunching glass and dying plants, I couldn't go to him with any help. No one could. I put my hands up to my head and wept.

Chapter Thirty

Numb with shock, I sat alone in my room until dawn streaked the grey skies with a grudging light. Outdoors, a rising storm was moaning. What misery the day would bring. . . .

Jared's wife was dead. And he had reacted with unmistakable love and grief. Perhaps he hadn't realized how much he cared until he held the beautiful dead woman in his arms. Once he must have had a deep, passionate feeling for her. Perhaps it had never really died and was only obscured by the agony of hurt pride when Katherine refused to be a wife to him any longer. In his loneliness, he had turned to someone else. A nurse who had aroused his gratitude and returned his kisses with surprising ardor.

This realization only filled me with a weary sadness. I was too drained, too empty for more intense emotion, though I knew it would come later. My tears slid silently, hardly noticed.

I had changed into a dark merino dress and thrust the green silk into a corner of the wardrobe. I would never wear that gown again. The masquerade was over.

Surprisingly, Miss Grey had proved to be a calm, efficient rock, though her face was wracked with grief. She had taken charge completely, herding everyone back to the parlor for the buffet after the accident, and then urging a quiet dispersement to their rooms. In the morning they would depart.

Miss Grey had only spoken a few heavy words to me. "Will you see to the child? I think the father has forgotten her in his grief. And guilt."

I was too numb to take offense and merely nodded. I looked into Harriet's room and saw that she and Annie both were sound asleep, so I did not disturb them. Time enough to tell them in the morning. I returned to my own room for a lonely vigil through the night, not even considering the thought of sleep.

At last a knock sounded at my door and I flew out of my chair. *Could that be Jared?*

But Bascom stood on the threshold and entered wearily, dropping uninvited into a chair. "Cripes, it's cold." He shuddered and rose to kneel down by the grate. In a few seconds, he had started a crackling fire.

I hadn't even been aware of the lack of heat, but now I stretched my hands gratefully toward the blaze.

"That's more like it," Bascom grunted. He looked at me with red-rimmed eyes and rubbed his hand across his face. "Some shocker this night's been, eh? she's dead, too, y'know—Lady Sylvia."

Dead?" I echoed, starting up from my chair.

"Aye. Tried to escape down the cliff and some loose rocks fell on her. She slipped. And that was that." He stared into the flames.

I sank back, drawing an unsteady breath. "Have you

told Mr. Warwick about Sylvia?"

"Naw, I'll talk to 'im later, poor bloke. Real cut up 'ee is. I sent someone to bring the coroner and coppers from the mainland."

"Did—did Sylvia speak before she died?"

"Said she 'adn't done so much. Just tried to scare Jared so 'e'd quit the bloody book. Swore she loved 'im. Cripes, some love!"

"Her uncle was behind it all."

"Eh?"

"He's a man of many names, very corrupt. He learned that a writer named Verite was digging into his housing project in the slums, and, when Sylvia found out from Katherine that Verite was Jared Warwick's pen name, a plan was hatched. Sylvia immediately cultivated Katherine and became a frequent houseguest."

"I know about the notes and so-called accidents. Jared 'ired me to keep an eye peeled right after the kid got 'urt. But that countess was pretty foxy. We didn't suspect 'er."

"Yes, she was clever. She did everything except the stabbing and the shooting at Lingrove. I guess her attacks on Jared weren't fatal because she really cared for him."

Bascom snorted. "She loved the bloomin' money more. Wonder what 'er next move woulda been?"

"We'll never know. I guess my note held up her plans. She had to find out what I knew."

"And do you in, too, most like. Just as she killed James, who was tryin' for a spot o' blackmail. That bloke spied on everyone, but with Sylvia he hit the bull's eye."

At that moment, the maid announced that the constable had arrived, and Bascom left to talk with him. I knew I would also have to see the police and make a statement about what had happened in the greenhouse. There would be a lot of publicity about Sylvia, the housing fraud, and Jared's book. Undoubtedly, there would be an investigation in the slums, and perhaps some good would come from this horrendous night. But would it be worth the price? Three deaths and a family left in tragedy?

The house was stirring now. Footsteps sounded in the hallway, doors opened and closed, voices rose. The guests must be departing. I could hear someone talking in the room next door, and I knew it was time for the heart-rending task of seeking Harriet.

When I knocked and entered, Timothy was there sitting in an armchair holding his young cousin. Both were crying as he tried to explain and soothe the child, and I remembered that he had loved his Cousin Kate and had once considered marrying her.

Harriet lifted a grief-streaked, puffy face and stretched out her arms. "Oh, Margaret, you were there. Tell me about it," she sobbed. "Why did Mama have to die?"

Tears welled into my eyes as I sank down by her chair and pressed the wet cheek to my own. "Your mother died because a terrible evil came into your lives. When your mother learned that it was Sylvia who had done all these things and nearly made you lame for life, she flew into a rage and tried to prevent her leaving."

I paused and looked at her soberly. "Did Cousin Timothy explain why Sylvia did these things?"

When Harriet nodded mutely, I continued. "Lady

Sylvia wanted to escape, so she fired a pistol and ran down the cliff. The shot broke the glass in the greenhouse and a piece drove into your mother's heart. She died instantly, my darling, and didn't feel a thing. I was there."

Harriet continued weeping, but not so violently. "So Mama did truly love me — and she loved Papa, too — that's why she fought with Sylvia. Isn't that r-right?"

I didn't hesitate. "Of course. She loved you both and hated Sylvia for what she had done."

"Why would Sylvia do those awful things to us, j-just for money?" Harriet gave a watery hiccup.

I sighed and stroked back her hair. "Remember *Lady Pamela's Fortune* and how her childhood friend tried to hold her for ransom? Sometimes there are false friends in real life, too. But it doesn't happen often, thank goodness."

"It's so hard to believe," Timothy muttered thickly, placing his hand across his eyes as though to blot out the terrible pictures from his mind.

Harriet slid out of her cousin's lap. "I want to go to Papa. Ring for Annie, Margaret, so I can wash and dress. I don't have anything in black. What should I wear?" Her lips trembled, but the tears had ceased.

"You don't need black today. Later, perhaps. White will do for now, my dear."

Out in the hallway, Timothy spoke to me in a low tone. "This news about Sylvia's activities certainly was an awful shock. Gad, I never had the slightest inkling. How could she? I mean, she always made up so to Jared. What an actress!" He gave a bitter grimace.

"Bascom told me just now that Sylvia died climbing down the cliff," I told him in a low tone.

Timothy sucked in his breath and stared at me. "My God! Well, perhaps it's best that way."

After a minute, he squared his shoulders. "Well, I'll see what I can do to speed the guests' departure. I'm going to stay on a while until after—" He swallowed. "Harriet may need me."

"I'm sure she will." I was very glad that Timothy hadn't been involved in any of the vicious events. Had he found my note? What had he thought about it? That it was just a prank of Harriet's? I would probably never know because I certainly was not going to ask him.

The guests, still shocked and talking endlessly about the tragedy, could be heard moving off in jingling carriages while the caterers removed all traces of the party. After a while, the constable questioned me, and I told him that I had confronted Sylvia with my suspicions and the countess had admitted her guilt in front of the agent, Bascom, Mrs. Warwick, and myself. Bascom had then tried to apprehend the countess, and, in the ensuing struggle, a gun was fired by the culprit, causing a shower of falling glass, which killed Katherine Warwick. The police wrote out a statement and Bascom and I both signed it. Jared did not appear, but the constable said he had spoken to him.

I knew that Jared didn't want to face me, and I determined to leave without delay. I packed my things and said farewell to Harriet.

"Don't go, Margaret," the girl wailed. "We need you."

"Timothy will help you, darling. You must go back to school as soon as possible. I'm afraid if I stay on tongues will wag, because I don't really have a job here anymore. Also, my presence now would just be a sad reminder to your father that perhaps my meddling helped to bring it all about."

"No, no, never! How could anyone think that?" We clung tearfully, but finally I broke away, Harriet insisting that I give her an address where she could write to me and begging that I come back "later."

Without much hope, I said that I would try.

Back in my room, I sat down to compose a note to Jared. I thought about the other notes I had written recently. *Had* I been responsible for Katherine's death? If I hadn't forced that confrontation in the greenhouse, would Katherine be alive today?

Or was that only morbid reasoning? I had only been doing what I could to halt the recent terrible events. I sighed, wondering what had become of the sensible woman I used to be? Practical, hard-working, fearless, and independent?

But that was all before a black-haired man had called me beautiful and sealed my love with his mouth on mine. He had brought me to a new sense of throbbing life I never had imagined.

Alas, how brief that time had been! Was it ended? Shattered like the greenhouse, with all its flowers dead, killed by the cold wind tearing through the broken roof, alone, deserted, and forgotten?

Through a blur of tears that I had to constantly wipe away, I dipped my pen into the inkstand and wrote my note:

My dear Jared: I will be gone when you read this, since I fear there is nothing I can do to help you, and my presence would only be a reminder of the recent tragedy. If my meddling caused more sorrow than it was worth, I will regret it all my life. Harriet will eventually be all right, and I pray that you will, also. My deepest sympathy.

After that I signed my name. But in my heart I added: "With my undying love."

Chapter Thirty-one

That summer it was very difficult for me to be in London. Besides the heat, the smells, and the crowds thronging to the exhibition, I was reminded of Jared Warwick on every hand.

The daily *Observer* shrieked with headlines about the housing scandal, which Parliament was now investigating. Henry Verite's newest book was not yet on sale, but it had been widely publicized as being responsible for the investigation and the arraignment of the leading culprit.

Only one letter had come from Jared and it was stiffly worded, weary-sounding, and told me little, except that he was embroiled in very public matters and it would be better if I stayed in seclusion.

I waited for another letter, but, as the days faded into weeks and there was no further sign from him, my hopes began to fade. I had been afraid of this— Jared blamed me for Katherine's death. And perhaps he now regretted the life he had forced his wife to lead on the lonely, remote island that she hated.

The guilt he felt for this might never leave him.

I often wept when I was alone on my cot beneath the eaves, knowing full well that tears were a foolish luxury, but I was unable to erase the sense of bitter hurt and loss. More and more, I withdrew into my work at the hospital, hoping to obliterate my memories of the island rising from the rock-bound bay and the man who had aroused my love.

Harriet wrote to me. She was back at school and now so far behind that she had to have a private tutor. She said that Papa had to go to court and do more writing on his book, as now it had a different ending.

With a heavy sigh, I realized that they were both too busy now to miss me. Octavia often heard me sigh, and one day she looked up sharply from her sewing. "I wish you would get out of that hospital for the summer, Margaret. You are liable to catch something. You don't look too well, you know."

I brushed my hair back with a hand that had grown much thinner. "I guess it's the unusual heat that's giving me so many headaches these days." I didn't mention the dizzy spells and wracking stomach pains, for which I had been dosing myself with salts volatile.

"No cholera in the city, is there?" Octavia asked anxiously.

"Not yet," I answered grimly. "But hardly a summer goes by without a lot of fatal cases."

"You should go back to Brendan's Isle. Now, don't shake your head. I guess you had to leave after all that happened. I only thought, later, perhaps . . ."

"I can't, Octavia," I muttered dully, stretching my

aching shoulders.

Octavia bent her head over a client's garment, which she was turning on the other side by picking out the tiny stitches. "I thought when Mr. Warwick was here — the way he looked at you — and the way you spoke of him — I mean, of course, after a decent interval . . ."

"No, Octavia."

"But why not, child? You said that you admired the man, and I suspect you felt much more than that, didn't you? He'll be free now —"

"He never will be free from his wife's memory, or his sense of guilt. If you could have seen his face when she died, Octavia, you would know what I mean. Katherine was the loveliest creature I have ever seen. No man who had known her could escape her spell. I think Jared will take a long time to recover. It may be never."

Octavia shook her head, and, adjusting her spectacles, applied herself silently to her picking.

The next day was the hottest one on record. The stench of the polluted waters of the Thames drifted on the air for miles. Flies swarmed over piles of refuse in the gutters, and in the hospital insects were a terrorizing menace. No one could decide if it was better to shut the windows and try to keep them out or open the windows and coax a stray breeze into the odorous, close wards. The grey stone floors were washed down regularly now that more young women were employed. The rotting bandages and the slop pails were removed, and the food, no longer spoiled or burnt, was served in clean white dishes.

I gave myself a little credit for these reforms. It was rumored that a young woman named Florence Nightingale, who had studied medicine in Germany, was going to open a training hospital just for women in the near future, and I thought I might apply there. Perhaps I might oversee the newcomers in some department and share my own experience. I would have to do something with my life. There was no future for me otherwise.

But today, thinking in the wards took too much effort. All I longed for was a breath of air. Recklessly, I pushed the window open, suddenly feeling deathly ill. A flame streaked through me and I screamed and clutched my stomach. As an aide ran toward me, everything fell away in a rush of terrible pain and faintness.

Dimly, I was aware of being carried to a bed, where a whirling delirium rapidly engulfed me. I had a raging fire within, alternating with teeth-rattling chills. The grey stone walls came closer, closer . . . then they moved far, far away. . . .

The voices so faintly heard, the flashing lights in pits of darkness, the salted water forced between my lips — all were objects in a nightmare. Hours of muddled consciousness faded into hours of complete blankness.

"Is it cholera?" I whispered to a nurse in a lucid moment, knowing there was no cure, no drug for it.

"Nobody's sure yet. It might be only something they call 'summer fever.' There's been a lot of that. Now, don't worry," the nurse said soothingly, "we're doing all we can — lots of water and cool sponge baths. Drink this now—"

Images passed like wavering grey ghosts. Octavia? Yes, it was! "Please go home, dearest," I insisted, trying to struggle up. "You—might —catch—something." A cloud erased the vision and I fell back, sinking down, down, far beneath the bed, the floors, into the very earth. I tried to scream and couldn't.

Another time, I felt a flood of joy. *Jared!* Jared, large, dark, looking so masculine and yet so helpless as he leaned above my pain-wracked cot. I tried to move my fingers to touch the beloved face. But my hand possessed no life. Maybe I was dead and didn't know it. . . .

Sometimes I heard disjointed words:

"Where is Brendan's Isle?"

"Doctor, how much longer—"

"Drink this, dearie."

"Octavia, can't we move her?"

One day, I heard my cousin clearly. "She doesn't know me anymore!"

And clearly I replied. "Yes, I do, Octavia. Why are you crying?" I was flooded with amazed delight. I had spoken aloud at last. "I'm alive!" I whispered joyously.

"Oh, dearest, yes, yes. And you're going to be well now. I can tell the fever's broken. I must get Mr. Warwick."

"Jared? How can . . . you . . . do . . . that?" The effort to speak was exhausting; thinking was even worse. I was too tired. I let myself fade away in sleep.

The next awakening was better. Octavia was

gone, but a big, dark-haired man slept in a chair beside the screen that separated me from the ward. His hair was roughly tangled and a beard shadowed his unshaven face.

"Jared, Jared," I croaked and tasted tears upon my lips.

Instantly, he roused and bent above me, his hands trembling on my own. "You're better, darling, thank heaven!"

"How—how did you get here?"

"I came as soon as I heard about your illness."

Holding his hand, I drifted off to a blissful rest.

The next time we talked, I felt much stronger. "Oh, Jared, I—I didn't think you wanted to see me anymore."

"Foolish girl!" He drew his chair close to the cot and took my hands in both of his. "I came as soon as possible. I also have been ill, or I would have come much sooner. Before that, there was so much publicity, I had to keep your name out of it."

I fastened on one word: "Ill? You have been ill?"

He nodded. "Just fatigue and misery and yearning for you. I sort of collapsed after the inquest, the fevered rewriting, and so forth. Harriet wrote to your cousin when we didn't hear from you, and it was then that we learned of your own illness."

"Oh, Jared, if I'd only known, I would have come to take care of you. But before that, I felt so guilty—"

"You had no need for that, my dearest. I was the guilty one. I hadn't loved poor Katherine for years, but her death was a horrendous shock. I felt I had no right to any happiness until I had paid a debt to

Katherine's memory. But now I intend to take you out of here as soon as the doctor agrees to let you go."

"Where, Jared?" Weak and bewildered, I clung to his hand, half-afraid that he might vanish like the other ghostly visions.

He bent and kissed me gently. "You're coming home with me, beloved. Octavia will come with us to take care of you. I'm taking you to Brendan's Isle where you belong. To stay with me forever as my wife."

Chapter Thirty-two

"Octavia wants to be our housekeeper now that Miss Grey's gone," I said, taking my dear husband's arm as we strolled about the garden. The brick path was deep in golden leaves, and the waves were strong against the jagged shore where only the bravest seabirds lingered now. But here in this walled area, the sun still shone warmly, and every day Jared accompanied me for an hour's stroll.

"I can help Octavia with her duties," I added. "I am in exceptionally good health these days."

"Yes, you're positively blooming, my love, completely recovered from your illness," Jared said. "But I have other things for you to do."

"Such as walking in the garden—"

"Also talking, dreaming, making love . . . ah, I have so many things for you to do, it will take us several lifetimes." Jared dropped a fond kiss on my hair.

I seldom wore a hat, as he liked to see my auburn hair caught casually at the back of my neck. I had gained weight since my illness, and never had I felt so vibrantly, so thankfully and deliciously alive.

"My bride," Jared whispered possessively. "It's just two months today. I was afraid it might be too soon when we got married."

"Well, it was rather. We caused quite a scandal by not waiting the prescribed year."

"I meant too soon after your illness to submit to an importuning husband."

I leaned my head against his shoulder. "That was not soon enough."

Jared laughed, sounding triumphant, proud, and happy. He pulled me up against him, and we kissed as rapturously as we had that first time on the beach.

When we resumed our stroll, Jared pressed my fingers, which were tucked into his arm. "I know we didn't wait the prescribed time to get married, but I wanted you so much and I couldn't pretend to mourn any longer for poor Katherine."

We had spoken of this before, and I now understood his feelings of remorse and regret when Katherine died. It had not been love that I had seen on his face that terrible night, only pity.

Hastily, I cast around for a more cheerful topic; there had been enough of sadness in the past. "We are lucky to be so happy now. I love it on this island; you have your work, and Harriet seemed delighted when I came back to stay. Did I ever tell you what she said to me the day that we were married? 'Now I can call you Mama, can't I?' Wasn't that sweet of her? Do you think she'll mind another one who will call me Mama next year?"

"Not at all. She has already informed me that the first child must be a boy. She wants to call him Timmy."

"And if the baby is a girl?" I asked.

"Then we'll call her Tammy. That will be close enough. Agreed, my love?"

"Don't I always agree with you, my lord and master?"

Jared chuckled, but didn't comment. It was just as well. He was learning to be a wiser husband every day.

SENSATIONAL SAGAS!

JEWELLED PATH   (1504, $3.95)
by Rosalind Laker

In the glittering turn-of-the-century settings of Paris, London, and Monte Carlo, Irene was as unique as the jewelry she created. Two very different men, drawn to her emerald eyes and lustrous pearly skin, forced her to choose one as her destiny. One stirred her body, and the other her heart!

WHITE NIGHTS, RED DAWN   (1277, $3.95)
by Frederick Nolan

Just as Tatiana was blossoming into womanhood, the Russian Revolution was overtaking the land. How could the stunning aristocrat sacrifice her life, her heart and her love for a cause she had not chosen? Somehow, she would prevail over the red dawn—and carve a destiny all her own!

IMPERIAL WINDS   (1324, $3.95)
by Priscilla Napier

From the icebound Moscow river to the misty towers of the Kremlin, from the Bolshevick uprising to the fall of the Romanovs, Daisy grew into a captivating woman who would courageously fight to escape the turmoil of the raging IMPERIAL WINDS.

KEEPING SECRETS   (1291, $3.75)
by Suzanne Morris

It was 1914, the winds of war were sweeping the globe, and Electra was in the eye of the hurricane—rushing headlong into a marriage with the wealthy Emory Cabot. Her days became a carousel of European dignitaries, rich investors, and worldly politicians. And her nights were filled with mystery and passion . . . .

BYGONES   (1030, $3.75)
by Frank Wilkinson

Once the extraordinary Gwyneth set eyes on the handsome aristocrat Benjamin Whisten, she was determined to foster the illicit love affair that would shape three generations—and win a remarkable woman an unforgettable dynasty!

RAPTUROUS ROMANCE
by Wanda Owen

ECSTASY'S FANCY (1467, $3.75)

From the moment Fancy met Nicholas Dubois aboard the *Memphis Belle*, his flashing white smile haunted her dreams. She knew his reputation as a devil for breaking hearts, yet when he took her in his arms she gloried in the sweet ecstasy of surrender . . .

THE CAPTAIN'S VIXEN (1257, $3.50)

No one had ever resisted Captain Lance Edward's masculine magnetism—no one but the luscious, jet-haired Elise. He vowed to possess her, for she had bewitched him, forever destining him to be entranced by THE CAPTAIN'S VIXEN!

TEXAS WILDFIRE (1337, $3.75)

When Amanda's innocent blue eyes began haunting Tony's days, and her full, sensuous lips taunting his nights, he knew he had to take her and satisfy his desire. He would show her what happened when she teased a Texas man—never dreaming he'd be caught in the flames of her love!

GOLDEN GYPSY (1188, $3.75)

When Dominique consented to be the hostess for the high stakes poker game she didn't know that her lush, tantalizing body would be the prize—or that the winner would be Jared Barlow, the most dashing man she had ever seen. On first glance at the golden goddess, Jared couldn't wait to claim his fortune!

MORE BESTSELLING ROMANCE BY JANELLE TAYLOR

SAVAGE CONQUEST (1533, $3.75)

Having heeded her passionate nature and stolen away to the rugged plains of South Dakota, the Virginia belle Miranda was captured there by a handsome, virile Indian. As her defenses melted with his burning kisses she didn't know what to fear more: her fate at the hands of the masterful brave, or her own traitorous heart!

FIRST LOVE, WILD LOVE (1431, $3.75)

Roused from slumber by the most wonderful sensations, Calinda's pleasure turned to horror when she discovered she was in a stranger's embrace. Handsome cattle baron Lynx Cardone had assumed she was in his room for his enjoyment, and before Calinda could help herself his sensuous kisses held her under the spell of desire!

GOLDEN TORMENT (1323, $3.75)

The instant Kathryn saw Landis Jurrell she didn't know what to fear more: the fierce, aggressive lumberjack or the torrid emotions he ignited in her. She had travelled to the Alaskan wilderness to search for her father, but after one night of sensual pleasure Landis vowed never to let her travel alone!

LOVE ME WITH FURY (1248, $3.75)

The moment Captain Steele saw golden-haired Alexandria swimming in the hidden pool he vowed to have her—but she was outraged he had intruded on her privacy. But against her will his tingling caresses and intoxicating kisses compelled her to give herself to the ruthless pirate, helplessly murmuring, "LOVE ME WITH FURY!"

TENDER ECSTASY (1212, $3.75)

Bright Arrow is committed to kill every white he sees—until he sets his eyes on ravishing Rebecca. And fate demands that he capture her, torment her . . . and soar with her to the dizzying heights of TENDER ECSTASY!

Available wherever paperbacks are sold, or order direct from the Publisher. Send cover price plus 50¢ per copy for mailing and handling to Zebra Books, Dept. 1650, 475 Park Avenue South, New York, N.Y. 10016. DO NOT SEND CASH.